THE SWORD OF STONE
THE SHATTERING SERIES
BOOK ONE

by

KD Johnson

AKUSAI
PUBLISHING

To my dad,
who bought me my first Final Fantasy game
after a dentist appointment.

The Sword of Stone: The Shattering Book I

THE SHAPING

It is never a simple act to shape the will of the Elders. Yet this was his goal.

The Shaper sat down in the dark red stone room. The room was built circular giving the feeling of disorientation to anyone who entered. Some shapers loved this feeling, of being lost, unsure of where one was. It was better for the Inspiration, they said. Those invisible masters who commanded from the "On High", demanding that they seek the future for this King or that King. For Emperor of the Yarcho Kingdom—he was particularly demanding.

His body felt disoriented from the darkness and lack of direction. It was believed in the Citadel that darkness led to absolute concentration.

This just proved to the Shaper that no one—even his own people—understood him and his abilities.

There were several people in this world who had what they called "gifts," the gift of sight and art inspired from the Elders themselves.

Few could claim such a strong connection. This particular Shaper, however, felt the connection at a small age. He was summoned for his gift, an ability to shape events in the future through concentration.

His favorite medium remained clay. He found the textures, the pliability, the smells to be much more comforting than paint or ink. Those Shapers who worked with other specific mediums were often messier, higher end.

He, on the other hand, held his powers like a noose around his neck. It was something that he was led to believe was his gift to the world, his responsibility.

What it really was, was a gift, a lingering voice and image that sat within his brain and poked and prodded him into action.

A wooden door opened from the outside. "What are you doing?" asked a voice.

"I am preparing for today's shaping," he said.

"We have a specific assignment for you," said the voice. The Shaper could not recognize its owner. Still, any command that came from the On High were the voice of reason and the law. "We need you to report your shapings immediately."

This was not an unusual request, but it struck the Shaper odd that he was told to do this explicitly. The other Shapers had been struggling recently. The future had been harder to foretell since the Dallheim Wars. It was an unusual and rather stressful situation to be in: to have a skill and not be able to use it, no matter how hard you tried.

"I will report them at once," said the Shaper.

The door closed and once again, the Shaper was left in silence.

He sat, cross-legged and waited for the inspiration to come to him. His eyes lifted up behind his eyelids. He felt the usual relaxation of his cheek muscles, the feelings of tension leaving his body.

Then, he felt something he had not done in years: an image, an intense image of fire, death. Of a white mountain collapsing.

The Shaper opened his eyes and gasped. The feelings and images were too intense. Too strong, but were familiar. They were dreams he had before that resulted in shapes that were thrown away.

The Summoner and the On High disliked their materials to go to waste. The Shaper took many a beatings to preserve his secrecy. Punishments and torture at the hands of sick, bored, and demented monks that relished in anything that gave them the slightest bit of power.

For while they were treated like kings and gods in the outside world, inside the Shapers were chattel, treated with very little dignity, if any at all.

His hands searched the lowered stone pedestal before him. The clay smelled like salty mud and created bubbles in his hands as he squeezed it playfully.

This was always the best part.

The Shaper began to create his images. He took the clay apart, creating three sections: one of them a box, the other a long oval.

The Shaper's hands worked quickly, rolling and twisting the individual pieces into things that no longer resembled themselves. People often said that his shapings were art, both a pleasure to look at and functional representations of the future.

The Shaper's hands moved quickly, creating something small enough to fit into the palm of his hand.

He opened his eyes.

What he witnessed surprised him.

"Summoner!" the Shaper screamed.

The door opened, but no light crept in. "Are you done so soon?"

"I am, but I must speak with someone from On High immediately."

"That is impossible. You know that. The On High take your shapings, you go back to the Citadel."

"That is not acceptable. They must see this." The Shaper held up the palm of his hand. In it, a little bassinet. Inside, a little baby.

"A child?" said the voice. "You wish to speak to the On High for a child?"

"It is important."

"Children are born every day," said the Summoner. "You are wasting time," he said.

The Shaper crawled to where he believed the door was. In the darkness, in this large room, the echoes were often deceiving and finding one's own location in that room proved difficult.

"You have shown us that your abilities have not come back," said the voice. "You are to return to your cloister immediately."

The door shut, the sound of the lock being released and finally a faint light of a torch lit up the room. "Come with us," he said.

The Shaper stood up, leaving the mess of dried clay. "As you wish." The Shaper's steps dragged along the ground. His sandals were not made for comfort, but only provided for convenience.

"Hurry up!" the voice commanded.

The Shaper nodded, but did not pick up his pace. His mind settled on the picture of the child, a little girl, in the bassinet. It nagged at him, this girl who would be the one responsible.

For the Shattering?

Was it possible that a little girl would be responsible?

"You took too long," said the voice. "To the Citadel."

The Shaper nodded and proceeded down the long, darkened hallway. Nearly every building in the Shaperate was built using a dark red stone. It held the darkness in and kept light out, the way that the On High preferred it.

Darkness led to Inspiration as far as the On High knew.

"I know the way," said the Shaper. "I am among the eldest here. Maybe I walk myself to the Citadel?"

The Summoner paused.

The Citadel was a short walk across a bridge away. The legends surrounding the Citadel speak to it being a sacred place among the Elders when they once inhabited the human lands. The Citadel sat along the eastern edge of the lands, only a few days' ride away from most of the cities to which they reported. The highlands held beautiful pastures that were said to please the Elders and yet allowed for safety to watch their creations.

To the Shapers, safety was key. Far too often had the kingdoms called upon the Citadel for their own personal Shapers. But the gift of prophecy was denied to all. The Shapers were never permitted to leave the castle, though no one had tried in centuries. The instinct of following rules had been thoroughly enforced and fed. Those who paid attention to the rules were given extravagant things. Food, clothing, even their own servants.

The Summoner gave it some thought. The Shaper had been betting that the Summoner was tired of his duties. The sky had been dark, clouds crossed over the full moon in waves that gave the illusion that the night sky had a nightmarish flicker about it. "You may go by yourself," said the Summoner. "Peace be with you."

"Thank you, Summoner." The Shaper did not turn around to face his escort, but bowed anyway. The disorientation had not fully left him, it seemed.

The Shaper continued to walk slowly. He secretly listening to the other end of the hall. The Summoner's footsteps were heavy and flat, each one slapping the stone beneath him.

As the footsteps were only an echo, the Shaper walked briskly down the hallway. The doors to the gates should be easy to get to, he thought.

But the guards were lazy, but attentive. He would have to be cleverer to escape.

The food carts. They received weekly shipments from the nearby towns, tributes from the kingdoms that surrounded them.

If he could ride with them, then he stood a chance to warn the village.

The Shaper's rounded features remained hidden under his hood, drawn up to protect him from the sight of the others. The brown cloak he wore covered most of his body, held together only by a small belt made of a red leather. It would keep him warm, he hoped, in the cold night during his travels.

The Shaper walked down a long winding staircase of stone to the dining area. There, he exited the building and stepped outside. The moon illuminated the darkness of the night sky, thin wispy clouds passed overhead, reflecting and absorbing some of the moon's light further. The air smelled sweeter and filled more of his chest.

There, by the expansive road that led to the rest of the world, sat a cart. It was covered by a thick burlap tarp. Only pieces of boxes and some larger fruit remained visible. The Shaper kept his vision straight ahead on the cart, to look like he belonged, had a purpose and wouldn't be questioned.

With no one stopping him—no doubt everyone was inside and resting—the Shaper climbed into the cart with some trouble and rested snugly between a box of red raspberries and an empty crate.

The fit was tight, but enough for the Shaper to fall asleep despite the rapid beating of his excited heart. Soon, he would taste the freedom of the outside world and find his way to Vamori Village, home of the most dangerous girl in the lands.

This Shaper, however, had rebelled against the world itself, refuting his own visions and denying their authenticity to the others.

But this image, however, the baby—this girl child—was something he could not ignore. It was not the first vision he had of this auburn-haired child.

"Could it be the Shattering?" he asked himself. The thought twisted his stomach.

The Shattering was legend, myths told by kings and mayors to keep the world in line. Even the Sacellum had often shared their own versions of the stories: death, rebirth, the end of the world as all knew it.

But as the Shaper had given it occasional thought from time to time, the evidence began to add up into something too much sense to ignore. His fellow Shapers were losing their own touch with the Inspiration. The weather changed frequently. Wars destroyed towns and villages.

The legend of magick, it was told, was wiped off the face of this earth. Rumors still reached the Citadel by way of traders, however, of people with special abilities. People who could tame nature and destroy with but a thought.

Even the Shaper's own creation, a child of a seemingly innocent face in a bassinet, filled him with dread. The physical manifestation of his visions created the art of a child. The images, however, he could never explain to anyone: scenes of fire and stone and shadow.

There was a connection, he knew it.

ONE

The hooded figure pressed his hand against the door to Hibert Kaisar's throne room and pushed it open.

A tall man dressed in a red leather and cloth uniform—red with the green stripe of the Vamori Village army across his chest—answered the hooded figure's call. "You are not permitted without a summons," he said. "Return back outside or be returned."

The figure withdrew his hood, revealing the dark skin and bald head of his people. "It is important that I speak with Hibert."

"Hibert is otherwise indisposed." The guard motioned to the front door. "Now if you'd please."

"Please, you have no idea what you're doing to your village if you turn me away."

"Is that a threat, little man?" The guard reached for the handle of his longsword and held it still. "I'll not ask you again. Return back outside."

The bald man peered from side to side and then held up a cloaked hand. The robes of his people demanded that most of his body be covered to prevent exposure to prying eyes. It was true that he was not supposed to be out this far—indeed he faced death if anyone found out.

"Maybe this will help to convince you," said the bald man. He held up his hand and, with his other hand, pulled back the sleeve.

The guard gasped. "You—you're—"

The bald man nodded solemnly. "If I may speak with Hibert now, please."

The guard said nothing more, but motioned for the little man to follow him. To prevent further eyes from prying, the man covered his head once again and followed the guard down the short but bright hallway. The natural lighting in the hallway reminded the bald man of his cloister. In the citadel he and his fellow people were sheltered away from the rest of the world. This, they claimed, was not to harm him and his kind, but to protect them.

The one thing the man always found comforting, however, was the bright lights and warmth afforded to him by the thick rays of light that crept in through the large hallway windows.

They came upon a thick door. A dark wooden door that appeared held firm by dark metal hinges and a round knocker held tightly by a metal claw. Perhaps a dragon. Maybe a griffon's. "If you'll excuse me," the soldier said. "Your audience is coming shortly."

The man nodded and held his hands together. He stood there as a ghost, clothed and silent. Only gazing that the simple surroundings and fearing that his words will go unheeded.

It was even a miracle that he had found this place to begin with.

"Your audience with the Chief is ready."

The wide doors opened and revealed the strong and solid stature of Chief Hibert Kaisar. The man had recognized the chief immediately. It was just as he had envisioned him, sculpted him. The only thing missing, naturally, was color, and so the red hair of the war hero Chieftain drew the bald man's eyes.

"Your Chieftain," he said. "I am humbled by your presence."

"Cut the nonsensical shit," he said. "I know what you are, Shaper. Why have you come?"

"I come with great news," said the Shaper. He dropped the hood to expose his dark skin and bowed eyes. He knew not the customs of this village, but bowed his head and knelt down on one knee anyway.

"Get up and answer my questions," said Hibert. "Why have you come again?"

"The time is coming closer," said the Shaper. "You are heading toward disaster. It is important you move this village."

"Move the village?" Hibert let out a laughter that rattled the Shaper. "Do you see how large this village is? One does not simply move a mountain." Hibert laughed again and stood up. "Your warnings were taken into counsel before, Shaper, I do not see a need for your return."

The Shaper stood up and forced himself to connect eye-to-eye with the Chief. "By ignoring my message you are damning your village, Chief Hibert. You willingly walk into such destruction?"

"Your ways are suspect, Shaper. Your people are beyond their uses. You claim inspiration from the Elders that have forsaken this world. Take a look around." Chief Hibert opened his arms wide, exposing his massive chest and strong arms. His face beamed with pride. "You came sixteen years ago with doomsday warnings and we still stand!" Hibert stepped down the tiny set of stairs that separated him from his guest. "Your warnings are pointless myths, your prophecies old dogs with no teeth. They mean nothing and bear no threat to me and my village."

The Shaper, "I understand your—"

"This conversation is ended." Hibert's voice thundered through the halls. "I wish you a wonderful stay in my village." Hibert dismissed the Shaper with a wave of his hand and turned to exit the room through a side door.

The Shaper watched as the frustrated Chieftain exited. The guard grabbed his arm. "If you will, sir, please follow me." The Shaper followed the guard's motions and left the room. The door shut loud behind him, followed with a metal bar fixed across the latch.

The Shaper's shoulders sunk low. There would be no way to convince the Chieftain now. He had ventured nearly two months' distance to reach this place. He had hoped they would heed his warning. If Chief Hibert refused to listen to his warnings, then the weight of the world fell upon his shoulders.

"Excuse me," he said, motioning toward one of the guards. "Where might an old man find your village's best food?"

TWO

Leanah Kaisar tossed stale bread at the center of a group of birds. These pigeons—the rats of Vamori Village by everyone's account—flocked to the new pieces, fighting and trampling on each other for food.

"Calm down, boys," she said. "There's plenty for all of you." Leanah ripped another piece of bread from her stale loaf, leftovers from her dinner the night before—and tossed it away from the birds toward the smaller chicks at the outside of the group.

The scene of bobbing feathered heads, the chirping and grumbling of stomachs made Leanah smile. She loved observing the birds' movements as she fed them. The way they struggled to get the last crumb, the last hope for food, inspired and amazed Leanah.

How any animal could stand on its family to get food was beyond her. Leanah had never had to fight for food or security: Her father was Hibert Kaisar, the Vamori chieftain and hero of the Dallheim Wars twenty-five years ago. This, of course, meant that

Leanah was considered the progeny of a beloved war hero, a fact that drove Leanah crazy at every bit of reminder.

These thoughts, however, fell away as a young pigeon chick, still a soft downy gray, approached Leanah's bare ankle and yipped.

"Did you want some, little guy?" she said. Leanah ripped a large piece—larger than she usually reserved for the birds—and placed it gently at her feet.

The chick hopped backwards at first, bowing its head down as if ready to pounce on her hand or run for cover. As Leanah pulled her hand back up to her lap, she watched as the bird hopped forward on its twig-thin feet and prodded at the bread with its beak.

"It's okay," Leanah said. "It will not hurt you."

The bird seemed to understand and snapped at the large crumb. It yanked, putting all of its young birdy strength into the tug. It was met with some success. Though the chunk of bread had not relinquished a crumb small enough for the chick to eat, it did move ever so slightly toward the bird's direction. Leanah only laughed and watched. It was important, she thought, to let the bird struggle.

It needed to learn to struggle on its own, if only to experience what it's like to bite off more than you can chew.

"Leanah!"

She sighed, as she recognized the voice immediately. Deciding that it may be best to not pay attention to the voice—that maybe it would just go away—she tossed another piece of bread at the flock of birds and laughed.

"Leanah! Don't you dare ignore me!"

The voice, Leanah knew, belonged to Ciaran.

"What do you want?" she said.

"You know darn well what I want, madam. You were due in class nearly an hour ago. What happened?"

"I got," Leanah tossed another chunk of bread at the hungry flock, "distracted."

"So I see," said Ciaran. His skinny frame cast a long shadow over Leanah's squatting figure as she sat on the boulder. "No matter," he said. "We can do this right here, too."

"Go away."

"You know I can't do that," he said. "I was paid to ensure you gain a rightful education for a future chieftain."

Leanah barked a quick laugh. "You seriously think they'll make me chieftain?"

"Those are the rumors at any rate."

"Why does everyone whisper and have rumors about me?" she asked. The chick at her feet chirped, asking for more food. Leanah dropped a small crumb and turned to look at her tutor. "Why am I the center of attention?"

Ciaran sighed.

"Of course you won't answer. No one answers me." Leanah stood up and dusted off her hands as the last of the bread crumbs were consumed by the zealous and hungry pigeons. "It's only my life we're talking about. Excuse me," she said. "I'll see you tomorrow." Leanah started toward her house. "Maybe."

Leanah counted to five with her footsteps. It would only be a matter of time before she was stopped and asked to turn around.

This routine was predictable because Leanah found all adults predictable. Not wanting to disappoint, they could eventually be coerced into talking about anything, even if it meant lying through their teeth.

"Leanah!" cried out Ciaran.

Jackpot. Leanah stopped, shielding her smile from her tutor.

"Come," he said. "Let us talk."

"It's about time I get some answers," she said and crossed her arms. "But only if I get the truth," she yelled back.

"I promise nothing," said Ciaran.

"Then I'll see you another time."

"Leanah, you know I cannot—"

"All or nothing, Ciaran. I am unwavering on this."

"Fine," said Ciaran. "Come, have a seat."

Leanah followed Ciaran to the table which he sat. The table had been etched nearly fifty years ago—long before she was born. Stone had been the most prominent resource around Vamori. As such, one could not find anything that was not made out of stone. Homes, furniture, and even eating utensils were all made up of the hard rocks and stone found littered around the area.

This table was created out of a gray stone with orange-red swirls. The swirls, Leanah believed, came from the fire of the volcano from which it came. In the not so far distance, Kaverano, a fiery mountain named after Kaverin, the elder fire god of old, had been the source of raw materials for the entire kingdom.

The kingdom, however, no longer existed. It, too, was destroyed in the Dallheim Wars. The last of the kingdom stood as a single village, Vamori. Leanah's birthplace and home to a wonderful legend.

"Do you really want to know the full extent of the rumors?"

Leanah became annoyed at the question. "That was what I said, was it not?" Leanah felt her temper flare, a heat rising from her chest to her face. Even when promised a straight answer, Leanah had learned that rarely anyone ever followed through.

However, this time she sensed a deep sadness in Ciaran, a

hesitation that she could not see in many of the adults around her. This, she believed, was because Ciaran was not originally of this village. A refugee from the Wars nearly fifteen years ago, Ciaran had come to the village to seek a new life. Somehow, he had become the village tutor and responsible for shaping Leanah into a powerful and intelligent ruler.

"If this is what you command, I cannot hold it from you," said Ciaran. He stared off into the distance. Leanah attempted to trace his line of sight to catch a glimpse of his distraction. She saw nothing.

"Well," she said. "Out with it!"

"I take no responsibility for this message, my student. Just be aware that these words have been in existence since long before you were born."

THREE

Ciaran shifted his body opposite of Leanah and stared directly into her eyes. "Long ago, when the world was young, a new group—The Elders—existed in these lands.

Much of what we see and know now were different then, with many different animals and lakes and rivers existing that do not exist now.

These Elders took great care of the lands, helping themselves and doing what they needed to survive under one primary rule: it hurt nothing else in the entire world.

But some of the elders were not okay with this rule. They sought power and dominance over the world and over each other. This led to a war, a war of elders that resulted in the death of a many great people.

Massive destruction laid waste to the world, for these Elders had a power that was mostly lost to the people of today."

"Mostly?" asked Leanah. "What do you mean mostly?" She paused, then slammed her hands on the table. "And just what does this have to do with me?"

"Patience," Ciaran said. "If you want to know the truth, you must go back and understand its origins."

"You're testing my patience," she said. "But go on."

"When I say mostly, child, I refer to the fact that in some places, the gods still exist in different forms."

"Nonsense. Does my father know you fill my head with lies?" Leanah demanded. "We all know that the gods do not exist."

"Of course they do," Ciaran said. "The Elders exist. They have always existed. They always will exist. Power and life and energy will always find a way to exist, young child. Sometimes it must take a different form to survive, but it will always exist."

"And what does this have to do with me?"

Ciaran smiled and leaned over the table toward his student. "I will get to that, Leanah. Patience."

Leanah sighed but Ciaran ignored the frustration.

"The conflict came to a head, with each faction of the Elders arming themselves with sacred magicks and weapons and armors. These were miraculous weapons that could destroy mountains with a single swing. Dry out lakes completely with a touch. These weapons were powerful, but necessary, for each Elder knew that this battle would reshape the lands, possibly even destroying all in existence."

"But we're still here," Leanah said. "So they failed."

"Not exactly, child. The fact is, the war lasted for years, decades. As soon as one side looked like it would win, the other faction took over, seizing arms and armor and subverting the other faction. That is, until finally, an Elder made of stone," Ciaran paused. He waved his hand over the horizon and pointed at the distant mountains, "the same stone that makes up the lands you see before you, led a final battle against the Conquerors, the elders who believed that the lands were theirs to do as they pleased. The Elder of Stone, Kragg, led his fellow Elders into a great battle. The battle lasted only a few days, but Kragg and his army was victorious, but at a great cost. The world had been saved, but the lands were no longer in the same shapes. For the first time, islands were formed. Mountains formed where there was only flatlands. Lakes and forests burned away. Others grew in opposite lands. Even the sun grew hotter and deadlier.

But the greatest loss came in the form of Elders' lives. All were lost, and even the great Kragg had lost his physical form.

What remained of the flesh of the Elders came to the lands transformed, scattered across the lands. Your village, Leanah, holds an important artifact, a remnant of the Elder Wars."

"The Stone Sword?" she said.

"The same. The sword in your village, it is believed, belongs to the village and protects it. And once every fifty years, a chieftain's son must take the sword and feed it the blood of the Shadowed Wing, an ancient being that once fed the Elders themselves. Once the sword has been fed, it must be returned until another fifty years."

"A chieftain's son?" said Leanah. "But my father never had a son."

Ciaran sat backwards, unblinking. "Exactly." He crossed his arms and looked unnecessarily comfortable considering the news. "Hence the rumors, you see."

"What happens if the sword is not fed? You did not tell me that part."

Ciaran stood up and fixed his cloak across his shoulders. "I've said too much."

"Too much?" Leanah demanded. She stood up and clenched her fists. The temptation to grab Ciaran's cloak and pull him across the table was too much for her handle. "You've said too little!"

"I've said more than I should have," Ciaran stood backwards, protecting himself from Leanah's impending anger issues. "I apologize, madam," he said. "I believe today's lesson is over." He turned and started for the center of the village, toward his tent.

"But what happens to the village?" Leanah shouted. "You must tell me!"

"It may be best you ask your father," said Ciaran and threw his cloak over his shoulder.

Leanah watched as Ciaran disappeared around a corner and left her by herself with her thoughts.

Leanah's first instinct told her to rush to her father's side and demand answers, but this, she knew would not do.

She walked home. The sun had already crossed over half of the sky. It would be safe for her to return home without having to answer questions about being early or raising suspicion about her activities.

To get to her home, one of the largest in the village, Leanah had to cross through the village center. The center could be described as the busiest part of town. Everything from the tavern—the only one allowed in the village—and the many different shops pointed toward the village's center. The center was also the stage area, a place where many of the announcements, ceremonies, and celebrations were held in honor of the harvesting feasts.

The center had served the village well as a meeting place and social area. Leanah never felt the urge to socialize with the other villagers, but nonetheless felt comfortable being lost in the organized chaos of the village center, watching as her people bustled from shop to shop, gathering berries and meats for their evening dinners.

It was here she learned about other family customs, learned what fighting was. Here she watched the boys take their sticks and spar, twirling them around their heads, hacking and slashing at one another.

Leanah envied the boys and their ability to take their frustrations out at one another.

"Can I learn to sword fight as well, Father?" she had once asked. Hibert answered with a harrumph and left the room. Leanah had never worked up the courage to ask again and the matter had been settled. Instead, she opted to watch and study on the sidelines, hidden from view as the boys beat each other senseless.

Despite all of these moments of being lost in a crowd, today Leanah felt the center of attention. Ciaran's story had disturbed a deep part of her. She felt the others turn away as she looked at their faces, ashamed of staring at her. She watched as they made faces of disgust, of fear, of hate—these faces she had never witnessed before. Was she blind to this all along? Was she truly that oblivious to the feelings of her people? If she can't even sense their worries and frustrations, how could she be a great leader in the future?

Was she to blame for the fate of her village?

Leanah hung on to these thoughts and hastened her pace to her home. If anyone would have an answer for her, it would be her mother. She had always been honest in the past. If pressed, Leanah was sure she could get the truth one way or another.

Leanah stopped at the doorstep. Her hand rested on the door's handle, but it shook from fear and anticipation. The deepest part of her longed for an answer to the question. What happens if the sword is not fed? And if it does not feed, will it be her fault?"

Leanah held her breath and shoved the door open. "Mother?" she cried out. "Mother?"

Her words echoed off the walls and felt hollow in her chest. No sign of her mother in the house. At this time of day, she was usually preparing their evening meals. Her stomach grumbled in fear of not having dinner later that evening.

"Mother?" she cried out.

With the kitchen and the house seemingly empty, Leanah decided that she must be in the throne room. The room was not aptly named. Instead of being a room with a throne in it, it housed a wooden table—wood brought in from the oak forest just south of the village—and a series of stone chairs covered in the comfortably soft pelts of local wolves and bears.

Leanah traveled next door, but paused when she heard the heavy and deep thud of a staff walking toward the door. A voice muffled through the door muttered what sounded like a solemn warning and then the door cracked open. The man—bald and dark skinned—froze in place, just as frightened by the sudden appearance of Leanah as she was by the bald man.

At once, the man's face relaxed and smiled, his dark green eyes reflecting a sense of joy that Leanah had almost forgotten.

"I do not know what to tell you, but your stories and your worries are uncalled for. As you can see, everything is perfectly fine." The voice was her father's. She recognized his deep, thunderous voice anywhere. And nowhere could it sound more powerful than in the empty halls of the throne room.

"Clearly," said the bald man, grasping his gnarly wooden staff with his right hand and feeling about for a step below. "I'm sorry to have wasted your time."

"Under the circumstances," Hibert said, "I understand

completely."

Leanah stood to one side and watched the man leave toward the village entrance. His white robes turned dark, dusty, and orange where it dragged along the dirt ground. His sandals kicked up little dust. If Leanah had not known any better, she would have thought the bald man a ghost or apparition.

"Who was that, Father?"

"Leanah!" The bass of Hibert's voice shook Leanah's shoulders. "You are not to be here. Go on home."

"I was home, but no one was there. Where is mother?"

"I'm here," she said, stepping out of her husband's shadow. "I was needed here, Leanah. I did not mean to worry you."

Leanah's eyes narrowed as she watched her mother try to mask her concern. "What's going on here?"

"Nothing that concerns you," said Hibert. "Go on home. We'll follow."

"Why do you all treat me like I don't exist?"

"Don't be so insulting." Hibert's coarse red hair fell upon his shoulders. His beard glowed a fiery red when exposed in the sunlight. Hibert had been known as the Son of Kaverin during the Dallheim Wars, so named for his flaming locks of red hair and beards that hung from his face like a upside down torch. Red hair had been a sign of valiance, of being touched by the Gods—if you still believed in them.

Leanah had envied her father's hair. She—like her mother—had a light brown hair, held tight against her head in a taut ponytail to keep it out of her face. In the wind storms that frequently attacked Vamori in the summers, it was always best to keep your hair out of the way, or be faced with the sudden pain of being whipped across the cheeks and nose. Leanah had noticed, however, that hair had a reddish tint, the color of rust when the sun's rays had reflected just right.

"We treat you like the future chieftain, Leanah." Hibert's rather large feet and long legs meant that Leanah had to practically jog to keep up with him during walks. "Because you just may be."

"Maybe?'

"I'm sorry," Hibert said. His giant hand grasped Leanah's bare shoulder and squeezed tightly. "I meant will be."

"What do you mean maybe?" she asked. "And why is everyone staring at me funny? And who was that guy back there? And what happens if the sword isn't fed?"

At the last question, Hibert stopped walking and grasped his daughter by the shoulder again, squeezing tight and pulling her close. "You will keep your voice down, Leanah." He whispered this solemn command with a dangerous concern in his eye. Leanah noticed her father's eyes twitch, keeping track of the people around them. Then, a sudden switch in personality and Hibert stood up and smiled, patting her on the head. "You must be careful not to spread harmful rumors," he said. "Your people will trust you to be strong for them."

"But you didn't answer my question," Leanah said. She attempted to pull away from her father's grip, but failed. The tighter she pulled, the stronger her father's grip, a grip developed with decades of battle practice wielding broadswords, axes, and other heavy weaponry. Leanah relaxed her shoulders and followed her father's footsteps, making two for every one of his—back to their home.

"Leanah, be a dear and go out back. Choose a chicken for tonight. I'll be there presently to help bring in turnips for our meal."

Leanah nodded. To continue the discussion would only result in more chores and more ways to get rid of her. A much better tactic would be to play it close, to stick around and wait for the discussions to resume when they believed that she was out of listening distance.

The chicken pen out back, Leanah had noticed, was getting barer and barer. There would be few—if any—new chicks being born in the coming weeks. The hens simply were not laying eggs with the speed they used to. She had brought this to her father's attention once before, but he dismissed her with a wave of his hand and a command to go walk the village and get a feel for her people.

However today, the evidence was indisputable. Leanah counted a total of ten hens, down nearly five from last week. Death lingered in their animal pens, death from hunger and lack of rains these past few weeks.

All of this stood strong in Leanah's mind as she counted the hens and cocks. She was torn on the subject: Leanah felt the chickens needed to grow more, but her hunger lay bare in front of her. As her stomach growled, she closed her eyes and allowed for her pointing finger to wander from side to side, eventually settling by chance on a skinny bird huddling in the shadows against the chicken coop's wall.

"Have we found our dinner for tonight?" Leanah's mother asked. Serah, her mother, was a robust woman of little words—a perfect match for her husband. She stood cloaked in thin cloth that was not unlike those of the other women in the village.

Male visitors to the village, it was said, frequently confessed their interests in pursuing her affections. These rumors, however, Leanah never believed. She could not envision Hibert allowing such disrespectful behavior to continue in his presence. Still, she saw why her mother was considered beautiful. In the intense sun, her mother's skin was soft, a natural blush making her cheeks glow pink as if dusted with magical dust. Leanah had also inherited her mother's bright hazel eyes, expressive eyes that could boost your spirits with a smile or make you wish for death in dismay.

Leanah was familiar with both of these emotions. It was once said that Serah's own gazes and stares of disappointment could fell a dozen armies at once. And though it was all said in jest, Leanah knew the truth of her emotional hold on people.

"I am hesitant to choose one, mother."

Serah smiled and patted her child on the head. "There is no reason to be hesitant. Just pick one for dinner. We must do it soon so that we have time to clean and cook it."

Leanah closed her eyes and pointed in the corner, the same corner where the red female lay huddled against the wall.

"A fine choice, dear," Serah said. With that, she stepped into the coop while ignoring the clucks and concerned haws of the chickens. She approached their future meal and seized its head, spinning the body around twice, and letting it droop, lifeless."

Leanah looked on with great interest. The death was quick and clean and often amazed her. What amazed her even more was her mother's stoic demeanor as she took the life of their animals. Leanah found a comfort in watching her kill the chickens. This was a woman who was unafraid of doing what was necessary to feed her family. She remained respectful while practical, a trait that she often tried to emulate.

"Take this, Leanah, and take it inside." Serah offered the chicken to her daughter and high-stepped her way out of the chicken coop.

"But what do I do with it?" she asked. "Leanah, you're fifteen years of age. You should know how to prepare a good dinner for your future husband by now."

The term future husband felt distant and strange in the forefront of her mind. To have a future husband, did she not first need a current boyfriend or any male friends?

"Take the chicken over there and being pulling out the feathers."

Of course. First the feathers, she thought. Leanah sat on the ground and grabbed a fistful of bird's red feathers. They felt coarse in her hand, rough the way her father's hair felt. These poor chickens, even they were not getting the nutrients they needed to be a strong, healthy dinner for her family.

"I'll be back to see how you are doing," Serah said with a smile. She stood at the doorway to observe for a mere five seconds before disappearing into the darkness of the house.

This was her chance, she knew, and Leanah slid her bottom along the rust-colored ground. Her mother would yell at her later for being so reckless with her clothing, but Leanah was glad to take the consequences later. She needed answers now.

"We must find a way to tell her, Hibert. If we do not, she will become an enemy of her own village."

Enemy? Leanah thought.

"We cannot tell her," Hibert's voice thundered. "You cannot imagine what that would do to a little girl."

"And you think you know the heart of a little girl?" said Serah. "She is very much like you. Strong-willed and stubborn. She will survive if she knows the truth."

"And what then? We tell her and let her become an enemy anyway? We are already doomed to be destroyed by our own curse, Serah. I do not see how frustrating my little girl will help us save our village." Leanah poked her head into the doorway of the kitchen and watched as the distant shadowy figure of her father sat down, burying his head in his hands. "This is my penance, Serah. My penance for the crimes during the War."

Serah's own shadowy figure sat down beside her husband and gave him a hug. "You know that is not true. The Gods have rewarded us with a beautiful daughter and a thriving village."

"We thrive, yes, but for how long? We have no rain. No food. Traders will not come to the village. We have naught but rock and dust to make due, Serah. Like it or not, we either move the village or welcome our destruction."

Leanah hands slacked at the thought of moving all four to five hundred people in a massive caravan. The uprooting of so many people would cause even more destruction, more damage. She could not leave her home, her people.

The chicken's almost bare skin made a wet slap against the cobblestone floor of the kitchen.

"Leanah?" Serah called out. "How are you doing, dear?"

Leanah struggled to grab the chicken by head—its eyes staring direction at Leanah, seemingly asking her not to eat it—and go back outside to play pretend.

"I'm sorry I forgot about you, dear," Serah said. "Your father and I just needed to talk."

"Who was that man, mother?"

"What man?" she said. Serah took the chicken from her daughter's grip and checked over the body. "You did pretty well, Leanah." She flipped the chicken over and checked its belly. "Although it looks like you missed a spot here." Another pause as she inspected the body. "And here. And here." Serah smiled. "Well, at least you got most of it off."

"Mother, that man, at the throne room. Who was he?"

Serah's eyes seemed to turn a dark brown as they peered

downwards at the chicken's corpse. "Your father would be angry if I told you."

"Who is he?" Leanah asked. Her voice cracked as she said this. "I need to know. I can feel the danger, mother. Look at the chickens. They don't thrive the way they used to. Dust covers everything, our ground is so dry. The skies have not let loose their rains in weeks, if not an entire moon cycle." Leanah swallowed, hesitating. "Our village is heading for catastrophe, isn't it?"

Serah placed the chicken on the ground and seized her daughter's quivering body. "Of course not, dear. We have gone through difficult times before, and things tend to cycle around. Do not worry, my dear, sweet daughter. We will survive. Vamori will survive as we have survived in the past."

"Mother? Who was that strange man?"

"He was a Shaper, dear. Your Shaper."

"Mine?"

Leanah had heard about Shapers before from her studies with Ciaran. Shapers were monks, cloistered away in a far-off citadel. To be a Shaper meant a life of solitude and loneliness. At least this is how Ciaran had presented it. Shapers were forbidden to interact with the outside world.

"Why do I have a Shaper?"

Serah paused, peering into the Leanah's eyes. She detected a hint of sorrow, maybe hesitation behind her mother's eyes. "Because you are important, dear."

"But why is he out of the Citadel?" Leanah said. "I thought they were forbidden to leave."

Serah's laugh sounded uneasy. "That's nonsense, dear. Can you imagine anyone being held up in their world, away from everyone else?"

Leanah felt the shock of having such truths strike deep into her chest. She felt similar, kept away from the realities of the world. Locked away from politics.

The words made perfect sense to Leanah's sensibilities, but something felt wrong in her heart. All of this information conflicted with her lessons about Shapers from Ciaran—an outsider. Her mother was a local and could not possibly benefit from lying to her daughter.

"Can I meet him?" Leanah asked.

"You already did." Serah smiled. "Just then at the throne room."

"I mean a proper introduction. May I visit him? Or maybe we can send for him? I have so many questions for him!" Leanah's voice picked up speed with excitement. She felt her head spin with questions and words and wonders that no other adult would ever, ever answer. Then, a sudden halt as one big question entered her mind. "Has the Shaper said anything about the fate of our village?"

"There is nothing to worry about, Leanah." Serah's voice felt like a cool drink of water to Leanah's dry, thirsty ears. Comforting and gentle. Serah pulled Leanah closed to her chest and squeezed her tightly. "I promise."

And with that, Leanah's fears fell to the wayside as she listened to the soothing beat of her mother's heart.

FOUR

After dinner, Leanah chose to visit the chickens in their coop. The sun had begun to set behind the gray and orange Kaveranos Mountains to the west. The air had already begun to carry a deep chill into the village. It would no doubt be another night for fur blankets to keep warm.

The chickens huddled together inside the roost, built by her father to ensure a warm place for the chickens to hatch their eggs. No warmth meant no new chicks and, potentially, no new meat. Their source of bulls and calves died nearly a year ago with the latest outbreak of disease and infestation.

As Leanah studied the formation of the stars, she remembered the last time she was allowed to sit outside undisturbed. These moments came to her rarely, if at all.

The last time—Leanah had thought she had buried these memories—was during the last cattle outbreak. To keep her protected from the disease and from the sight of such pain and frustration, her father commanded that she remain at the house, held away from the realities of the village.

She did as she was asked, but only out of respect for her mother. When they had arrived back at the house, Leanah greeted them with excitement and anticipation of stories, neither of which was returned by her parents.

Her father sent her to bed, her mother brought her a drink of water.

"We'll talk later," her mother lied.

That night, Leanah went to bed with the deep feeling in her gut that everything was wrong. The sun felt warmer, the nights colder. Animals were falling dead from diseases no one had cataloged. Indeed, it was the first time Leanah understood the meaning of dread.

Comparing that night with this one, Leanah looked upon the chickens, keeping warm and sharing their body heat with each other. "At least you are all free," she said. Leanah sat down on the rust-colored floor and attempted to catch a glimpse of the entire flock inside the roost. "And none the wiser of your plight." She leaned over, forcing her eyes to squint and focus into the darkness of the covered roost. "But you know, don't you? You feel it coming, too." Leanah sighed and looked back up at the stars.

The twinkling jewels set against the black velvet of the sky, the moon a giant pearl shining her brilliance back to her face, Leanah felt comfort in these things, that something larger than her remained consistent. No matter what happened around her, she knew that something would stay the same. Safety in familiarity.

But all of the clues pointed toward the same thing: the lands were changing, falling apart and threatening all life.

The sword. It seemed to be the answer to everything. Her village's beloved savior and protector would now be the end of everything she knew and loved. She wished she could just grasp the sword in her hands and destroy it, kill it before it killed them.

She laughed.

How can you kill something as old as a God? If Ciaran told the truth, how can you destroy a God but with another God?

She was no God. At least she did not feel like any God she knew about.

"Leanah, it's time you came in. It's getting dark and cold."

"I'm fine, Mother," she cried out.

"Listen to your mother." Hibert's voice boomed, even outside. "Get in the house."

Leanah stood up and stared into the sky. She spotted her favorite star, the one in the far east that twinkled pink and red during the sunset. "Please, Elders of old. Please do not let famine and destruction come to my village. Protect my people and protect my family. I beg of you."

"Who are you talking to?" Hibert stood by the front of the entryway. "Get in here."

"No one, Father," said Leanah. She bowed her head and smiled. "Straight away."

"Leanah!" called out Serah. "You have a visitor."

Leanah rested a tired, unsuspecting foot onto the ground and felt for her skin rugs. The chill of last night had just begun to disappear, the sun's rays acting slower than normal to warm the day.

"Leanah! Are you up?"

"Yes, mother. I'm up."

Leanah remained unsure if she was truly being heard all the way out into the meeting room, but the noise from her mother ceased. This, she thought, was a good thing.

"You have a visitor, now hurry up and get dressed." Leanah's mother burst into her room, pushing aside the red cloth that hung as a door between her room and the hallway. Wood had been too scarce, the Oak Woods too dangerous, for lumber to be used in the village as anything but front doors and tools. This meant almost no privacy in for Leanah, who had a yearning for solace and silence much more than normal these past few years.

"Who is it at this hour?"

"This hour?" Serah laughed. "My dear, you've slept past the morning. The sun is already at its highest."

"Midday sun?" Leanah stuck her head out the window and into the streets. "You let me sleep that long?"

"You must have needed it," Serah said. "Quickly, now dear." She clapped her hands together twice. "Get dressed."

Leanah threw on a new tunic and leggings and left to meet her visitor.

Midway down the hallway, Leanah spotted a silver shine beam into her eyes. "What are you doing here?"

"You did say you would see me tomorrow." The voice paused and cleared its throat. "I do believe tomorrow would be today."

"Ciaran, you incessant—"

"So glad you could come wake her up," Serah interrupted. "I was afraid she would stay in bed all day."

"Is that a crime?" Leanah asked.

"It ought to be. Just look at how beautiful it is outside. There are even clouds outside and winds are picking up. There may be hope for rain yet."

Leanah smiled and glanced upwards at the sky. Her lips mouthed the words "thank you" to the sky and then she returned her glance to Ciaran. "Fine," she said. "Lead on."

Leanah picked a strand of yellow straw grass and rested it between her lips. She closed her eyes and focused a stream of gentle air across the top of the blade of grass. The blade fluttered in her hand before finally falling to the ground. "In the past, I used to make these whistle."

"Ah, you would need far greener grass than this," Ciaran said. He knelt down and grasped the straw grass with his hands, yanking up a handful still clung together by its roots. "This is barely fit enough to feed a bluhorn."

"Fortunately, we don't have many bluhorn left."

The bluhorn population did not remain untouched by the recent drought and influx of strange diseases. These hoofed, mountain goats thrived well in the Kaverano Mountains, feeding on the plant-life and remaining safe in the mountaintops. It is believed that the bluhorns' only natural predators are man and Shadowed Wings.

Over time, Vamori found a use for the creatures, harnessing their strength to plow and build farmlands. Some took in a bluhorn as pets, though the massive animals could easily eat a family into poverty.

Thus, the sudden drop of bluhorn had impacted the Vamori village's ability to maintain farmland and keep pets.

"Leanah, I feel I should apologize for yesterday." Ciaran's eyes refused to meet Leanah's. "It was inappropriate to spread these rumors to you and allow you to feel blame for something so far outside of your control."

"You have no reason to apologize. It was the truth."

"But I overstepped my boundaries. My job is to teach, not to manipulate."

"You were teaching me about our history. Let's leave it at that." Leanah extended her hand to Ciaran. He grabbed it, shook it twice and then stuck his hands back underneath his brown cloak. "So now tell me, what is it we are learning today?"

"I thought maybe we can continue some of our history lesson from yesterday."

Leanah shot him a glance, hopeful at first, and then damning. "What else am I responsible for?"

Ciaran raised a thick eyebrow. "No, please do not misunderstand me." He smiled to disarm the situation. Leanah's tension did not relax. "I mean to simply extend the story about the Elders."

"What is the point of spreading such rumors?" she said. "We both know that the gods have never existed. They are dead, gone."

"Not true. Not true at all." Ciaran pointed to the left at the fork, motioning them to go further down the fields. "You see, the Elders, when they fell from the sky, they came to our lands as a different object, different shapes. They hide among us."

"You lie."

"Do I?" Ciaran smiled. He seemed entertained by the challenge. "How do you know?"

"Have you ever seen an Elder?"

Ciaran rested his hands against his chin and thought for a moment. "Yes, I suppose I have seen many."

"Many?"

"Yes. Many. In my travels from land to land."

"Where have you gone?"

"I've been all around. Here and there. Looking for this and that." Ciaran smiled and pulled his cloak closer to his body. "You know. The usual type of journeys."

"Why is it so difficult to get a decent, straight answer out of anyone's mouth in this forsaken town?"

Leanah stomped ahead of her tutor, breaking free and running about, tumbling and rolling around in the crispy grass.

"You have quite the skills there, Leanah. I know I did not teach you that."

"I like to watch the boys spar in the town center." Leanah stood up and adjusted her ponytail. "I've learned a thing or two from watching them."

"You seem like a natural."

"You think so?" Leanah beamed from ear to ear. "Do you honestly believe I'm a natural?"

"A natural? Sure. Humans are born to fight, to struggle, to kill."

"We are born to live," Leanah corrected. "Not kill."

"I have seen many things in my journeys, little girl. Things that would scare your wits from you. Things that would make you refuse to go to bed at night. Things that would destroy your hopes, shatter your dreams."

"Is the whole world so dreary?"

"No, of course not. In some places, there are young women like you, strong. Outspoken. Brave."

Leanah scoffed.

"You are indeed brave," he said. "You brave the penalties of admonishment when you sneak around the town. You brave the people here despite what you know they think of you."

Leanah felt her shoulders slump.

"And above all, you feel the urge to be into battle, to jump and roll and hit. These are not actions of cowards. These are the actions of bravery, of a person who will not settle with defeat, with failure." Ciaran grasped Leanah's chin and raised to face for his eyes to meet hers. "You are a special young lady with an interesting future ahead of you."

"What do you know of my future?" Leanah broke free of Ciaran's grip. "What do you know of me, anyway?"

"I know much more than you think, Leanah. I know that you are destined for greatness, as are many spirited ladies around the realm."

"So you try to woo me?"

Ciaran laughed. "You are like a daughter to me, Leanah. I could not woo my daughter." He barked another laugh, this one deeper, but shaky with anxiety. "You are my pupil, and I your teacher. That is the extent of our relationship."

"I would not want to see my father's reaction were to tell him that you looked upon me as woman and not your daughter."

"I would not want to see your father's hands around my neck were you to share that information."

"You have no worries about that, as long as you remain truthful in your tales."

"I am being as honest and truthful as I can be."

"Then tell me," she said. "What happens to the town if the sword is not fed?"

"There will be certain and inevitable destruction."

Leanah took a step back. Her chest felt tight, squeezing her lungs to the point of near suffocation. It was one thing to suspect it, but another entirely to hear the words from someone else's mouth.

"Don't tell me you're surprised," he said. "Look around you. The heat, the mountains, the deaths. You mean to tell me that this is not the will of the gods? A way to punish Vamori for not following through with its rituals?"

"Then why don't we follow through? Why do we wait?"

"Basic tradition demands it," he said. "We must follow the rules or we are doomed to failure."

"And what, exactly, are the rules?" Leanah stood in front of Ciaran, held her feet steadfast into the ground. She would not allow him move, or her to be moved. "Tell me. Now."

Ciaran looked away, then pulling his cloak up over his head, he said, "The ritual is fairly simple. I've never seen it myself, but legend has it that the male son of the chieftain must take the sword on a journey, to a distant land, the Swamps of Mrondir, and slay a Shadowed Wing. Only when the sword has quenched its thirst will it go back to sleep and protect your village again."

"And if we remove it? Take it away before it wakes up?"

"Sudden ruin. Do you not think that has already been tried? Centuries ago someone decided that the sword was too much of a burden to the people. There were attempts to rid the village of it. All attempts failed when there was a massive flood that washed away people, cattle, bluhorns. All suffered because their stupidity and refusal to listen to the gods."

"You go back to this question of the Gods, but tell me, why would they turn on us? Why make it that we must go out of our way to serve them, when they do nothing in return? You're so smart, a well-traveled man. Tell me, why would they use us so?"

"I fear I do not have an answer for that, Leanah. It would be unfair for me to assume the nature of the will of the gods."

"Pfft," Leanah said. "Will of the Gods. The gods seek to

destroy us. Nothing more. Nothing less." Leanah knelt down to grab another handful of straw grass. "Look at this!" The grass flipped over itself, fluttering back to the ground. "The grass, once green is now yellow, dry. Dead. Even the land itself is dying. And this serves the Gods' purpose how? How does this make things better?"

"Leanah, I believe we need to calm down here."

"What purpose does it serve to destroy those who revered you? Why would a mother or a father slay its own child? None of this makes any sense," she said. "None of it." Leanah felt her chest heave with the pressure of her words, the stress of knowing that deep down, she felt she was right.

"Many before you have attempted to solve this same problem, Leanah. In all my travels, hundreds of learned men attempted to determine the will of the Gods, to plan for their whims. All of failed, ending back at the primary question. Why do bad things happen when the Gods are supposed to care?"

"And their answers?"

"Their answers ended in failure." Ciaran's voice quieted down, solemn and regretful. "That, I believe, is one of life's greatest mysteries. That all-powerful, mysterious question: Why?"

"And here we are, suffering," Leanah said. Her hands let loose the rest of the straw grass, letting it tickle her palms as it fell to the ground.

As she did this, darkness blinked over them. "The clouds are traveling faster, covering the sun, Leanah." Perhaps we should begin to head back.

Leanah nodded and followed her tutor back toward the village.

"Ciaran," she said. "Do you believe we will ever discover the will of the Gods?"

"I believe that one day we may stumble upon it, but if we do, it will only be by accident."

Upon reaching the outskirts of the village, Ciaran waved goodbye to Leanah and returned to his home. Leanah began walking home, looking forward to playing in the rain and watching her chicken friends drink of the fresh rain water.

The skies had gotten dark, the clouds hanging low and heavy with—what Leanah hoped—rainwater.

"Great!" shouted the voice of a boy not much younger than Leanah. As she crossed the center of the village, Leanah found the boy shouting this at her. She knew not his name, but had frequently observed him practicing sword fighting with his friends and teacher. She had seen him spar many times. He had better skills than his friends, as evidenced by the fact that many of his friends wore bruises and cuts and scrapes like one wears a tunic or sandals. "Please, Leanah. Go away so it can finally rain."

"What's that supposed to mean?"

"You're a curse to this village. My uncle says so."

"You're uncle's a drunkard!" Leanah shouted back. In truth, she had no idea who his uncle was, but it was worth a shot.

"And you're a curse to this village. You'll be the death of Vamoril!"

"Take that back!" Leanah demanded. Her foot stamped the ground in front of her. Her hands and arms stretched out to her side, tense, fists clenched. "Take that back or I'll beat it out of you."

The boy laughed and pointed at her. "You couldn't beat me. A girl? You have funny jokes, girl."

"Take it back!"

"I will not!" The boy pointed his wooden practice sword into the sky. "Look at that? See how those clouds move quickly? Even they see what curses you bring to them. It will not rain because of you. You have doomed this village."

"Enough of this talk!" Leanah picked up a rock, sharp against her fingertips and stared at her target: between his eyes.

She grit her teeth, kept her eyes focused and let the rock fly into the air. It flipped over itself, rotating in a circle until she heard a loud click of the rock bouncing off the edge of the boy's wooden sword.

"Not a bad shot," he said. "But you can't just throw a rock at me and expect it to hit."

"I can this time!" Leanah screamed and let loose another rock. This one fell smack into the boy's forehead. The hit shocked him at first, causing him to step backward and regain control. Then, without such warning as a grunt or a yell, the lowered his head and rammed forward into Leanah's gut. The force threw both of them to the ground, kicking up orange dust.

Leanah gasped for breath. Her lungs felt heavy, deflated. The boy grasped hold of Leanah's tunic and pulled back a tight fist. "Stupid witch!" he exclaimed.

Leanah felt the warmth of blood rush to her face. The boy had probably cracked her nose bone, though she felt too much rage and frustration to stop and recognize the difference.

"I'll kill you!" she said and flipped the boy over her with her knees. Next she flipped over and slammed her knees into the boy's stomach. His face turned pale as he spat on his own cheek.

"Stop!" the boy cried out, but Leanah could not hear the words. She felt nothing but the rush of her knuckles against his cheekbones.

"Leanah! Stop this instant!" Ciaran's hand gripped Leanah's shoulder and pulled her backward. "This is not how you deal with problems!"

"He started it!" she said. Leanah stepped toward the accusing young boy, only to be held back by the surprisingly strong hand of Ciaran.

"He started it!" she yelled. "Tell him to stop!"

"Run along. Now," Ciaran commanded. The boy's face turned downward, unsure of just how much trouble he could really get in. "Or I shall have to tell Hibert what you did to his only daughter."

The boy did not need to be told again. He turned and ran into the distance, hiding among the distant houses along the far eastern edge of the village.

"What was that about?" he asked.

"He called me a witch!"

Ciaran sighed and pulled Leanah closer to his chest. "You cannot go off the handle whenever there is someone who accuses you of a great evil. You will find that many people will accuse you throughout your life. You cannot kill all who come your way."

"Then what do you suggest I do?" she asked. Leanah wiped away tears, welling up not from pain but frustration.

"You become the strongest person you can. In strength lies confidence and power to make a difference."

Leanah nodded. She only understood half of that sentence. "How can strength lead to power? Isn't strength power?"

Ciaran grinned, then shook his head. "In time, Leanah. In time. Now let's get you back to your home."

Leanah returned to her home with her head hanging low. In her head, she played out the scene already. If anything, her father was predictable.

Ciaran knocked on the door.

"Why hello, Ciaran. Leanah, what happened?"

Ciaran waited for Leanah to respond before finally saying, "Your daughter had a bit of a mishap. A fight, really. It seemed that a young boy taunted her into a struggle."

Serah face turned south as she seized her daughter from Ciaran's loose grip and held her close. "Are you hurt?" Serah's hands ran over her daughter's face. "Have you been injured?"

"Just blood," Leanah said. She pointed to her nose, but it stung too much to touch it. "Nothing big."

"Nothing big?" Serah gasped. "Thank you, Ciaran. I hope you know who this little runt was?"

Ciaran smiled. "I would not worry about it. It's been handled."

Leanah buried her head into her mother's shoulder and let the tears flow willingly from her eyes. Nothing Ciaran could say will save her from the wrath of her father.

"Thank you for bringing this to my attention," said Serah. "I do not appreciate you handling the situation on your own. It was not your responsibility."

"Oh, but you entrusted Leanah under my tutelage. If anything she is my responsibility, madam." Ciaran looked up and bowed slightly. "If you won't mind me saying so, of course."

Serah smiled. "Yes. Of course. You're right."

Leanah noticed a marked lack of emotion from that last statement.

"If you'll excuse us," said Serah. "I need to get her cleaned up."

"Of course," said Ciaran. He rested his hand on Leanah's shuddering shoulder. "We'll continue our lessons tomorrow, then?"

Leanah nodded her head while still buried in her mother's side.

"Excellent. Take care, Leanah."

"If your father found out, he'd have that poor boy killed," Serah said. She pulled Leanah to backyard and dabbed a cloth in the chicken's drinking pond. "Out of respect for you, I'll withhold this from your father's knowledge. But if he finds out, I will do nothing to keep you from his punishments."

"Mother!" Leanah cried out. The skin on her face pulled downward with each aggressive stroke. The combination of damp skin and dry winds made her skin feel rough, raw as exposed muscle. "You won't have to tell him." Leanah swallowed. "I will."

The rag smeared across Leanah's upper lip harder, more aggressive. "You will do no such thing!" her mother said. "You must keep your mouth shut. This behavior of yours, it is unbecoming of our future chieftain."

"Mother, look at me!" she said. "Am I really fit to be a chieftain?"

"You will make a fine chieftain," her mother said. "If you wish to be."

That was the question, Leanah thought. If things were to work out according to her parents' plan, then it would be necessary for her to answer that question. "Where is father?" Leanah held her mother's hand still, the rag dripping dark round spots on the dusty ground beneath them.

"Your father is out with the hunts. They need more eyes to find meat for the village," she said. "He offered." Serah freed her hand and wiped away the last of the dirt away from her daughter's cheek. "You know how much your father missed the wars. Hunting mountain elk is the closest thing to war he will get at his old age."

"He's not that old, is he?"

Serah's laughter shook the hand that grasped Leanah still. "Oh dear, when you get older, you will understand."

"When I get older," Leanah whispered.

FIVE

Serah had banished her daughter to her own bedroom until her father came home.

Leanah, however, did not see it so much as a punishment. She pulled out the bones and her skin cloth. Stretching out the cloth as wide as it will go, she tossed the bones out into the cloth and watched where they lie. The bones, according the trader who had stopped in her village nearly three years ago, belonged to the hands of ancient magi. These magi had worshipped the dead gods. The trader had made a big deal about offering these to Leanah. "You have great skill," he muttered in a low whisper. "The magicks of a mage come from their hands, and so it is their hand bones that contain great power."

Leanah felt a certain solace in acknowledging that she might have something special within her.

The bones fell in a significant distance from each other. Each of them, parallel to the other, not touching and far-reaching across the cloth.

"This is," Leanah grasped for ideas in her head. "I don't know what this means!" she said. In frustration, she scrapped the bones across her room and listened to them clink against the far wall.

"That boy," Leanah muttered. "That boy did this to me."

Her hands grasped the windowsill. She pulled herself up to peer out at the rest of the world. Down below, the salty, succulent smell of dinners wafted into the airs. Leanah smelled the hints of spicy meats and vegetables, grilled and charred in the hearths of the people in their smaller houses. Leanah listened for the click click click of her own mother's knife cutting the potatoes for tonight's dinner.

She heard nothing.

Out of hunger, Leanah stepped down the hallway and into the kitchen. Instead of hearing the sizzle of food on the fire, her ears detected the squeal of happiness coming from the village's gates.

"Mother?" she asked.

Leanah left the house—she'll face the consequences later—and walked the short distance to the front gates of the village. A small crowd gathered as the women and children huddled in groups to welcome home their men.

For some reason, Leanah had thought about feeding the pigeons just yesterday.

"They come with meals!" a woman cried out. "Look!"

The village women cheered in unison as the group of hunters trudged closer and closer to the village gates. "Open the gates! Let them in! Let them in!"

The gates opened wide, but slowly, as the teenage boys too young to go hunting grasped the ropes and pulled. Leanah, fearing that it would take them too long to open the gates for her father, grabbed hold of the end of the rope and yanked harder.

The boy in front of her—as if by magic—appeared to be the boy she had so harshly beaten not an hour ago.

He flinched as Leanah grabbed the rope to help. "Don't flatter yourself," she said to him. "Now pull."

The gates opened with a slow, steady motion, eventually wide enough for the fifteen men of the village to return, half of whom bore the carcass of a hooved animal from the mountains.

"Are those bluhorns?" a woman whispered. "Surely they are not bluhorns! The Elders will ruin us for sure!"

"Nonsense!" another woman exclaimed. "The horns are short and flat. These are a new species."

"But the markings on the fur! They must be bluhorn!"

Leanah listened as the voices spread rumors and questions faster as the men got closer and closer. Soon, they all had passed the door and the children pushed the gates closed.

The women gave in to their instincts and abandoned all propriety, running to their husbands and kissing their cheeks and faces.

"Father!" Leanah cried out. "Why did you not tell me you were leaving?"

"You were away with your studies," Hibert said and patted her on the head. He turned his head to face the crowd and raised both of his hands into the air. The crowd hushed each other, eventually a wave of shushes and silence overcame the people.

"Beloved Vamori!" he cried out. "We were blessed during our hunt and today we bring seven offerings from the Kaverano!"

The crowd cheered and stomped its feet.

"Today, we feast like the days of old. Together and victorious! Let us celebrate!"

The crowd broke into a wild cheer and the corpses of the goats were pulled away into the distance, toward the village center.

"Hibert," Serah said, "you look sad."

"It's nothing, Serah. Look at how much food we brought back!"

"Hibert, what is it?"

Hibert looked at Leanah and pressed her lightly against her shoulders. "Run along and feed the chickens. We'll return shortly."

Leanah nodded and knew what that command really was. "Of course, Father." Leanah ran a few steps toward her house but slowed her pace and ran to the side, hiding behind a cart to listen to her father and mother.

"Serah, I fear for our village."

"But our bounty today!" Serah said. Leanah recognized her mother's tone, the one meant to boost spirits. "We'll be fine tonight."

Hibert shook his head. "I commanded that those beasts be prepared for dinner because we did something inexcusable, Serah. Those beasts we slew were our own bluhorns."

"Hibert." Serah paused, then took her husband's strong hand and led him to the village center. "Allow them to eat. They won't know the difference."

Leanah's heart sunk deep into her chest. Despite her mother's best attempts to remain cheerful, Leanah witnessed the destruction of her village one day at a time. Today, it was eating their own work animals. Tomorrow, who knows?

Leanah gathered these secrets in her heart and traveled back to her house. As she crossed into the house, her thoughts shifted to the sword. Everything could still be saved. If only someone could slay the Shadowed Wing.

Leanah heard footsteps behind her. She rushed to the backyard and stood by the chicken coop. Maybe it was just a trick of the light, maybe her own pessimism, but the birds appeared shallower, smaller. Their clucks excited at the sight of her and the handful of grains she sifted into their grains.

One. Two.

Leanah counted the chickens as they bustled around the coop, fighting for feed.

Three. Four.

"Where are you, little guy?"

Leanah knelt down and peered into the coop. The youngest, a white with red spots, lay on the floor of the enclosed shelter. Its breathing looked fast, afraid. "What's the matter, little one?"

Leanah knelt closer to the opening, closing one eye, then the other, to get a better look inside. The young cock had not come out to eat. Waiting for it to come out, Leanah decided, would not make it come out any faster.

It, too, would be dead soon. Leanah stifled back tears and turned to see her mother stand at the doorway. "Come, help us with the meat." Serah's eyes turned to concern. "Come here, what is the matter, child?"

Leanah shook her head and said nothing, instead taking the few steps and landing in her mother's arms once again.

The men gathered around the fire as the women worked to cut the meat into responsible portions for the village. With five hundred people, the seven corpses, even stretched thin, would not offer enough meat to make everyone happy. Still, it was more than they had seen a long, long while.

Leanah had broken free from the gossiping women. She grew

tired of being shoved off to the side, being in the way of everyone no matter where she stood or what she was doing.

Instead, she watched as the men sat around the fire, the orange glow flickering shadows across the flat dirt lands. They cheered and shared stories in bursts of drunken, hearty laughter. Leanah not understand much of their stories, but she stood hidden behind them all, listening to the suspense of attacking goblins, elk, and giants.

These were the stories she wanted to know, the knights of old.

"Hibert!" Fronir shouted above the rest of the men. "Tell us again about the Dallheim Wars! About that time you slew those magic-using sons of bastiches!"

Hibert laughed, his face turning a color of heat exhaustion and dripping beads of sweat from the fire. "It's been too long," he said. "I don't remember much."

"Nonsense!" Fronir exclaimed. "You know you remember. A battle that ferocious!" Fronir held his mug high into the air. "Never you mind! I'll tell the tale!"

All laughed and cheered as Fronir hopped on the stone table and knelt down, as if ready to pounce out on the villagers.

Leanah watched the faces of the boys and men circling the fires. She knew of the battles, but never the fine details. These battles, her father would say, were not important. What kind of man it made out of him was.

Leanah, however, never paid much attention to the results of the battle. Her heart was in the battle itself. She longed for the conflict and struggle. She wanted—no, needed—to know what success in battle felt like. Leanah had imagined it like a fiery burst in her chest, an explosion inside her heart. The kind of fierce joy that she witnessed in the boys at sword practice nearly every morning.

"Leanah!" Hibert said. "Come."

Leanah stood up and held her head low. She had seen someone speaking to him earlier, and the look on her father's face going from happy and cheerful to disappointed and angry. Leanah had hoped that she get a bite to eat before she was sent to her room again.

"Yes, Father?"

Hibert's large hands waved for Leanah to come join him, and upon reaching him, grabbed her shoulder and held it tightly against his side. "This is one of the fiercest warriors yet!" he shouted. The other men laughed and jeered.

"No, no!" Hibert said, holding his hands up to silence the cynical crowd. "Hear me out." Leanah felt the squeeze of Hibert's forearms on her back. "Just today she entered into battle and defeated the young Avaya boy!"

The crowd laughed and turned to Adrian Avaya, who sunk lower into his seat. "From what I hear, she has quite the warrior's spirit, just like her father!" he said.

Hibert's face turned still and emotionless. "Your son was begging for the beating, from what I understood."

The crowd grew silent and through his shaking forearms against her own body, Leanah felt her father's frustration and anger.

Adrian stood up. "And if your girl wasn't so cursed, we would never have been in this mess." He looked over to the crowd, but his eyes focused and stayed on the face of Leanah. "Your daughter is the possessed spawn of the dead Elders themselves, cursed to ruin this village."

Hibert's knuckles popped in quick succession as he formed a tight fist, large and tight as a small boulder. "You forget your place in this village, drunkard!"

"Father, please!" Leanah said. "He's had too much. Leave him be. He means nothing by it."

Hibert, however, shoved her off to the side, paying no attention to his daughter. "This daughter of mine will grow to be a fine warrior some day and lead this village to great victory!"

"She'll be the ruin of us all!" Adrian shouted. "We all know it."

The air grew cold, the crowd stepping back as if in silent agreement.

"We just sit and wait for the cataclysm that we all know is coming. And when we do, we will offer your daughter to save our pathetic hides!"

Hibert stepped forward and grabbed Adrian's face with his hands. His hands had been so large, Adrian's entire face lay smashed against the palm of Hibert's hand. "Say that again," said Hibert. His hands squeezed on the top and sides of his hand. "Please, I do not believe I heard you the first time."

"Father! Stop!" Leanah cried.

"Hibert, release him this instant!" Serah demanded. She carried a white stone plate of charred meats to the table. "You and your drunken escapades! What village will we have left if you kill all of our villagers?" she said.

The crowd broke into a drunken laughter, even Hibert's stone cold face gradually shifted from the stoic, angry red to a happy, glazed over smile that came with pint after pint of ale.

"Now eat before it gets cold," Serah said. She sent a wink at Leanah and then motioned for her to come help with serving of the food.

Leanah moved cautiously through the crowd, her legs feeling weak and flexible, as if the bones had been removed. Never before had she heard them speak so openly about her.

The rumors, she knew about, but now, so did her father.

Were they getting more daring? More angry with her?

Leanah attempted to lose herself in the serving of meats, as if nothing had happened, as if her father had not tried to squash the head of Adrian Avaya.

Everyone happily took a slice of meat from her and chewed on it contentedly.

This must be what it felt like to be her mother, a devoted keeper of the home. She loathed the feeling of being in service to a group of bumbling, drunken idiots.

"I saved you a piece," Serah said. She held a small white stone plate with both her soft hands. "For you."

Leanah looked at the meat and waved it off. "I'll be okay without it," she said. "You have it."

"Leanah, please. Do not be rude. Take this and eat it."

"No, I will not, Mother."

Hibert stood up. His shadow danced over Leanah's body. "Do as your mother told."

"I will not eat that."

Adrian's voice sounded over the crowds. "Sounds like your daughter has sworn off meat!" The crowd laughs. "What future chieftain refuses to eat meat!" Hibert's face grew a cold expression again.

"I will not be embarrassed by you again," he said into Leanah's ears. "You will take the meat," he said and seized the meat from his wife's hands. "And like it."

Leanah's hands held the plate, thrust into her hands by her father, and stared into the angry gaze of her father.

"I will not eat bluhorn," she said.

Some women near the fire gasped. The sound of men resting their plates on the stone table echoed into the night.

Hibert remained stoic, even stronger than before, and stepped so close to Leanah, she believed he might squash her with his giant boot. "You will return to the house and remain there until I am ready to talk to you!" Hibert's hand pointed at the house.

"You should be ashamed of yourself!" she said. "We do not eat our sacred animals!" she cried out. "It will surely bring more ruin to our village."

"No more than you've already brought upon us," Adrian said.

With that, Hibert lifted Adrian up into the air with his thick, muscled arms. "I thought I told you to be silent!" he screamed at him. Leanah watched as her father turned into something she had never seen before. An angry creature, twisted, darker than the father she knew before. "If you want to remain in this village, you will stop spreading this filth and lies!" Hibert looked away to Leanah and shouted at her. "Go! Now!"

Leanah felt her face and body feel warm from her nerves. This feeling, this is what she felt before attacking the Avaya boy. Leanah clenched her teeth tight and trudged along to the house.

In the far distance, Leanah heard the crashing of Adrian Avaya against the woodpile across the center. "Leave us, now!" her father roared at Adrian. "You are not welcome here."

The words, Leanah felt, echoed true to herself as well.

Leanah walked to her room, but stopped just short of going inside. The celebration would be going on for maybe another hour before the nighttime cold comes in, and so decided that she would rather spend her time with the chickens out back.

But when she went outside, nothing greeted her. The chickens lay huddled in the middle of their shelter. No doubt trying to stay warm.

Leanah sat outside and tried to peek at the chicks inside. She grabbed at her own shoulders to keep warm. The night had grown chilly despite her own fiery anger and rage inside.

"I thought I told you to remain in your room!" Hibert had found her sooner than she anticipated. "If you do not listen to me, you will only embarrass your family and yourself."

"I am the embarrassment?" she shot back. "You come home, hiding the true source of food from your own villagers? Is that what I'm supposed to learn here? To lie to my people?"

"You are too young to understand."

"And you go back to your usual defense. I'm too young to understand. I'm too young for this. Too young to learn how to fight."

"Your job is not to understand what I do, but to listen and do as I say!" Hibert stepped into the night sky, his face red and slick with sweat and frustration. "You challenge me in front of my own people, spread rumors about the meat and then defy my orders even now? Just who do you think you are, Leanah? I raised you to be a respectful leader, a child of compassion and honor. Your actions speak to none of this."

"You raised me to be a doting shadow in the back of the house. You raised me to do be the son you never had," Leanah said. "I know about everything, Father. I know about the village's destruction. I know about the dangers of not fulfilling the prophecy. I know how we will come to ruin." Leanah fell back on her feet. "It's true, isn't it?" she said. "It really is all my fault."

Hibert towered over her daughter. He moved as if he wanted to kneel down and comfort Leanah, but stopped short. "You will not disrespect me, my position as Chieftain, and your family. It is entirely uncalled for."

Leanah wiped away tears, sobbing into the arm of her cloth sleeves.

Hibert turned away to go into the house. His strong hand gripped the side of the doorway and paused. "Leanah," he said. "It was never your fault." His breath came out in a heavy sigh. "If anyone is to blame, it is me and my crimes during the War."

Leanah listened as Hibert's footsteps disappeared into the house.

"Ciaran!" Leanah shouted. "Ciaran!"

Ciaran opened the door to his hut and peered outside. "Leanah, you will get both of us burned at the stake with your shouting. Get inside!"

Leanah did as he commanded. "Tell me about more about the village traditions!"

Ciaran thrust a tired finger into the corner of his eyes to wipe away the dust of sleeping. "And which traditions would those be?"

"Don't play with me, Ciaran. The sword tradition. What is to be done with the sword?"

"Leanah, can this wait until tomorrow?" Ciaran's skin seemed bright, even paler than Leanah had remembered. Even in this darkened night, she had never seen him appear so weak.

"No, this cannot wait until tomorrow. Our village is falling to ruin! We cannot find enough to eat. Did you know we have fallen to eating bluhorns? Bluhorns!" Leanah gasped for breath before continuing with her tirade. "We need to be saved, and surely our savior and protector, the sword of stone, must be fed or this village will waste away into nothingness! Even the chickens are dying!"

Leanah thoughts she noticed the gleaming of a toothy smile, but looking again, saw nothing but a smug look on Ciaran's face. "Why do you ask this now?"

"We need to be saved," Leanah said.

"And you are the one to do this?"

"If I must."

"Leanah."

"If I am the cause, then maybe I could cause something good. Cause some fortunate for our people."

Ciaran paused and crossed his arms. "The legend goes that one must take the sword to the Swamp of Mronir, slay the Shadowed Wing and feed the sword its blood."

"What does it mean, feed?"

Ciaran shrugged. "It means what it says, I suppose. How one feeds an inanimate object is beyond me." Ciaran turned away and entered the kitchen. "It was to be done by the chieftain's eldest son, however."

"And if it was done by the eldest daughter?"

"You would be the chieftain's only daughter."

"Only daughter, then?"

Ciaran arrived with a cup of a steaming liquid and offered it to Leanah. "The legends are quiet on that matter. You see, women were not to go into battle in the past. So naturally, the potential of having a woman handle the sword has never been discussed."

Leanah smiled. "Then there is always a first time."

"You do realize that if this doesn't work, you can bring the village to ruin?"

"And if it does work? What then?"

"If you remove the village's protector, you risk the village meeting certain danger. Rivals, death, pillagers. Then of course, you risk having your father look for you." Ciaran paused and leaned against the wall. "You have not thought this plan through, have you?"

"We have not the time to do so, Ciaran."

Ciaran smiled and nodded. "This," he said, "regrettably, is true."

"I will not sit back and allow my village to come to ruin."

"So it would seem," said Ciaran. "I cannot permit you to go alone."

"If we both go, then my father will have you hanged for sure. I must go alone."

"Then I will stay here and distract him, allow you for some time to escape with the sword tomorrow."

"There is no need for that," she said. "I'm stealing the sword tonight."

SIX

Ciaran had cautioned her against just walking up and taking the sword, but he said nothing against sneaking in and stealing it herself.

Leanah snuck through the silence of night to her father's throne room. As she crept through the darkness, she began to dig through buried memories—treasured memories—to determine just how she was going to steal the treasured relic.

As a child, Leanah remembered sneaking in and out of the room past the guards. Her footsteps made less sound then, being nearly half full-grown. Whenever she wanted, she was able to sneak into the throne room, hide behind a pillar and watch as her father conducted business and met with other local officials. The day-to-day business affairs made no sense to her. Worse yet, they bored her to death. But the thrill of sneaking in, of being a silent spy with her father being none the wiser, that was what she sought.

It wasn't until she grew older, however, that she realized the guards had been giving her leeway to sneak past them. Playing her game, it would seem.

This moment of sneaking past them, into the treasury room. This would be her moment of reckoning.

One of the other fine secrets her father shared with her was the secret escape. Her father had always had a contingency plan should he be attacked during negotiations, or if one of his subjects got a wild hair during a public meeting.

His plan? A secret escape for his family and valuable nobles who could not fight. Rarely, if ever, was Hibert afraid for his own life. The Stone Fist of the Dallheim Wars would surely never run from battle. It would be a disgrace, an embarrassment.

You will not embarrass your family.

Hibert's words echoed in her head as she sneaked around the largest building in Vamori. She had only known about the passage coming out. Never had she experienced going into the throne room.

"This is for you, Father," she whispered to herself, and held her hands flat against the wall. She pressed hard and spread her fingers out, searching for the crevices of a secret door or hidden entrance.

"Where are you?" she whispered. The guards, if she remembered correctly, watched over the area in far distances from each other—easily thirty to fifty paces each. This was enough for her small frame to sneak past without causing notice.

But, first thing first: she needed to sneak in.

"This is ridiculous," she mumbled to herself. Leanah took three steps to the right, trying to remember just where she exited during her father's initial instructions. She only remembered a small passageway and bright, piercing light.

And a smell. Something putrid. Sour.

Like animal dung.

Leanah stopped, allowing her head to flip from side to side. Where were the animal pens? In her years of living there, she did not remember any animal pens around the area. The animals were held off to the west, toward the loftier and greener pastures toward the mountains. Letting the water travel from the mountain sides to the drinking bins required the least amount of effort.

The west. Coming downwind. Leanah followed her view of the mountains to the building. Her eyes landed on a ledge just three large steps away from where Leanah stood. "Jackpot."

Leanah side-stepped to that side of the wall and pressed her fingertips against it. There, she found a ridge, a long ridge, that traced into the shape of rather large, man-sized door. With her fingers, she pried into the edges, looking for something to open up the door. She pressed every rock and bump she could find. One particular crevice, however, stood out more than the others. She wrapped her hands around it, pulling with all of her might until she very nearly had her feet against the wall, pulling out.

It would not budge.

Leanah, exhausted, leaned against the wall and peered around. The guards had not witnessed her sneaky activities, and for this she was feeling blessed.

This was a message from the Gods, even if her father did not believe in them any longer.

"Come on, please," she said, looking up into the sky. There, she found her three stars, the ones that made a shape she viewed as a dog, two feet and a bright star for the head. "Please, help me save my village."

Leanah rested her head against the wall and closed her eyes. She needed rest if she was going to pry her way into the doorway again.

She took a deep breath, her chest rising up deep, holding in the fresh, cool air, and exhaling.

As her lungs released the air, she felt something move behind her. A portion of the wall had begun to give way under her weight.

The central panel of the door pressed inward and the door shifted, releasing dust and dirt into the air. Leanah coughed, but tried to hold it in. What came out was a muffled harumpth that she swore would get her caught. She paused, waiting for something to stumble her way, to check on the sound.

After a few heartbeats had passed, Leanah dug her hands into the doorway and pulled. It opened with surprising ease, a fact that she felt her father should know about. But probably not until she got back from her journey.

Leanah crept into the building and pulled the door closed behind her. As she did so, the light disappeared into a thin line, then disappeared completely, engulfing Leanah in a darkness that left her paralyzed and cold.

No torches and nothing to light the way, Leanah stumbled down the hallway with her hands against the wall for support. Her footsteps were small, no bigger than a young infant learning to walk. A frustrated scream curdled in Leanah's throat, but she swallowed it. At this rate, it would take her too long to reach the sword. She would get caught, be in even more trouble, and watch as her village died around her.

Leanah held fast against the wall, braving larger steps as she moved forward, or so she had hoped. In this extreme darkness, even pausing once to rest against the wall could leave her disoriented and moving backward. With her luck, she'd be traveling back and forth all night.

Her feet stepped onto something soft, squishy beneath her feet. Her sandaled foot pressed down on lit lightly at first, noticing it give way and stretch outwards.

It was a small body. A dead rat by the size.

Leanah shuddered. Trying to keep her feet near the ground, she let her foot slide off the rat's corpse and onto solid, rocky ground. Leanah moved her toes around, feeling for anything slick. Maybe blood leaked into her toes.

Her foot felt cold and dry, the only time she felt thankful to be such.

Her journey reached the end after two more long strides, her nose almost coming into contact with the stone cold wall before her.

Every inhale brought more dust into her nose, that sour, slimy smell of fungus filling her nostrils. Leanah held her breath and reached around, grasping at anything that appeared as a handle or button. The technology in this area was ancient, older than many of the towns before them. It used to be a central worship center for the Kaverin, and the priests and priestesses had access to knowledge that was lost long ago to her people today.

She remembered the first time she went through those caverns. The button, her father called it, was located in the center of the doorway.

Leanah's fingers once again traced the door's outlines. Then, measuring as well as she could in the darkness, she pressed her hands in the middle of the doorway and searched around.

Something sharp pressed into Leanah's palm, and rather than shout or squirm, Leanah raised her fist and pounded it into the doorway.

Something appeared to shift, making a hollow clicking noise

before the door popped open slowly. Leanah once again pulled the door open and poked her head inside. Her eyes met with moonlight. Moonlight from the windows of the Treasury.

Leanah bit her tongue to keep from squealing in delight. She never imagined being able to make it in here this easily, thankful that her memories of her childhood had remained intact.

Leanah stepped past the stacks of precious ore and shiny metal objects that her village had procured in the past. The riches had come to this vault thanks to the Dallheim Wars and the victories of Hibert's men. Another reason that Hibert had become so popular despite his aggressive and secretive nature.

When the villagers realized they had the wealth to bargain with the other villages, they immediately granted him access to the Sword of Stone and allowed for him to feed it. His successes came back with the understanding that he would-be ruler.

This room's precious glow was owed to her father. More legends and pressures to live up to.

Leanah snuck toward a metal strongbox. The box had been closed, but not locked. It hadn't a lock on it since Leanah had first discovered it. The original logic, her father had told her, was that the Sword of Stone belonged to the village, and thus all people should have access to it.

"But why is it held in a treasury and guarded with soldiers?"

Her father never answered, brushing her away with a sweep of his hand.

"Come to me, my darling," she said. Leanah needed both hands to open the lid of the box, which squeaked as it opened on its hinges. No doubt the thing had been kept closed for nearly five decades. Anything longer than that and she would never be able to open the box.

"Come to mama," she said and reached inside. The sword felt heavier than she anticipated. In her own private practices, she had only felt the weight of a practice sword, made from the lightweight wood of weakened trees. The swords were not to be taken seriously, just practice. It was not important to practice hitting hard, but technique. "To be able to bludgeon something to death did not need a sword," she overheard the sword master tell their male pupils. "The sword requires a finesse, a will to cut and slice and flay. If you want to beat something to death, have some honor and use your fists."

The handle of the sword felt cold, even through the leather straps that were wrapped tight around it. With great care, she wrapped both hands around the hilt and pulled it out of the chest. The weight of the sword nearly pulled her forward, into the box's lid, before she could press her foot forward and maintain her balance.

"How did anyone use this thing?"

Leanah flipped the sword around, holding it upward and took a few practice swings against an invisible opponent. She imagined goblins, short and rotund, and slicing into their green-gray leathery hides.

The sword traveled through the air with great ease, but its weight made it nearly unmanageable. For now, she had the sword. How she was going to use it and kill the Shadowed Wing Leanah would have to figure out later.

Leanah let the sword drag against the cobblestone floor when she walked back toward her exit path. But this would not do.

She searched around. If she was to travel great distances, she would need to find something—maybe a bag or satchel—to carry it in.

Amidst the stacks of ore, Leanah spotted a brown leather sack. It appeared to be made of cowhide, a rare and expensive animal to upkeep in these parts. Inside it contained precious, green multifaceted gems. Leanah took out each of the gems one-by-one and rested them in the corner. To be sure, she hid them behind a statue of a golden woman, maybe a goddess or a wife of a hero. She had no time to trace back the steps.

As Leanah rested each of the gems behind the statue, she heard something that sounded like a cough, or maybe even something bumping against the floor.

She paused and listened. For extra silence, she paused her breath and waited for the sounds to continue or stop.

It seemed to be the latter. Nothing else made noise, so she hurried and turned the bag upside down. Taking her time could cost her moonlight, and her escape would be nigh impossible if she could not make it out of the village before her parents awoke.

"Come on, come on." The last of the gems trickled down onto the floor. Leanah placed the bag on the floor and allowed for the opening of the bag to remain open. Then, she dragged the sword over onto the bag and slid the blade, inch by painful inch, into the opening of the bag.

At once, the sword slid into the bag and dropped out of her hands. The fabric of the bag muffled the sounds of a metal sword hitting cold, hard cobblestone, but Leanah held her breath anyway.

She paused, listening for footsteps outside. She peered toward the door, her eyes directed underneath it and watching for shadows pacing back and forth. Nothing, which meant she was temporarily in the clear.

Leanah stood over the bag, grasping her sides and taking a deep breath. The sword had been too heavy to grasp with one hand. She did not look forward to lugging that thing all the way to the Swamps of Mronir on her back, but it had to be done.

Leanah grasped the bag's straps and lifted the bag with both hands, using her weight as leverage to get better lift.

What happened next astounded her, nearly knocking her backward.

The bag felt light, as if nothing were in it. In her haste to lift the bag up with a focus on her strength, she had thrown the bag up into the air and caught it as it fell back down. The bag, it seemed, may have been enchanted, making the heaviest of objects appear light as air.

"This...," she said, looking up to the windows of the treasury and smiling at the stars. "Thank you."

She threw the bag straps around her shoulder and retraced her steps back outside.

The path outside felt faster, more natural, than before. Her first inclination was to rush through, but felt that rushing would lead to carelessness, something that would cost her the village if she were to get caught.

So Leanah tiptoed out of the hallway and back outside under the starlit sky. Leanah bowed her head and pressed her hand to her chest. "Thank you, Kaverin," she said, then paused. Something had made a noise as before.

The kicking of something around her. Maybe footsteps or a voice. She was unsure if she wanted to find out.

Leanah's feet dug into the dirt and kicked her toward the front door. She ran from shadow to shadow, feeling the cold air breeze through her brown hair and wishing for a moment she had thought to bring a heavier cloak.

When she reached the village gates, a cloaked figure sat, legs crossed, hood drawn. Leanah clutched the bag on her shoulder tightly with both hands. They would have to take this bag over her cold, dead body.

"You have no idea what you enacted, girl," said the hooded figure.

"And who are you to tell me?" she said. She took a few steps closer to the figure to keep from shouting. Attention—any attention—would bring about misfortune. Leanah's muscles in her shoulders and arms felt tense, ready for action should she need to attack this mystery man.

"I am one who sees many things. I see that you are going to bring about great ruin if you continue down this path, Leanah. Your destiny is not a happy one."

"Who are you?" she said. "Tell me, or I slay you where you stand."

"Your words are empty," said the figure. He stood up, rested his hands in his sleeves. "I see what you can and cannot do, little girl." His hood raised up, bright blue-green eyes staring into Leanah's soul. "You cannot undo what you are about to put into play. Return the sword."

"If I return the sword, we all die," she said. "I will not have that."

"Then you will have the death of the world?"

Leanah shrugged him off and walked a direction around the hooded figure. "Leave me be."

"You will fail without my help," he said.

"First you want to stop me. Now you wish to help me?"

The hooded figure fell silent, then dropped its hood, revealing dark-skinned, balled head.

"You?" Leanah said.

"I have been here waiting for this moment. Please, Leanah. Allow me to help you."

"I do not need your help."

The Shaper smiled, then bowed his head. "You do not understand. I am a Shaper. I have knowledge you need. Knowledge that could very well serve your purpose and save your village."

Leanah weighed the words in her head. "Fine. Come if you must, but you must not impede my journey."

The Shaper pulled his hood over his head and withdrew his hands back into his robe. "Then if you will lead the way."

The idea of having a Shaper at her disposal entertained her. Leanah pointed at a rope ladder often used by the guards to climb and sentry the bridge. "This, here," she said.

The Shaper and Leanah climbed the ladder and slid down the less perpendicular aspects of the gate. While the gate was excellent at keeping most marauders from getting in, it could do little to keep from getting out. Particularly with uneven areas such as this one, which allowed for an easy slide down to the outside world.

The Shaper slid down with less ease as he grasped his cloak and held it near, trying not to let it fall prey to splintered wood or stray pieces of lumber.

Leanah's feet touched the floor in a puff of dust. The lands looked open, though the road to Vamori had been nearly wiped away flat.

"Have you knowledge of where the Swamps of Mronir are?" Leanah asked.

The Shaper nodded and knelt down onto the sand. His finger traced a map, a large land area and then traced an X. "This is where we are," he said. He created a line with his fingertips, twisting back and forth along a curvy path to nearly the edge of the area. "We are to go through the Forests, following the river to the Swamps at the end of the continent."

Leanah nodded. "What's a continent?"

The Shaper smiled and nodded. "You have much to learn, little girl. I hope you know what you are doing."

"That's what I have you for, is it not?"

As the two set forth, Leanah paused for a moment, feeling the pressure of pins against her neck. With an intense curiosity, she turned around. Surely someone had been throwing something at her. Maybe insects. Mosquitos, maybe.

She smacked her neck, searching the air for buzzing globs of bugs. What she found was pure darkness and a fresh air. But still, something felt dark, a gloom of something watching over her.

"Shaper?" Leanah called out, but he had already started to pass her up on the roads.

Leanah turned back toward her village with the knowledge that she would have to come back successful, come back with the knowledge and power to save her village. Something caught her eye, a twitching. No, a blinking. Leanah squinted into the shadows that lined the walls. Something blinked.

"Leanah! Come, we waste moonlight!" called the Shaper.

Leanah looked over her shoulder to see the Shaper making more distance between him and herself.

Eyes?

Leanah looked back and searched the shadows yet again. Something yellow—no, white—blinked, then disappeared.

SEVEN

The Shaper's fists clung tight to the staff, holding up his skinny frame, but just barely.

"Have you any idea where we are going?" asked the Shaper. "I fear we are no longer following the map I laid out for you."

"I'm looking for water," said Leanah. She stopped and turned around. "Unless you have any other better ideas."

"Water is always good, my lady."

Leanah felt snug under tunic. The sun had become to shine nearly a quarter into the sky, the heat still remained bearable. "It's best we find water before the sun reaches its highest peak."

The shaper sighed, but continued to follow in Leanah's tracks. "Water flows downhill, my lady. Why are we going uphill?"

Leanah paused, pressing her hand to her head to show thought. "Because I believed the lake to be up here."

"And which lake is this? I am unfamiliar with this area."

Leanah paused. "A lake, you know. Where Vamori gathered its water for the year.

"You do not know the name of the lake?" he asked. "I do not mean to disparage you, my lady, but this does not bode well if we are unfamiliar with the locations."

"But you know of the Swamps of Mronir?" Leanah paused again, pointing her finger directly into the Shaper's chest. "Tell me, baldy, just how does that work?"

"I know many things, Lady Leanah," he said. He pulled his cloak tighter over his head. "You would not understand the source of my knowledge."

"Try me."

The Shaper pressed his hands together and then stopped, pausing for effect. "You cannot know. Not now."

"Fine," she screamed at him. "Keep your secrets, but do not dare speak to me about knowledge. Do not make me feel like I'm the source of your problems. You came with me, remember that!"

Leanah gripped the straps of her pack and tugged it tighter around her shoulder.

The Shaper watched her storm off. "My lady, if you will. You're still going uphill. We should perhaps head south, toward the forests."

Without firing a single syllable at the Shaper, she turned around and stormed in the other direction.

"Are you coming or not?"

The Shaper formed his right hand into a fist, extending only his thumb, index, and middle fingers. "Dear Elders, please watch over us, steering our direction."

The Shaper concealed his hands back into his cloak and pressed on. "My Lady, maybe it would be best to make it to Deckal first. For supplies."

"That's exactly what I was thinking," Leanah shouted back.

Her footsteps stomped high, her arms swung back and forth as if she were a woman on a mission, determined to march all the way to the Swamps alone. "You read my mind."

"I'm sure I did," he whispered to himself and followed along.

Hours passed without a single exchange between the two. Leanah felt she had many questions for the Shaper, but did not know how to form them. He had already corrected her twice. It would have been thrice had she not thrown her hands up and demanded his silence. Her stomach had begun to growl, her feet felt tender. Every rock must have been sharpened for the sole task of destroying her will to accomplish her goal.

These tasks, these problems, all of them were tests from the Gods, she told herself. These were things that she could control, had she the time and the effort. For now, she just needed the sword.

That was all. The sword and the Shadowed Wing.

"Just how far is this Deckal?" she said.

"Again, my lady, I am unfamiliar with the geography of these parts, but it must be south still, where the two rivers meet."

"Rivers? They have answered my prayers!"

"The forests should be just beyond the town," said the Shaper. "If my memory is correct."

Leanah's pace seemed to hasten to the Shaper. The hope that there was water propelled her along her path with a speed and excitement that was befitting of a young girl.

The Shaper watched, took notes. This girl, this was the girl he remembered seeing on his first visit to Vamori.

"How much further south?" she called out, nearly ten paces

ahead of the Shaper's slow strides.

"Of that, I am not sure," he said.

Leanah made some sound, a rude one that offended the Shaper though he knew not why. He felt the urge to apologize, but decided to reserve his strength, for the sun had begun to climb to the mountain tops. In a few short hours, it would descend behind the mountains, bringing with it uncertainty and darkness.

"We should perhaps begin looking for a safe place to camp out," he called out.

"But you said we were almost there." Leanah's pace slowed.

"I am not—"

"Familiar with these lands, yes, I know." Leanah searched along the sides of the road for a safe place away from the roads. Camping on the roads, she thought, would be pure suicide, inviting anyone and anything to come camp with them.

That seemed the most dangerous of options.

"Where should we camp?" she asked.

"We may set up camp, uh—" He peered over to the far western side of the road. The roadways here consisted of dirt, packed into the ground from hundreds of travelers and hooved animals. The well-worn paths had created the roads as a natural path and were not maintained by any such powers.

Indeed, no such powers had the money to keep up these roads. When one traveled in these parts, you did so on faith and little skill alone. In the cities, however, all was different.

"I'm afraid I will be no such help," said the Shaper. Without warning, he wandered to the west, toward the hills that began to take form into the mountains, some five hundred meters from where they both stood.

"Where are you going?" Leanah called out.

"I'm looking for safety," said the Shaper. His staff hit the comfort of the softer ground, mushy and pliable from blue grass that clung to the moisture in the soil. This brought a smile to the Shaper's lips, but the smile was short-lived as he watched the sun's bottom half touch the tips of the Kaverano Mountains. "We must make haste, Leanah."

"You are not leaving without me!" she cried out.

The two traveled until half the sun was consumed by the mountain tops. "Can we stop yet?" Leanah asked. Her breaths became short, intense pauses between each of her words. "I am hungry and I grow tired."

"This will work for now," said the Shaper. He stood atop the hill and squinted out east. The roadway was still in view, but not close enough to draw attention. "This will not be the best of security," he said, "but at least we can see any potential thieves and looters if they approach."

"Let them come," said Leanah. She dug her hand into her pack. "I have the Sword of Stone with me! Let them defeat that!"

The Shaper smiled, comforted that at least her spirits were high. It had become apparent that neither one of them knew the truth of this journey, and knew lesser still of the dangers. This, the Shaper feared, would be their undoing.

"Do you even know how to use the sword?"

Leanah stood up. "How dare you!" she cried. She seized the sword with a quick grasp and nearly fell over. The sword, she had forgotten how heavy it felt before. She tried a second time, grasping the hilt with both hands and letting the pack slide off the blade of the sword. "Of course I know how to use this," she said. "I just choose not to."

The Shaper held in his laughter, making it sound more like a cough. "And I'm sure you could do great damage, my lady."

Leanah gripped the sword and attempted to flip the blade over, to brandish it the way she had seen the warriors and fathers of her village. The blade, however, proved a slave to gravity and tilted forward just enough to force Leanah to tumble down the hill.

The Shaper could not contain his laughter at the sight and allowed it to roar into the chilling nighttime air.

"You will not laugh at me!" Leanah said. With her hands still clutching only the rounded pommel, but just barely, she dragged the sword up the hill. The blade traced a thin line into the ground, a line that wavered due to Leanah's inadequate strength. The weight of the sword soon overtook her again, and she fell to the ground, sliding backward on her behind.

The Shaper, against his better judgment, burst into laughter yet again.

This time, Leanah could not help it herself, and joined in on the laughter. After the Shaper had brought her the pack, Leanah slid the blade back into the pack tucked it back into the bag. As if by magic yet again, she slung the seemingly light-weight sword over her shoulder and marched back up to the camp.

"Shall we gather something to eat?" she asked.

"We have a slew of berry bushes and some bugs that are available." The Shaper dug his staff into the soft, grassy ground. A line of insects—small and six-legged—marched out of the hole and attacked his stick. "But I do not think there is enough to truly whet our appetite."

Leanah watched the ants attack her companion's staff and took a step back. "Berries it is, then." She lay the pack near the agreed upon camp spot and traveled into the nearby bushes.

The small leaves and sharp thorns held round berries, pink ones, that appeared tastier than usual due to her day's worth of hunger. At no other time would she even bring herself to eat something so raw and so tiny as these morsels. But beggars, she had determined, could not choose in times of dire need.

"I found some berries over here," she announced, picking through the sharp thorns and prickly leaves. As she gathered a small handful of berries, she grabbed hold of the leaves, massaging them between her fingers. The leaves felt smooth and thick. Snapping them in half revealed a fleshy, light green inside that shined with liquid.

"I found some leaves as well!" Leanah's excitement caused her to gather as much as she could without thought of how to bring them to the Shaper. She gathered a small group of berries in a crevice between her stomach and her elbow, then to make matters easier on her, she snapped a piece of the twig off the brush.

"Come!" she called out. "I have berries and leaves!"

Leanah dropped the berries in a small space, carved out in the darker, wetter soil. She beamed from ear to ear, proud of her accomplishment. She had single-handedly brought her and her companion food and sustenance for the night.

"This is wonderful," said the Shaper, less than enthused. "But a waste of time."

Leanah eyed the berries, then squished one of them between her fingers. The pink juices dripped down her fingers. As she brought her hand closer to her mouth, the Shaper slapped it away with the edge of his staff.

"If you want to stay alive, I suggest we toss the berries."

"But this is the best part." Leanah covered the berries with her arms, protecting them from his staff. "I don't want to die of starvation."

"You will not die of starvation. Not yet, at least." The Shaper nudged Leanah off the stack of berries and mashed his staff into the pile, making a thick pink sludge on the edge of his staff. "Those are poisonous berries. The bright colors appear to animals as warnings to not eat them."

"But they smelled so delicious."

"And that smell would have gotten you killed," said the Shaper. "I'm sorry, but I do not wish to drag your corpse back to Vamori."

Leanah sat back on her feet and looked at the staff. She wiped the juices on the ground beside her and smelled her fingers. The sweet scent of the juice, the herbal undertone, the simple thought of eating it made her mouth water.

"So what now?" she asked.

The Shaper nudged the twigs that Leanah had brought back. "These, however," he said, pushing it closer to him. He knelt down and picked up a twig. He brought it closer to his nose and sniffed.

"What are you doing with that?"

The Shaper stuck out the tip of his tongue and licked the bark, taking a second to smack his tongue against the roof of his mouth, then licked the bark again.

"Are you really going to eat that?" Leanah winced. The Shaper had taken a third, then a fourth lick, then chewed off the edge of the bark.

"It's really quite good." He smacked his lips. "And good for you." The Shaper bit off another piece and chewed it between his back teeth, a small piece sticking out between his teeth like a toothpick. "It tastes like cinnamon."

"This is disgusting," Leanah countered.

"But it's food," said the Shaper. He bit off another piece. "And good is what we need for our long journey tomorrow."

"Long journey? Just how far is Deckal?"

"My guess is just a few hours' walk." The Shaper swallowed his bark. "Should we perhaps just return to the village and return the sword?"

Leanah grasped the pack and held it closer to her. "Give me that branch," she said. Keeping her eyes firm on the Shaper's own bright blue eyes, as if answering the challenge, she chewed a thick piece of bark off the bottom of the branch. Without hesitation, she chewed it quickly with the sides of her teeth until it had felt just soft enough to swallow without poking her throat. "There," she said.

Leanah handed the piece back to the Shaper and walked back toward the bush with the pink berries.

The Shaper, however, said nothing, just preferring to watch her motions.

The young woman grasped a handful of branches and tugged. They gave way with a surprise, loud snap. Leanah stood holding the grip of branches—twigs, really—and studied the bumps and irregular colors of the brownish gray bark. They did not look appetizing, nor did they taste of cinnamon, but they weren't bad. Not as bad as it had looked. Leanah licked the bark once more. At once, her stomach rumbled upward. A sign of a deep hunger that she had not felt since she was a child.

Leanah searched the stars for her three stars, the Dog. Finding the head, she closed her eyes and held her hands to her chest, crossing her palms atop each other. "Thank you for this opportunity," she said. Bowing her head, she said, "Please watch over us."

Leanah opened her eyes and felt a tear drop down the sides of her nose. It tickled enough for her to wipe it away. But soon, more came. She felt the prying eyes of her companion and wiped them away.

"These are great!" she shouted out to him. The branches felt prickly against her lips, but she chewed the bark off them anyway. "Mmmm," she exclaimed, then swallowed.

The Shaper nodded and forced a smile. Using his staff as balance, he sat down on the ground and crossed his legs. Then, he drew up his hood and laid the staff across his lap. It balanced, then rolled nearer to his torso. With his hands, he dug into the dirt with his fingertips, allowing for them to soak in the moisture of the dirt around them.

The soil had such a marked difference here when compared to the soil of the Vamori Village. If there was something to be said of the traditions, then that village and the lands it stood upon were dying by the day. Soon, nothing would be left.

The Shaper brought the soil closer to his mouth, letting the tip of his tongue meet its strong acidic flavor. To the Shaper, it felt more nutritious, able to sustain life.

The Shaper rested his neck muscles, allowing for the cool air to caress his hairless head. For a moment, his focus lay on the air currents around him, then the vibrations of the earth beneath him. Before long, he opened his eyes, seeing only a white light. Not blinding, not bright, but an aura of pure white.

His hands dug deeper into the soil and cupped it, bringing it to his lap in small piles. With no control over his body, his hands grasped the soil, seizing it and plying it into shapes. First, a round circle. Then smaller circles. Soon, the Shaper felt less connected to his body, his arms and fingers working on command from someone else. A higher power.

He relaxed, allowing the force to use him. Tomorrow, he

would know what he was making, shaping, for the coming travels. Exhaustion traveled over his bones, making his muscles heavy, his thoughts drifting away into those of slumber.

"Are you eating mud?" asked Leanah. She held out a brown-black circle, crumbling in her hands. "Is this a mud pie?"

The Shaper rubbed the dirt from his eyes and blinked to regain his focus. "Mud?"

Leanah let the smell of the mud pie drift under his nose. "This," she said. "What were you making?"

The Shaper rubbed his eyes one more time and then glanced at his creation from last night. "I—I do not know."

"How do you not know?" she said. Leanah brought it closer to her nose and let the tip of her tongue rub against the side. "It tastes of goat droppings."

"And you would know the taste of goat droppings?" The Shaper reached for his staff and used it to stand up.

"I was a child," Leanah said, then dismissed the thought. "We're talking about you, here. What is this?" Leanah cupped the object, round with some ridged craters dug into the surface. "It looks like a rock we use to find at the volcanoes."

"I am unsure of what this is," said the Shaper. "I only make these things—shape them, if you will. I am not always privy to their meaning."

"Meaning?"

The Shaper nodded. "This is a gift from the Elders."

Leanah shook her head. "Bah, the Elders are gone. Dead."

"But yet you pray?"

As Leanah stood still, studying the intricacies of the round object, the Shaper placed some of the previous night's twigs into the pack.

"This is really, really good," Leanah said, offering the item back to the Shaper. "Whatever it is."

"We cannot take it with us."

Leanah raised an eyebrow. "And why not?"

"It does not belong to us." The Shaper threw the pack over his shoulder. "Shall we get going?"

"Only if we get to bring this."

The Shaper seized the mud sphere from her hands and allowed it to fall from his grip to the ground. It crumbled into pieces, splattering into the ground.

"That was uncalled for," said Leanah. "I thought it was rather nice."

"It belongs to the earth now," said the Shaper. "We must get going. Deckal is near." The Shaper brought the conversation to a close with a few brisk steps down the green hill toward the more familiar dirt road.

"As long as I get to carry the pack!" Leanah exclaimed.

The roofs of Deckal appeared just over the horizon. The image excited Leanah, who quickly began to skip, then jog, then run toward the walls.

The Shaper, pleased at the sight himself, picked up his pace.

"We're here!" Leanah shouted. Her stomach growled when she approached the front gates—left wide open for incoming travelers. "We must get us something to eat."

"We have no money, young one," he said. The Shaper pressed on with his walking staff, using most of it to carry the weight.

Leanah's feet refused to stand still, he noticed, giving cause for her to pace back and forth along the strong wooden walls. Each piece of wood appeared to be a full tree trunk, stuck together with a combination of ropes and a sticky adhesive mud. The combination, when dried together, created a method of fortifying the contents of the town.

"This is amazing," said Leanah. "Have you been here before?"

The Shaper nodded. "Once, yes." He pulled his hood over his eyes. "But they are not the nicest people you will ever meet."

"Nonsense," Leanah said. Her hands gripped the pack's straps along her shoulder. "It's just because you're so dark compared to the rest of us. No one in these parts has such dark skin as you." Leanah paused. "Just where are you from, anyhow?"

As the Shaper approached Leanah's location and the entrance to Deckal, he heard and felt the rumble of his unhappy and very hungry stomach. "Looks like we both could use something to eat, no?"

Leanah stood, waiting for an answer that she could not seem to get just yet. The Shaper's walking stick clicked against the hardened ground, occasionally banging onto small rocks and pebbles until coming to a cobblestone road nearly ten feet into the village.

"One of these days, you'll answer one of my questions!" she shouted to him.

"One of these days," said the Shaper.

The two traveled into what looked like the market district of the town. "How do we suppose we get food," asked Leanah.

The center bustled with the urgent wants and needs of its villagers. Leanah had never seen such a large group of people going in so many directions before.

"Excuse me, little girl," said a woman, pushing past her with a basket made of twigs and straw. Her accent surprised Leanah. The way they spoke, with short, quick vowels sounds, words coming in rapidly and without apology.

Leanah stepped forward and closer to her friend. As she looked behind her, she watched the woman walk away briskly. Even the woman's dress, maroon that flowed like the waves of a pond, looked foreign to her.

"This will be harder than I thought, isn't it?" She took hold of the Shaper's elbow and squeezed tightly.

The Shaper attempted to comfort her with a gentle caress of his fingers. They felt surprisingly soft and cool to Leanah's warm, nervous skin. "I would not worry just yet," he said. "We'll be fine."

Leanah felt a truth behind those words that allowed her to relax, but only enough to let go of her traveling companion. "Perhaps we should get our food the old-fashioned way?" Leanah held up her hand and wiggled her fingers.

"You mean to steal our food?"

"Have you any coin?"

The Shaper shook his head and said something in another language.

"Well, then it's settled." Leanah looked down both ways of the market district. The crowds moved in no predictable pattern, no flow or current to this river of villagers. "If we split up, perhaps we may reduce our chances of being caught."

The Shaper nodded his head in reluctance. "We meet here after we have procured food. In whatever means necessary."

His words carried a dripping cynicism that Leanah felt unnecessary. Desperate times, however, needed extreme measures, and she was certain that if she were left hungry, no one would be happy for the rest of the trip.

"Agreed." Leanah patted the man on the back and turned left, heading down toward the smell of fresh sourdough breads and fruits.

Leanah's small stature became more of a problem for her as she traveled up the current of people. Being smaller than many of these villagers, they bumped into her, rattled her and very nearly stepped on her when she was not careful.

The street, though much larger than any roads she had seen in Vamori, seemed tight and contained due to the massive traffic of people. Leanah had never imagined the lands could carry this many people before.

Leanah stuck her nose to the air and let the smell of freshly baked bread carry her to the possibilities of food. Having nothing on her except her pack and the sword, Leanah was certain that she would have to grab and dash. Though with this amount of people, it could be possible to grab more food and simply walk away.

Beyond the large numbers of people, Leanah was also struck by the size of the buildings. Like the walls that protected the village, the buildings were constructed from large pieces of wood, cut into flat shapes and layered upon each other to form walls.

Nothing here appeared to be made of stone. Whereas nearly everything in Vamori was small, heavy and gray, Deckal was large, light, and brown. Wood. All of it.

Leanah smiled at the hidden meaning of having everything made of wood. They were close to the forest. Less traveling. Maybe they could be at the Swamps of Mronir and back within a week.

"Hey, Shaper!" she said, but stopped cold, looking around. "Right." She took a deep breath. "Looking for food."

A further look down the street revealed a series of open buildings, doorways cut half open in a manner that confused Leanah. Only the lower part of the door remained closed. The top half, open. The idea struck her as hilarious. Were the people to jump into every building?

Leanah looked at the physiques of the busy people that surrounded her. They were all shapely, but not build solid as her people. If placed into a test of strength, there was no doubt her weakest villagers could manhandle the strongest one here. These people in their soft clothes and soft buildings. They did not know the meaning of true work, true hardships.

In the distance, through the random pockets of people, the young girl identified something bright, delicious.

It had better not be more poison berries, she thought.

She crept, slowly, hiding in the middle of crowds to get to the cart that held green and red apples, bright orange spheres that smelled delightful and herbal.

Leanah's stomach grumbled. It, too, knew this would be a great feast if she could only pull this off. She decided that it would be best to take advantage of the large crowds, so she walked past the cart two, then three times to ensure she could get an adequate view of the scene.

If watching the boys fight taught her anything, it was that you always want enough room to run in the face of defeat.

With this many people, however, it should be an easy task. Leanah's fingers felt twitchy, eager. In the fourth pass, Leanah moved close enough to keep a cautious eye on the cart's owner.

He was a burly man, whose stomach was draped with a white piece of cloth, stained with a rainbow of juices nearly as bright as the fruits on his cart. He held out the orange spheres, shouting something that Leanah only half paid attention to. Her real focus was not on the cart keeper, but the food.

Leanah snuck close to the cart, hiding behind it slightly, just to the left of the cart's owner. As the man turned to offer an orange sphere, then a small green and red apple, Leanah seized her moment. Her hand swiped an orange sphere off the cart and landed softly in her lap.

She paused, daring to take another. The man had not seen her. From this side of the cart, she could see that he was not significantly taller than her, just standing on top of a hard wooden basket in the shape of a box.

"You there!" he shouted in a rough, scratchy voice that commanded little attention. "You, you look like you could use an apple! One bit each!" he shouted.

She had heard about these things: bits. The men coming back from their journeys into the forest, they spoke of these shiny bits, round and flat. The other women had called them coins. According to this man, she could trade these coin bits for the tantalizing fruit.

Leanah's heart beat intensely enough for her to feel it in her throat.

One more. At least. She knew she could do it.

She observed the man with the tenacity of a hawk studying its prey. She waited for the perfect moment, that moment he turned around and for just a second the cart was out of his sight.

She waited, then waited more.

Forget this. She needed more fruit and was running out of time. The Shaper, maybe he would appreciate one of these orange things.

She placed her fingertips on the edge of the cart, letting the fingers crawl like a spider to search for the tiny, rippled surfaces of the orange balls. She reached, feeling everything until, just directly in front of her, another orange. She scraped it with the nail of her middle finger. The floral and herbal scent reached her nose and her stomach rumbled again in response.

"No," she whispered to herself. The loud conversations of the shopping people were just enough to cover the sounds of her own rumbling stomach and self-warnings. She was thankful to the Elders. Should everything during this trip be this easy…?

Leanah reached for the orange ball and stood up, shoving it into her arm in a single motion. Her hand gripped the other orange ball so hard she felt the juice inside, briefly entertained by how squishy this little thing actually was.

She would enjoy this later, she was sure of it.

Leanah pranced out into the crowds. She had escaped unseen, the unsuspecting shopkeeper none the wiser. The Shaper, he would be so proud of her when she returned with not one, but two exotic fruits.

"There!" someone shouted behind her. "That way!"

Leanah ducked under the cover of a rather large woman in front of her. Attempting to stay in her shadow, she kept pace with each step despite how much the rapid beats of her heart screamed at her, Run!

Leanah's own instincts took over, though she questioned her own inner logic of holding her breath and slowing down when someone wanted to nab her for stealing fruit.

"Not that way!" a man screamed. "That way!" A shuffling of boots on the cobblestone street caused the group of people to stir, moving and pressing themselves against the buildings and shops that lined the road.

Even her cover, the large lady with a green dress the color of the grass outside, she had moved away, leaving Leanah to feel the heat of the sun on her neck as she ducked out of sight and, hopefully, out of mind.

Her eyes raised to the scene in front of her. The chaos and her would-be chasers, they were all behind her. She peered over her shoulder. A group of men—not in uniforms or official outfits, but regular everyday clothes—ran at top speed toward her.

"Run," something told her, and she did. Her arms flailed at top speed, keeping pace with angry men behind her.

Leanah felt fire in her lungs, the strain of having to run after so much suspense had drained her reserves. She had little to eat, and now she felt the full effects of not having a full belly in the last two days.

"It was just two orange balls," she said, though no one seemed to listen to her pleas.

"Help!" she screamed.

Her top speed was not enough, however, and she stopped, pulling herself to protect her body. She held her breath, listened, and waited.

Her pursuers overcame her position—and then ran right past her.

Leanah clutched the oranges that had fallen out of her grip onto the floor. "I'm sorry," she said. "They were only fruit."

But she appeared to be apologizing to no one. In front of her, the group of men disappeared around a corner. Leanah still felt the thunder of their movements, their rampage into the streets.

"That's right! You better run!" she screamed at them and picked up her oranges and continued to meet the Shaper.

Back at the town's busy center, Leanah found a location to spy on the rest of the crowd. She looked for the heavy, mud brown cloak of her traveling companion. Her stomach fluttered with butterflies. What she held in her hand—and the circumstances around it—caused her to be proud of her first thieving attempt. She had been successful, and yet had no one to brag to.

Just wait until she comes home and tells Ciaran all about it. Even he, she thought, would be proud of her survival skills.

The group traveled in crisscross ways, moving about from one location to the next, but something stuck out. A group of people, men—the same men that chased her—fleeing through the group, apparently chasing down another victim.

This victim, he must have done something really bad if he attracted this much attention.

Leanah squinted upon the crowd, trying to track the movements of the men. This part seemed easy: the men shoved everyone aside for their actions.

"You!" one of them screamed. Leanah followed the voice to a far corner. A hint of orange flashed before her eyes—a piece of orange clothing—and then disappeared behind a corner.

"What was that?" Leanah asked. The thrill of the hunt tugged at her. "The Shaper can wait for me," she said. "I must see more."

Leanah followed the group, staying on the outskirts of the ever-moving crowd. This path seemed faster.

Reaching the far corner of the town's center, she smelled something—something familiar. Maybe cooking? She had discovered more food! Leanah followed the will of her stomach. Her best bet would be to stay low, following the crowd but stay under their attention. But speed was key. If the men were also heading toward the food, then there would be nothing left when she got there.

The orange balls, they would be wonderful treats, but the smell of meat called to a deeper part of her.

Leanah licked her lips. The scent got stronger, as did the screaming, the further she went down into the alley. "Leon!" she heard a man scream. "You bastard!"

Leanah turned yet another corner—this town was too elaborate for her amateur tracking skills—to stumble upon a smoking corpse.

Leanah gasped. The corpse belonged to a human, on its back with his arms outstretched as if fending off an attack. Its hand turned inside, bent toward the body with fingers that appeared like crisp, black claws.

Leanah gagged. The smell of charred flesh that had tempted her hunger traveled from this very spot. Leanah grabbed her mouth to contain her inevitable scream.

In front of her, a circle of men standing around something, something orange and flailing, as they yelled at it, calling it a curse, a witch. With each kick of the men's boots, the figure in the middle yelped and grunted in pain.

"Leave him alone!" Leanah shouted.

The men ignored her at first, kicking and punching their victim with more forceful blows.

"What is this?" One of the men, the smallest one with the longest hair pointed at Leanah. "A little girl?" He pulled at his buddy. "Get a load of this!"

One by one, the group stood up and pointed at Leanah. The last man to stop beating on the flailing orange figure stood up, the largest one and judging by the gnarled look on his face, the angriest.

"Go home, little girl." He wiped the sweat off his face and snarled at her. With a giant fist, the man picked up the orange figure high enough for Leanah to see that it was a man. His own body had begun to give off a vapor, either steam or maybe a small dust cloud, she could not tell which.

"Not until you leave him alone!" she shouted.

The man dropped the orange figure and stepped forward in the crowd, clearly the leader. "Or what? You'll run and tell your father?" The men laughed.

Leanah gritted her teeth together and reached into her pack. The sword came out with ease, but felt a sudden heaviness that forced Leanah to allow the blade to drop to the ground. Again, her soft, weak hands seized the grip of the sword and dragged it toward the men's direction.

The tallest man belted out a laughter so hard he doubled over. "You cannot even lift that thing!" The man's face turned red as he struggled to breathe and laugh at the same time. "Come here, girl. Give me the sword. I wouldn't want you to hurt yourself."

"Just you wait until—" Leanah gripped the sword closer to its thick metal guard. As she did so, out in this daylight, Leanah noticed what looked like a face, scowling or asleep or both, just above the guard on the sword's shoulder.

"I grow tired of this," the tall man said. He pressed on closer to Leanah, stopping just one pace in front of her. "Give me the sword."

"Over my dead body," she said.

"That was the point," the man said. He extended his hand to Leanah, holding it only a finger's length away from grabbing her wrists.

"Leave us alone!" Leanah shouted. She tugged her upper body

upwards, whipping her shoulders back and pulling up the sword. A bright, silent light filled the area, blinding all in the alley—including Leanah. When the light disappeared, the man lay on the floor, grasping at his chest with both hands. His own dirty white tunic becoming soaked with fresh, dark red blood and sticking to his body.

"How—?" The man's words disappeared into a whisper as his body went limp. He had died.

"She's a demon, too! A witch!" another man shouted. "She'll kill us all!" With that, the men fled in different directions.

A cough from behind reminded Leanah that she was not quite alone.

"Are you okay?" she asked. Leanah tucked the heavy sword back into her pack and slung it over her shoulder. "Do you need help?"

The orange figure twitched, then rolled over onto its hands and knees. He coughed and spat up something onto the ground. Eventually, the man nodded.

"You are okay?" Leanah asked.

The man nodded again and rolled over onto his side. He extended a hand out to his savior. Deep beneath the shadows of his own orange robe, Leanah detected a friendly smile. "Please?" he asked in an accent that Leanah had never heard before.

She extended a hand out to the man and helped to pull him to his feet. He stood taller than her, his body covered in a combination of brown and orange garbs.

"Where are you from?" Leanah asked. "I have never seen anyone dressed like," Leanah held out a hand and motioned up and down. "It's so bright, but beautiful."

The man pulled back his hood and smiled. His own red brown

hair fell in front of his eyes, bringing Leanah's attention to his eyes, blue as a clear sky. Leanah's words came stuck in her mouth.

"My name is Grenseal," he said. "I am from," he paused, "abroad."

"I am Leanah. I am from Vamori, to the north."

"Nice to meet you, Leanah of Vamori." The mage extended his left hand out to Leanah.

Leanah shook his hand with her own left hand, a motion that felt awkward. "I always thought—" she began to say, but Grenseal interrupted.

He held up his right hand, revealing bruises along the back of his hand and crooked fingers. "I'm a little banged up at the moment," he said.

Leanah nodded. "Well then," she said. "It was a pleasure, but I have to go find my friend." She began walking back toward the center of the town when she heard Grenseal catch up to her.

"I'm trying to find a friend as well. Dark skin, about maybe your height. White hair?"

Leanah nodded. "My friend is bald but has dark skin."

Grenseal looked up toward the sky, thinking, then said, "No, I don't believe he would be bald. Not yet, anyway." Grenseal smiled at his own joke. Leanah, however, did not appear entertained.

"What was that flash of light back there?" Grenseal asked. "A spark? Fire, perhaps?"

Leanah shrugged. "What light?"

Grenseal panted as he struggled to keep up with her through the dense crowd. "Surely you saw it, too. The one back there, before the man was felled."

"That light? Yes, I did it," Leanah said. She wondered if she was maybe sharing too much information. "I think."

KD Johnson

"You think?" Grenseal said. "That was truly fantastic! Perhaps you could teach me that trick?"

Leanah paused, turning to Grenseal and grabbing him by the arm. "Just how far are you planning on following me?"

"You saved my life, young lady. I am indebted to you. If you will have me, I would love to share my knowledge and offer my services as a guide. I have some very handy skills that might work in your benefit." Grenseal's blue eyes seemed to gleam, reflecting only a beam of the sun's bright light overhead. "What do you say?"

"Skills?" Leanah asked. "I can take care of myself."

"I would show you these skills, but I fear we'll need a quieter location."

"How well do you know the area?" Leanah demanded.

"Well enough, I suppose." Grenseal smiled. He sensed that Leanah was coming around.

"Fine," she said. She continued on her way. "Come along then, but do not cause problems or I'll do to you what I did to that man over there."

"Oh, I believe we wouldn't want that," he said and rushed to join Leanah at her side.

Upon entering the town's center again, Leanah spotted the brown cloak of the Shaper. "This way," she motioned. Grenseal placed his hand on her backpack for balance and location. "What are you doing?" Leanah said. She pulled the backpack in front of her, clutching it with both hands. "This is off limits to you," she said. "My supplies."

Grenseal snatched back his hand. "I'm sorry, I was looking

for a way to keep track of you. The crowd—" Someone bumped Grenseal away from Leanah, and he fought his way back. "This crowd is unbelievable."

Leanah's eyes narrowed. "Keep your hands off my things."

Grenseal studied her eyes, then the backpack. He noticed the odd shape the pack made: long, loose at the ends.

Leanah sensed this and pulled back over her shoulder. "Do we understand each other?"

Grenseal nodded. "Understood."

Leanah's shoulders relaxed and without warning, rushed into the crowd toward the Shaper.

"Leanah! I apologize," he said, but then stopped when the orange man stepped out from the crowd. "Who do we have here?"

"Shaper, Grenseal. Grenseal, Shaper. I saved him from a crowd of angry men."

Grenseal held out his hand toward the Shaper with a welcoming smile. "Glad to meet you, Shaper."

The Shaper's eyebrows raised in concern. "Is he, um, coming with us?"

Leanah nodded. "He knows the area and is willing to serve as our guide in exchange for me saving his life."

The Shaper nodded. "Very well. But you know that means more mouths to feed."

"I'm fairly self-sufficient," Grenseal said. "I've traveled much myself and have tools at my disposal."

The Shaper's eyes studied the man, taking quick glances over the man's belt of pouches and skins. "Clearly." He turned toward Leanah. "As I was saying previous, I apologize, but I was unable to procure any food."

Leanah reached into her bag and pulled out the two orange

balls. "Here," she said. "I found these."

"Just found them?" asked the Shaper.

"Yes. On a fruit cart." Leanah straightened her back, holding up herself proudly. "You should have seen how took these with such great skill, no one knew they were even missing."

The Shaper peered at the oranges, studied them. "Then I suppose we are fortunate." He held one up. "How many did you take?"

"Two. Why?" Leanah's eager eyes traveled from the Shaper to Grenseal and back.

"What about our new friend here?" the Shaper held his orange out to the man. "Maybe we should acquire another one?"

"I can steal another for our companion, if you wish."

Grenseal held up his hands in protest. "No, no. Don't go through the trouble for me. I already ate." The group eyed Grenseal's protest, both taking attention to his hands.

"What was that?" Leanah said, pointing to his right hand.

"What was what?" he said. Grenseal looked at his hand and then held it behind him. "A cut, maybe a bruise." He began walking toward the entrance to the village. "I'm fine. Really."

Leanah and the Shaper trailed their new guide out of the village. "Did you see that, too?" Leanah asked.

The Shaper nodded. "Indeed."

"Was that—?"

"So, you never did tell me," Grenseal said, turning to walk backwards, "just where are we headed?"

"The Swamps of Mronir," Leanah shouted. "Heard of it?"

Grenseal smiled, this one not as generous and welcoming as the others. "Yes, I've heard of it. To the south. Through the Oaken Forests. Maybe a few days' walk away."

"We haven't much time," Leanah asked. "Can you cut that time in half?"

Grenseal closed his eyes, still moving backwards and somehow avoiding everyone. "Maybe. If we were to cut straight through the forests. We'd have to avoid some paths, but it's not impossible."

"Great!" Leanah shouted. "Let's do that."

"As you wish," Grenseal said and the group left the fortified walls of Deckal.

"Have you asked this Shaper if he's seen your friend, Grenseal?"

Grenseal's felt his face turn the bright red of embarrassment. "Um, no. I have not."

"Well," Leanah said. "Ask him."

Grenseal grinned, "Excuse me, um, The Shaper, have you seen my friend?"

The Shaper raised his eyebrow and peered over his shoulder at Leanah. "Must this sound so—forced?"

Grenseal shrugged.

The road out of the town of Deckal widened the further south they had traveled. A sign, they had hoped, of running into more people for help or supplies. Despite the widening and the hope, nothing else appeared along the sides of the road. Even the Kaverano Mountains had drifted away from their path, running further west into the far distance. The green hills that had housed their campsite a little more than a day ago had also flattened out into the yellow grasslands they walked beside.

"This seems as entertaining as anything else at the moment." Grenseal walked over closer to the group. "So, have you seen him?"

Leanah, trailing from behind due to her smaller legs and tiny stride, said, "Now, Shaper, you ask him what he looked like."

The Shaper sighed. "Ser, could you perhaps describe your friend?"

Grenseal paused. "He is about Leanah's height. White hair—more of a pale blond—and dark skinned. Sort of like you, but sun-darkened skin."

Leanah looked to the Shaper for his response. "I cannot say that I have seen him. I stayed in Vamori for the last few months."

"Why is your friend missing?" Leanah asked.

"We were on a mission. A search and destroy mission, if you will."

Leanah ran to catch up with her group. "Search for and destroy what?" Leanah's eyes widened as she uttered the word destroy.

"I'm afraid that it's a difficult question to answer," he said. "I'm not quite sure you would believe me."

"Try me," she said. Leanah walked briskly to cut Grenseal off from the continuing forward. "Well?"

Grenseal side-stepped Leanah and continued on the roads. "We have been sworn to secrecy on the matter." He shrugged. "I apologize."

"If you cannot tell us that, then why did those men want to beat you?"

This caught the Shaper's attention. "Beat?"

"I—" Grenseal stumbled over his words.

"If you are a wanted criminal, then you pose a threat to us," the Shaper said.

"I assure you, I am not a threat to you. Nor am I a criminal."

"Then out with it!" Leanah demanded. "Why were they after you?"

Grenseal sighed, then paused. "Fine. If you must know." Grenseal pulled back the sleeve of his cloak and revealed his right hand. "I was wanted because of this." A ball of bright orange, then blue flame erupted over the palm of his hand. The flames danced in the winds.

Leanah and the Shaper stopped, both disbelieving their own eyes.

"How did you?"

"Elders watch over us," muttered the Shaper.

Leanah rushed over the Grenseal's hand, grabbing it with hers. "What is this? How did you do that?" Leanah grabbed his hand and searched it, stopping at his palms. Embedded within it, a molten rock, ridged with small craters. "Shaper!" she screamed. "Come see this! It's that thing you made!"

The Shaper walked to the Grenseal. "I do not think that it is that thing I made, as you so elegantly put it," he said. "It can't be." His words froze in his throat as the witnessed the shiny rock, protruding only half a finger's width from Grenseal's palm. "You have—" said the Shaper. "This, this is a rock."

Grenseal nodded, pulling his hand back and putting it back into his sleeve. "Indeed. It allows for me to do things, things that some people consider a mark of a demon."

"Like that flame thing?" Leanah said. "Do it again!"

Grenseal smiled. "Not now," he said.

The Shaper grasped his own hood and pulled it back to reveal his entire head. "And you came upon this how?"

"It was—" Grenseal paused, searching for the words, "—a gift. Nothing more."

"This is quite a gift!" Leanah said. "Let's see your fire again!"

"I cannot. Not right now."

"Sure you can!" Leanah said. "Show us!"

The Shaper grabbed Leanah's shoulders and pushed her along the road. "Perhaps we should leave it be for now. Let's just be thankful that we have someone that can be of some help."

"What is he not telling us?" Leanah asked him. "Why hide it?"

The Shaper patted her on the shoulder. "Some things are best left unsaid for now."

Leanah grasped the pack, clutching it tighter to her shoulder. "I suppose so."

"To answer your original question, however," Grenseal said, "those men believe that I was responsible for the destruction of one of their houses. Someone had seen me use my abilities and immediately accused me."

"And did you?"

"Of course not!" Grenseal said. "I was passing through, looking for Luca."

"Is Luca your friend?" Leanah said. She looked over to the Shaper, who shrugged.

"Yes, he has been gone for three months now. We were to meet back in Deckal to report our searches."

"I don't know of any Luca in our village," Leanah said. "Do you?"

The Shaper agreed. "No, I'm sorry. But as long as you are with us, we can keep our eyes and ears out together."

Grenseal smiled. "I appreciate that, sincerely."

Leanah felt the chill. "There is a breeze coming in from the east."

"Agreed, there may be a change in weather soon." Grenseal raised his hood, casting a shadow over his eyes and cheeks. "We may have to rest soon before we continue. Maybe eat before we enter the forests."

"But we have little time! We must press on!" Leanah walked faster, picking up her pace to surpass her friends. "Come on!"

Grenseal looked at the Shaper, who returned the same glance of exasperation.

"Leanah! He is correct. We cannot go much further without first having something to eat."

"Eat what?" Leanah shouted. "Dry grass and bugs?"

"There are ground weasels in the plains. It would take some time to hunt, but it is not impossible to fetch a few," Grenseal nodded to the others. "It would be my pleasure."

Leanah slowed her pace, then stopped. "Fine, if you two are going to gang up on me. But just know that if my village dies, I will be coming after the both of you!"

Grenseal spotted a thin tree far from the path. Its sparse, skinny branches could not protect from much, but they could serve as wonderful kindling for a fire. The tree had been nearly a thousand paces to the west, but not so far as to exhaust the weary travelers. Upon reaching the tree, Leanah and the Shaper began peeling off bark and snapping off small twigs for firewood.

Grenseal left the group to travel further into the grasslands, promising to return with at least one creature ripe for eating.

Leanah and the Shaper watched with awe at his confidence. This man had been worth the danger of saving, especially if he comes back with meat.

"Shaper," she said. "Is he some kind of magician?"

He nodded. "So it would seem."

"But I thought magick had disappeared when the Elders had died."

"It was believed so, yes."

"Then does that mean—" Leanah's voice faded away, unable to end the sentence.

"It just might, my lady. Have faith. We might have found what we need just yet."

Leanah watched on as the orange mage turned into a bright orange dot in the distance. He knelt down, thrusting his hands into the ground and letting go a growl that fortified her faith in her new companion.

"Shaper?" Leanah said.

A large burst of flame shot up toward the sky from Grenseal's hands.

"Yes, Leanah?" The Shaper snapped a twig off the tree served as their campsite.

"I think I'm starting to like this guy."

Grenseal came back with the charred corpse of two long creatures. Patches of the bristly, gray fur had been singed off in some places, grilled in others. "I come bearing gifts," he said.

The charred bodies of the critters landed on the flattened grass in front of the seated Shaper.

"Ground weasels?" Leanah squealed. "Oh my goodness! Meat! Finally!" Leanah rushed to view the size of Grenseal's catch. "This will taste so delicious."

"We have no seasonings to make it more palatable," the Shaper said. "But this will do."

Leanah lifted the weasel into the air. Its black tail swing wildly in the wind, clinging to the corpse only by a thin strip of crispy skin. "You already cooked it."

"An unfortunate consequence of my methods." Grenseal smiled.

"Only two?" Leanah asked.

"I did not see a need for any others. You two may have one each."

Leanah dropped the weasel onto the ground. "We can have it? Won't you eat?"

"I do not eat animals," Grenseal said.

"That is unheard of!" Leanah said. "How can you not eat animals? How do you keep up your strength?"

Grenseal smiled, and as if he had been practicing this speech for some time, said, "I have been at the mercy of the earth for quite some time. I cannot partake of the flesh of another living thing. It is a sign of disrespect, especially when killed with these." Grenseal raised his hands up to his companions. "With these, whatever I kill seems distasteful, unappetizing. I do not, however, judge those who choose to eat the flesh of animals."

Leanah tossed a weasel to the Shaper. "But it's okay if we eat it?"

As the Shaper caught the weasel in midair, the tail flipped off and landed on the ground. "Are you sure you are okay with this?" he asked.

"Of course. It would not be right for me to eat this."

"But what will you eat?"

Grenseal reached into his belt of pouches and pulled out a small red berry, triangular shaped. "Strawberries," he said and sliced off the tip with his front teeth.

"Suit yourself, then," Leanah said. Holding her food by the crispy legs, she bit into the haunches and pulled a layer of dry, red meat off the animal. "More for us."

That evening, the Leanah and Grenseal sat around the campfire, created by Grenseal's very own hands. The Shaper sat nearly thirty feet from the group, in a trance and sitting cross-legged.

The sky grew dark and remained cloudless despite the threats of rain earlier in their journey. Leanah had grown accustomed to the dry air after only these few days. Water had been a thing of the past, needing to drink the dew off the leaves of trees they came across—few and far between—in the grasslands.

"You never answered my question honestly," Grenseal said.

Leanah sat backed up against the trunk of the tree. The bark was smooth with little nods that pressed into her back in just the right places, depending on how hard she pressed into it. "What question?" Leanah grabbed the bag and pulled it near her.

"What caused that white light?" he asked. "When you saved me."

"I know what you're talking about," Leanah said. "But I don't know."

Grenseal nodded, eyeing the pack. "And what do you hold onto so dearly?"

"This is from my village, and it is very important to me." She lifted it to her lap. "Leave it alone, okay? It's mine."

Grenseal nodded. "No worries there, then. It is yours. I am no thief."

Silence fell upon the group as they watched the fire's tongue flick in the air. Its shadows created dancing silhouettes against the campsite and its campers.

"May I ask an honest question, Leanah?" Grenseal said. He sat forward, gripping his knees close to his chest. "Have you heard of magi before?"

Leanah nodded.

"Do you know what they are?"

She shook her head. "I had heard that they are magickal beings, but we have no magi in the village. I have never seen such magic before."

"Are you afraid of it?" he asked.

Leanah took some time to answer, but settled on, "No."

Grenseal's appearance seemed to relax.

"I would rather you have this power and join us," she said. "It will be most useful."

"What is the manner of your quest?" Grenseal asked.

"I don't want to talk about it."

Grenseal's voice dropped. "When you asked about my powers, and why the men were attacking me, I was honest with you. You wanted to know if I would be a threat to you." He let go of his legs and sat forward toward the fire. "Now I ask you: Are you a threat to me?"

Leanah stood up. "And how would I be a danger to you?" she said. "I am not the one who is a stranger here."

Grenseal laughed. "My dear, you are a stranger to me."

"Stop laughing."

Grenseal continued, "And if I am to go along with your quest, I would like to know what it is we are doing."

"I just need for you to take me to the Swamps of Mronir. There is something that needs killing."

"Mighty words for someone who is so little."

Leanah picked up a rock and tossed it into the fire. "I know."

"You resent this?"

"I resent that I don't have the power to save my village. If I had powers like yours, maybe I could do something. Something important, and make sure that my people are not starving. That my chickens can thrive."

"My powers are both a blessing and a curse," Grenseal said. "You misunderstand entirely."

"You can do great things," she said. "No matter how you got your powers."

Grenseal nodded, agreeing.

Leanah sat up, her eyes widened. "You should come back to the village with me, to help. Maybe you're the key helping to rebuild!"

Grenseal smiled, but sat back. "That's nice of you to say, dear. But it's not practical. I need to find my friend. I only go on this search with you until I find my dear Luca. After that, I must go my separate ways. I have a quest of my own to tend to." He looked up to the stars, gazing at the twinkling beauty, these diamonds in the sky.

"You can always change your mind," she said.

"I could," he said. "But I cannot. I will honor my debt to you, get you to the Swamps. But after that, I must return to Deckal and await my friend." Grenseal laid back into the stiff, drying grass. "They sure are beautiful, aren't they?"

Leanah grunted in agreement. "Grenseal, why do you believe that bad things happen?"

Grenseal sat up. "That is a fantastic question," he said. Grenseal grew silent, contemplating in his head. "I do not believe that bad things happen at all. I believe purposeful things happen."

"You would not say that if you saw the desperation and starvation of my village."

"I have seen a great many things, Leanah. And in all of these things—famines, wars, death—there has been a purpose that has served the greater good. Ours is to trust in the process."

Leanah stood up and walked toward the tree, stopping

underneath its largest branch.

"Where are you going?" Grenseal asked. "To sleep already?"

She nodded. "We have a big day tomorrow. We must make it to the forest."

Grenseal nodded. "I am sorry if I offended you."

Leanah said nothing, but turned her back on Grenseal. "Good night."

EIGHT

The trek to the next village of Aaris was long and hard. Leanah had never left the safety of her own village before. Being the most inexperienced of her companions, she felt it easy to scream, "Are we there yet" every five minutes. She grew thankful for the next village coming toward them.

"Grenseal, are you talking to a ground squirrel?" asked Leanah.

"As I said, my lady, 'tis nothing but a sign of respect for the lands," he said.

"How do you understand anything they say?" she asked. "How do they understand you?" Leanah's eyes stayed on the squirrel that appeared to be chattering something to the orange mage. She watched as his large shadow passed over the little creature beneath him.

"It's as easy as being able to talk to you." Grenseal felt into his bag to reveal a small dark brown nut. The squirrel held out its tiny hands and took it and squeaked something.

"I started hearing things just outside of my home, and before

I knew it, I was hearing full conversations of animals of the lands. Concentration is always important, since some of these animals speak different dialects.

"What's a dialect?" asked Leanah.

"What does your tutor teach you, exactly?"

"He teaches me history. More importantly, our history of the Vamori people."

Grenseal rubbed the head of the little squirrel and then patted it on its back.

The squirrel squeaked something then disappeared off into the long grass of the plains.

"He says that something is amiss up ahead."

The Shaper smiled. "And the animals told you this?"

Grenseal nodded.

"No different from the Elders speaking to you," said the Shaper.

"I have an agreement with the Elders," Grenseal said with a grin. "They leave me alone, I leave them alone."

"How lost you must be," the Shaper said.

"What kind of problems are we going to meet?" asked Leanah. "Do we get to see battle?" Leanah flung her sword around, but feeling the weight increase again, she allowed it to drop with a thud to the ground. Carefully, she pulled it back into her pack and slung it over her shoulder.

"I still don't understand why this sword does this to me. I think it's broken."

"The squirrel said that we will run into another town up ahead, but the paths have been blocked by bandits, but different bandits."

"Different how?"

"The squirrel called them large, furry. Like him, but bigger and no tails."

Leanah shrugged, as did the Shaper.

"That means gnolls."

"I see no gnolls up ahead," said Leanah. She put her hands to her face and squinted. "There's nothing ahead of us."

"We won't hit that town until tomorrow. We are on our own for now."

The group came to a stop late that evening. As the sun went down they all felt the temperatures dropping.

However, they had traveled so fast and placed so much energy into their travels that each member of the group felt soothed by the cold against his or her skin.

As Leanah settled in for the night she had noticed that most of the animals were asleep and hidden. "It's going to be incredibly difficult to find anything to eat without any of your friends out here," she said.

The darkness and shadows that covered the forests were thick. Even a tiny morsel of squirrel or prairie dog was impossible to find.

That night the fire started to die down a little, reduced to only a tiny spark over the logs. Leanah twitched and rubbed her nose and then rolled over. When she had opened her eyes to see what was making a little noise, she spotted Grenseal kneeling down by the edge of the roads. His bright orange cloak draped over the ground.

"What is he doing?" she asked. The Shaper sat up from his rest, looking out over the roads.

"Talking to more of his friends?" he said. "I don't know." He rolled over to sleep.

"Why can't we eat it?" muttered Leanah.

It appeared from her view that Grenseal was doing something too clandestine for her tastes.

Leanah rubbed her eyes and squinted to see. The light of the fire would quickly disappear and the moon was not yet full. Still, it was pretty obvious that he was doing something strange. This was Grenseal, however, so strange was not so unusual.

When Leanah squinted her eyes a little more she could make out his hand petting a small animal. The animal was almost as high as Grenseal's knee and had thick brown fur. It was difficult to tell exactly what could have been. It sat backwards on hind legs, a fat blob of fur and meat. Perhaps it was a groundhog, she thought. Those are yummy.

The ground hog sat back on its dark brown hind legs and pushed its head down every time Grenseal's hand went down to touch it. The mage also appeared to be talking to the groundhog in a human language, something that Leanah still could not quite understand.

The groundhog responded to Grenseal's whispers, nodding and chittering back to questions asked. Whatever language they were speaking was not Common speak, that was for sure.

"Grenseal, what are you doing?" Leanah asked. Grenseal tapped the groundhog on the head one more time and reached into his pocket. It looked to Leanah as if he had fed something small to it. Then he stood up and turned around.

"Yes, Leanah?" he said. His voice was calm and cool and fake. He knew he was caught doing something.

"What were you doing?"

"Just planting something," he said. He reached into his pocket and took out a handful of seeds.

"In the middle of the night?" Leanah asked. She did not really care, but the oddities of his actions as of late led her to feel particularly protective.

"Some flowers grow best when planted at night. Sometimes the sun is much too hot during the day," he said. "It burns their leaves."

"You are lying," Leanah said as she rolled her head the opposite way and closed her eyes. "Go back to sleep," she said.

"Yes, ma'am," he said. Grenseal tapped his pouch once more and removed his cloak. Underneath he was wearing a red tunic and black belt. The tunic looked like it was glowing in the night and Grenseal suddenly became even more visible. "Good night, my lady," he said and rested his head on a log near the fire.

The group ran with a sense of urgency after packing up camp.

It was true that they needed to make it to Bray soon since they were running out of supplies.

The Shaper could tell, however, that Leanah had something else on her mind. Her eyes never left Grenseal, and the Shaper was almost certain it had something to do with last night. "He was not planting anything," she told him. For some reason, she had seen it fit to tell him most of her secrets. The Shaper, due to his quiet nature, should have been used to it, but the tone of her voice often led him to believe that she was being critical of him as well.

It had taken them nearly a week to reach the edges of the Bray village. The anger and intensity behind Leanah's eyes had motivated them to keep up with her task. She knew not when they would need to return. All she knew that it would have to be a quick feeding, for she missed her home.

Leanah, spotting a small ditch in front of her, took a running start.

"Leanah!" the Shaper had shouted out. "Leanah, that is too big!" He turned his attention to Grenseal. "So now we'll have to dig her out of a ditch, too."

Leanah's feet picked up a pace and ran faster, her legs pumping harder. As the she neared the edge, she leapt into the air. At Grenseal's first glance, it appeared as if she was flying momentarily.

Leanah landed on the other side of the ditch, her feet spread wide for balance, her hand held forward to catch herself.

"That was quite a show of agility," said Grenseal. He caught up to her side by crossing the wood and rope bridge that connected the two land masses.

Leanah only smiled and propelled herself faster. "How did you maintain that? Please do not take this wrong, but that was not human."

She growled at him and flashed her teeth. Grenseal flinched as he watched Leanah's legs move faster. She took off in front of him.

"A simple 'it is none of your business' would have been enough," the Shaper told Grenseal, finally catching up to him and wheezing.

Leanah looked back at her two companions. Her eyes appeared to turn gray, then returned to black. Each of Leanah's feet kicked up a small cloud of dust as she disappeared from their view.

The Shaper held his hand against his side, marveled at the speeds at which the little girl can run. He knew she was young, but even in his youth he was unable to acquire that level of speed.

"Where is that coming from?" said Grenseal. "I sense magic, but I fear where it's coming from."

The Shaper patted Grenseal on his back. "Me, too, my friend."

"We are almost there," she said back to her friends.

"What are we going to do?" asked the Shaper.

"First we eat, then we sleep." she said.

"And just how do you expect us to pay for all of that?" he asked.

"I have a sword that cuts things," she said. "If we must, we steal again." She seemed to say this without any sign of remorse. Not eating last night had driven her to more rash actions. "This is the food I was looking forward to last night."

"This ought to be fun," said the Shaper. He looked upon his orange-clad friend with a sign of sarcasm. Grenseal trailed behind them, but ran without a sign of stress or worry. His feet dragged now lightly against the ground underneath him.

The grass turned a dry, dark yellow as his leather boots made their impressions. If he were not careful, he leave a blazing line of fire behind them.

It had been hard enough to avoid getting in trouble so far for the group. They were inexperienced in the way of travel, the Shaper knew. Even his own caravan to the village had been comfortable for the average person's travels. It was one of the perks of being a sequestered monk in the world of richness and wonders. In the larger cities, glittering gold traveled from hand to hand without a single thought. Travel was done with servants carrying you from place to place on wheeled chariots.

The Shaper looked down at his blistered feet. How he longed for a wheeled chariot right about now.

After they had slew the darkened owlbear, the Shaper had begun to wonder just how much more had been touched by the evil. Had his travels—his current and his past to Vamori Village—all been in vain? Is this how the Elders had wanted the world to end?

Not that Leanah cared. She appeared to have nothing to fear. But the sword, the sacred artifact and protector of Vamori was still a great unknown, maybe even the key to the changes in the world around them.

No doubt Grenseal noticed this as well, and decided to stick around in order to keep a careful eye on it.

The Shaper could not agree more with Grenseal, however. With his visions and abilities fading lately, he craved certainty. With the prospect of freedom also came the threat of uncertainty and fear. The Shaper did not know which he feared more.

The Shaper had started this quest with a single intention to save the village from the terrors he had shaped in his time in the Citadel. Now, it was plain to see that changes were occurring, and everything fell outside of his control.

Leanah, for example, her mind was already getting clouded. There were signs, he had noticed, of her being more aggressive. Angrier.

"We grow closer to the Bray," shouted Grenseal. "But I do not see the troubles we were warned about."

"Maybe they are gone?" said Leanah. She began to slow down to a brief jog.

"I see no reason why the gnolls should have left," he said. "Be on guard."

"We can take them on!" said Leanah. "We took down the owlbear!"

"You were lucky, Leanah," warned the Shaper. "Nothing more."

"I am simply concerned," said Grenseal. "You are running incredibly fast. I just wish that you conserve your energy." Grenseal wiped the sweat from his eyes. "In case we need it."

"Speak for yourself," she said behind clenched teeth.

"I do, but I also speak from experience," said Grenseal. Grenseal paused and looked ahead. "I can feel them." He pulled his hands out to his side, to tell us to keep ourselves still. "Perhaps we can discuss this with them, get them through."

Leanah reached to her pack and pulled out her sword.

"We are not taking those types of negotiations," said Grenseal. He could already tell what she was thinking.

"What is the matter, Leanah?" the Shaper asked.

"They are here!" she told him without turning around. "Don't make a move."

"Who?" he asked. "Who is here?" His stance widened, taking his staff into his hands. He had never been trained in combat, but the gods had blessed him with incredible luck. Luck, he feared, he had been straining far too long.

"Creatures of the dark," Grenseal said. He looked at the sword again. "No, no feast just yet."

"Are you talking to my sword again?" Leanah asked

"Leanah, hush!" shouted the Shaper.

Up ahead, small dark figures gathered together. The warm air carried their heavy, guttural grunts back to the human's ears.

"Are we going or not?" the Shaper asked.

"Of course we are," said Leanah. She held up a heavy, clenched fist up at Grenseal. "Do. Not. Move." Grenseal crossed folded his arms across his chest and hunched forward a little.

"So be it," he muttered and sat down in the grass.

Leanah pulled the sword up to her face and she peeked at my eyes. "Are you ready?" she asked. Grenseal nodded.

"I prefer that we do this my way," he said.

Leanah took that as a yes. She gripped the sword tightly and began to run closer and closer to the village walls. As they got closer, however, they noticed there were not walls to speak of. Instead, a small cadre of dark-haired, muscular gnolls blocked her view of the wooden gates.

"Visitors," she shouted back to the snarling gnolls. "No one said that they would have a meal ready for us." Leanah simply grinned and looked back at the Shaper, who followed behind at a slow walked compared to Leanah's quickening charge.

Leanah's eyes narrowed as she measured up the gnolls from left to right. In all there were about seven of them. Someone had apparently been ready for their passage or they were mercenaries taking over a city's trade route.

Either way, Leanah was determined to make it into the village alive.

Without saying a single word, Leanah leapt into the air and flashed the sword before the gnolls' eyes. All sets of dark, bulging eyes widened at once as the Sword of Stone grazed into the first gnoll's shoulder. The battle had begun.

NINE

The gnoll fell to Leanah's knees before she could land back onto the ground. She brandished the blade threateningly and held this battle face to the gnolls.

They, too, held onto their weapons and pointed them directly at the companions. "Yours will be the same fate if you do not leave this village," she said.

The gnolls still stood there without a single twitch.

"As you wish," she said and ran toward the quickly scattering group. One of the gnolls grunted and seized his pikestaff. The long, wooden shaft was a dark wood, but the metal spearhead on the tip was glistening in the sun. The tip of the blade seemed to cut the air in half.

The pikestaff whirled in a circle around as the gnoll twirled it around his arms and shoulders. As fast as it had started, the pikestaff stopped moving in a flash in front of Leanah.

Leanah stumbled backwards, unprepared for the sudden point in her face. "What is this?" she said. The gnolls moved quickly, if not confidently, as they spread their weapons out and attacked the group.

Some along the far edges, sought refuge while others ran for the more passive members.

Grenseal stood up and prepared a small barrier of heat between him and the gnolls that ran toward him. He clasped his hands together and bowed his head. The wave of heat, at first invisible, turned to a shield of flame that covered the front of Grenseal's body.

The gnoll's head followed Leanah as her body rose into the air. She twisted around and landed behind it. "Hah!" she said and slashed into the gnoll's left shoulder. It roared ferociously and grabbed its wound.

"Tue wursit fuer toten!" he screamed at her. Drool and spit dribbled from the gnoll's teeth as he snarled in her direction. Its nose twitched, then it suddenly it turned around, grabbing its pikestaff. It spun it around in the air before bringing it down in front, hitting Leanah on the elbow. "Hah!" he screamed back, mocking her.

"That was nothing," she said. She spun the sword around her own head in a move that mimicked the gnoll's. The gnoll brought its pikestaff up above its head to block the attack, but Leanah surprised him.

Instead, the Sword of Stone swished in the air across, slicing into the gnoll's darkened leather tunic, across its chest. She stood over the body, watching it fall in half to the ground. Another nearby gnoll looked down, only to be smacked hard on the back of the pommel. The second gnoll was down.

Two other gnolls roared simultaneously and charged at Leanah. She flipped her body around quickly, twirling the blade around to keep all of the gnolls back. "This is more like it!" she screamed. Then a bright red fire grew around my blade.

Leanah looked to Grenseal. He smiled back. "I will not take a life, but I can help protect you," he said."

Leanah pointed the tip of the blade to the gnolls and gritted her teeth. "Hai!" she screamed out loud. Fire traveled from the tip of the blade to the gnolls in front of us.

They roared in pain together as the fire engulfed the entire plains in front of the gates of Bray.

The gnolls threw their hands up into the air and ran around to fan out the flames. Panic had made most of them stupid, trying to put out flames by fanning them further.

"No," said Grenseal, approaching the gate. "Stop and roll."

Oddly enough, most of the gnolls fell to the ground immediately and rolled around, panicking and patting themselves as they howled in fear.

"The smell of singed fur is disgusting," I said. Leanah's eyes merely glazed over in a heavy black fog as she grinned from ear to ear. Then she lifted one heavy foot and stomped it down in front of her, one by one, as she entered the gate.

Leanah pulled the gate open with the help of the Shaper.

"And where were you?" said Leanah, nodding toward the Shaper.

"I am not equipped for battle."

"You have a weapon, you kill anything that tries to kill us," she demanded. Her eyes were unwavering. The blood from the gnolls had begun to gather in the bottom of the pack, leaving a dark black stain on the outside where it had soaked through.

"But Grenseal is against killing!" he said.

"And he still helped."

The Shaper gripped his staff tighter and flashed a dark look at Grenseal, who simply shrugged.

The smell of burning fur from outside came into the village traveling in the western winds.

A villager came running from the streets toward the group. His dress seemed formal compared to the companion's, tighter clothes and much more restrictive. The man's vest flapped in the winds behind him. He grabbed hold of his vest and said, "I believe we owe you a thanks," he said. The man's voice sounded shaky, unsure.

"For that? Out there?" said Leanah.

The Shaper nodded, "It was our pleasure."

"You didn't do anything," said Grenseal.

The man looked confused at first, looking from side to side until he finally resting his eyes on the oldest of the group: the Shaper.

"We have been under siege for weeks while they watched our doors. They said they were working for someone, but would not name them."

The Shaper bowed his head. "We dispatched them for you. Hopefully your village will come under no more threat."

"This is most wonderful news!" he said. The man cupped his hand to his mouth and shouted to the rest of the villagers and the empty streets. "These fine gentlemen have rid us of the gnolls!"

A woman poked her head out of the inn across the dirt road. "Dead?" She came out of the inn, wiping her hands on a white apron with rather large dirty stains. "They are dead? All gone dead?"

The man nodded. "Yes! These fine men are to thank!"

"Men?" said Leanah. "I did most of the work," she said.

The man looked at her, then at Grenseal and the Shaper. "Yes of course you did," he said, rubbing along her hair. "I'm sure you did help!"

Leanah grumbled and shoved the man's hand off her head. "I did help," she said. "Tell them."

"She did do most of the work," said Grenseal.

"You?" said the man. He looked down at the girl. "Is this correct?"

The Shaper nodded.

"Well then, little girl, I believe we should bestow our thanks unto you as well."

Leanah smiled and puffed out her chest. "Thank you," she said.

"Surely you are tired travelers!" said the woman. She grabbed the Shaper's cloak and pulled him toward the doors of the Inn. "You can use a drink, maybe? Something refreshing and a warm bed?"

Leanah smiled and rubbed her hands together. "That's perfect!" she said. "See guys? Good deeds do pay off." Leanah pulled the lady's hands off the Shaper and instead led her to the insides of the Inn.

The woman, whom they presumed to be the innkeeper, showed the companions to a table. The air inside the inn felt thick, humid in their lungs. Candles that lit the area on every table and on sconces along the walls, cast a yellow-orange glow on the rest of the dark wood walls that made up the building. Few others sat at the bar;

most of the noise that filled the room came from the clanging of glasses and mugs from the bartender.

"Please," she said, her hands clasped together to contain her joy. "Please, have a seat." She released her hands long enough to show them their table and then turned to a man behind the counter. "Whatever they would like," she said. "On the house!"

Leanah leaned over the table. "On the house?" she said.

"It means it is free, darling," said the Shaper.

"Thank you, very much," said Grenseal. He stood up and wrapped the innkeeper's hands in his. "May She bless you."

"Gesundheit?" said the woman, confused and looking at Leanah and the Shaper for an explanation.

"Just go with it," said Leanah. She waved him off and then stood up on her chair. "This is exciting, isn't it?" she said. "It's like we're real heroes!"

"We only did what we needed to do," said the Shaper. "Nothing more."

"But we killed them all. Well, I killed them all. You guys sat there and did nothing."

The Shaper's face grew red. "I am not trained for this type of thing, and he," the Shaper pointed at Grenseal. "He can't seem to get his magic together."

Grenseal sat down at the table, leaning over the top. "Can't do what?"

"Your magic fiery thing," said Leanah. "You didn't do anything with that owlbear." She said, snapping up in the air trying to get the woman's attention. "Why?"

Grenseal gently pressed Leanah's hands to the tabletop. "Don't snap, Leanah, that's rude." Grenseal. Continued, "My powers didn't work because I did not want them to."

"That's a stupid reason," said Leanah.

To her surprise, the waitress arrived at the table. "What will it be?"

"Ale!" shouted Leanah.

Grenseal patted Leanah on the head and corrected her, "The little one will have juice. I'll have the ale."

"But I want—"

"You are too young for such things," he said.

"Just milk."

"Milk?" said Leanah. "Everything is 'on the house' and you choose milk?"

"In the Citadel, we were held from such things. They said it poison for our abilities."

"And does it?" said Leanah.

"I don't believe so. We used to sneak some when we were little boys," he said with a smile. "My abilities worked just fine." He leaned in over the table so no one else could hear. "I suspect they just wanted to keep it all to themselves."

"They?"

He nodded. "They," he said with a shrug. "Whoever they are. We received orders sometimes, to command. Make more shapes to predict the future for important rulers."

Leanah took her drink from the waitress and sipped it. The liquid tasted sweet that was quickly replaced with a sour aftertaste. "What is this?" she said. "I don't know if this is supposed to be sweet or sour."

"Both," said Grenseal. "It is grape juice. Probably old grape juice." Grenseal sipped his drink, let it linger in his mouth, then gulped it. "This, on the other hand, is real ale." He smiled and held up the mug to the waitress with a smile. "Thank you!" he nodded.

The waitress waved and smiled back.

"So your powers?" Leanah said.

"I was not supposed to use my powers then, so it did not happen," he said, then drank from his mug. "Most of my abilities are based on emotion," he said. "I must appeal to my emotions when I want to use the powers. But I don't believe in violence," he said. Another drink. "So my rock did not respond."

"That's the stupidest power I've ever heard," she said. She slammed down the rest of her grape juice and reached for Grenseal's ale.

Grenseal pulled the ale out of her reach and said, "Stupid or not, this is how things work. I must have the support to do the things I want to do. I did not see a reason to use my abilities, so I did not."

"So you're useless and you dress funny?"

The orange mage smiled. "These are the robes of my people in the South. Sort of a family tradition, if you will. As for my abilities," Grenseal paused, let out a sigh and then sat back, "well, I don't believe in violence. I have been blessed with this curse, to create destruction, to harm and kill. It's my burden, given to me by these Elders the Shaper is so fond of. I have hurt far too many people. And now that the Gods have been hidden, I have been destined to follow this path of destruction and mayhem."

"Are you calling me destruction?" said Leanah, reaching out for Grenseal's ale again.

"I am saying that your path is a twisted one. The animals and the trees, they fear you. What you stand for. The Elders are the true evil. They are the useless ones."

A woman's screech came from behind the bar. The waitress stepped out, high-stepping then climbing out onto the bar itself.

"Rat!" she screamed. "Rat!"

Leanah stood up, looking at the chaos at the bar. "They grow rats really big out here."

Grenseal popped over the table. "That's not a rat," he said. "Excuse me." Grenseal stood up. "Calm," he said and held his hands up. "Just calm down, I'll help you."

The waitress screamed, "Get him out of here!"

"It's not a he, it's a she," said Grenseal, then got on all fours to the meet the animal face-to-face.

"What are you doing, little fellow?" he said.

The rodent stood up on his hind legs and squeaked.

"I've seen that thing before!" she said. Leanah pointed. "I've seen that before!"

Grenseal politely scooped up the animal and carried it outside.

"I think he's made another friend," said the Shaper, taking a sip of the milk and passing it over to Leanah. "Want some?"

The skies had gotten dark as Grenseal carried the groundhog out into the city streets. "What is your message?" he said.

The groundhog squeaked something to Grenseal, who nodded and then fed it a seed from his pouch.

"You're quite welcome," he said.

Grenseal lowered the groundhog to walk alongside him down the streets of Bray. The groundhog's little padded feet tapped along the cobblestone road. After a few steps, she would stop and check on Grenseal to make sure that he hadn't wandered off, squeaking at him as if telling him to hurry up.

Grenseal, of course, apologized and followed along. At last, they arrived at their chosen location: a closed building, door wedged shut with only one window that faced the side street. The mage knocked on the door with a clenched fist. The groundhog waited by his feet, occasionally licking her paws and cleaning herself. "And you're sure they're here?" he said.

The groundhog ran around Grenseal's feet and squeaked.

"Okay, I'll believe you," he said. He knocked again. This time, someone appeared to have knocked back. "Hello?" said Grenseal.

"What?" The voice was muffled but rough, throaty with a hint of an accent.

"I am a friend of Luca's. He is here?"

"Who?"

"Luca?" he said, holding his head against the wall. "Is it possible to talk face-to-face? It's much easier to explain all of this."

"I ain't opening no door for you."

"But you said you knew about him?" Grenseal poked his head around the corner. No other entrances, no way to sneak through.

"We ain't knowing anything about a Luca."

"That's not what my little friend here says." Grenseal rested his hand on the door's handle and allowed for the heat to transfer through his arm.

"Yeow!" Something rattled behind the door. "What the hell was that?"

Grenseal let a subtle smile slip through his lips. "I know you're looking for us," he said. "I was told you had him."

A woman walked down the road. Her strapless dress and high skirt fluttered in the light wind that swept through the alley like a wind tunnel. "Hello, dear," she said. Grenseal smiled and leaned against the door, keeping his fist resting on the handle. "How are you this evening?"

"I'm good," he said. "Good."

The woman lingered the alley in front of Grenseal, taking small dainty steps toward him. "You look quite," her eyes wandered up and down the mage, "colorful tonight."

"These are the robes of my people," he said. Grenseal pressed himself up against the door even further.

"Who's out there?" said the man from behind the door. "What's this?"

Grenseal knocked on the door. "Can you just let me in, please?"

The lady took Grenseal's cloak by his hands. "Are you looking for someone, honey?"

"I am indeed. But, um, I do not believe you are able to help me out." He rested his hand against the door and allowed for the fire to travel through his fingertips. The wood of the door began to smoke, glowing into red embers within seconds.

"That's some trick," said the lady. She took a few steps back, holding her hands to her chest as if gasping in shock. "I'll just be on my way." The groundhog ran to the woman's feet, chittering and stomping on her feet. The woman squealed in terror! "Rat!" she screamed. "Rat!"

Her fleeting steps echoed into the hallways, slowly taken over by the sizzling of the door behind Grenseal. "I said let me in."

Grenseal's door shattered at a simple tap against the wood.

"You can't just do that!" shouted the man.

Grenseal entered into the door, the groundhog at his feet. The building was a home, or meant to be someone's home aside from a secret meeting place. The walls were a bare stone, no other furniture other than wooden chairs and a stool pulled up to the large wooden table at the center of the largest room. Inside, a series of guards, wearing white shirts with silver armor once sitting at a table. On the silver armor, a crest of a hawk. The guards grabbed their weapons, swords and axes, and pointed them at the invader. "Need to know about my friend," he said. "She says he was here."

"Who?"

The mage pointed at his feet, where a pudgy groundhog sat up on her hind feet.

"So where did he go again?" asked Leanah.

"Who knows?" The Shaper shrugged and raised his hand for another drink of milk. "If you are wanting to know, the legend that Grenseal gave you was close," said the Shaper. He sipped more of his goat's milk and set the mug down onto the heavy wooden table. "I believe there must be thirty, maybe fifty types of these stories coming around the world." He took another sip and let the taste coat his throat. "I will admit, it's almost as if there is no origin story to the world."

"How is there no origin story? Where did everything come from?"

The Shaper took his milk and thanked the waitress. "Things came from the Elders. The stars, if you ask me." The Shaper drank of the goat's milk.

"We don't have no one here by the name of Luca."

"A dark-skinned man. Light hair? Blue jerkin?" Grenseal held his hand up to about his shoulder. "About yea high?"

"We didn't see him," he said. "I promise."

"What is your name?" asked Grenseal. "I'd like to know who's lying to me." Grenseal's hand flared a bright red. The flare began to grow bigger into a ball that encircled his entire hand.

"Lance." One of the men stepped forward, pulling his hands out and dropping his weapon. "You can call me Lance."

"Then Lance, I know you saw this man I described. Where is he?"

"We saw someone like that, yes. But we didn't have anyone stay here, we don't know where he went." Lance looked over his shoulders to the men behind him. "He, uh, he said he was looking for someone who matched your description."

"So he was here." Grenseal rested his hand on a wooden beam inside the house. The beam immediately burst into flames, spreading quickly to the ceiling support beams.

"How did you do that?"

Grenseal turned to Lance. "You don't seem as surprised as your voice would suggest," he said. "So, you tell me how I did that." Grenseal turned around and walked to the door. He held out a hand and then pulled it back slowly toward his own chest. The fire pulled back as well, away from the ceiling.

"You gentlemen are lucky I swore a life against violence." He stopped and turned around, the fire's own light disappearing as he spoke. "I don't know who you are and why you are watching me, but you will leave us alone. You have no idea what you are starting."

"Tell me more," Leanah said.

"About what?" Grenseal said. He took his seat next to the

Shaper and peered at his ale, now half empty. "Really?" he said.

Leanah shrugged and wiped her mouth.

He turned his head from the door, then held it in his hand. It looked painful, the way his neck turned upward such a strange position, toward Leanah's questioning face and the nightlights of the sky.

"About the legends. The sword. Everything," said Leanah.

"I thought you did not believe in these lies," said Grenseal. His smile was crooked, like a wooden beam on an old cottage.

"If I am to be this evil creature you say I am, then I want to know more."

The Shaper leaned over the desk and whispered, "There is nothing else I can tell you, madam. Your future is your own. These are merely legends and prophecy. The tomes are not lies that we tell others to scare them or make them believe we are powerful warlocks. These tomes are the intelligence of the gods and the memories of the Universe. It is the story of Terra, the Elders, and the magick as we know it."

"Then how do you know that I will be a monster?"

"I do not remember calling you a monster. I said that you were destined to be twisted with evil, Leanah. You may become Leanah the Destroyer or Leanah the Savior. Your future is your future."

"So there is still hope?" she asked.

"No, there is no hope because you will not listen," said Grenseal. "Now stop with the chatting, will you?"

"Why does it bother you, you crazy old fool?" said Leanah.

"Crazy old fool? You have a lot of nerve to call me, your guide and friend—" Grenseal looked over for some confirmation on the subject of friend, but received none, "an old fool. I am your fate, your savior, and your weapon. You shall address me with respect," he warned her.

"You are a bumbling magician wearing weird clothes," she said. "Nothing more, nothing less."

"If that is all you think about me, then you may as well keep me here," he said.

"What do you mean?"

The Shaper leaned over the desk and touched Leanah's folded hands. "It means that if you have no respect for my power, then the sword will not work with you. How much more simple must it be for you?"

Grenseal sat himself up a little bit and rolled backwards. He crossed his feet in the air and then pulled them back down in front of him. "She does not understand because she does not want to understand, Shaper."

"It is proper respect for a remnant of sacred protection, don't you think?" the Shaper said as he bowed.

Grenseal paused, looked at the pack and smiled. "I think it just talked," he said. "Did anyone else hear that?"

Leanah smiled and pulled the pack closer to her side. "And what did my pack say?"

"Not the pack," he said. "The sword. It spoke. It said, 'I like you' and it laughed."

Leanah pulled his mug away from him to the far end of the table. "And that's enough ale for you."

"Why?" said Grenseal, attempting to sneak the Shaper's mug of goat's milk away from his side of the table.

"That's why, you drunk," said the Shaper. He quickly grabbed the mug by the handle and pulled it back, out of Grenseal's reach.

"They say that the sword is a rune, a rune of Stone. It was supposed to have rock, or strength, or durability, of stamina."

"Show me," she said.

"You will see them when you are ready to see them," said the Shaper.

"But I am its owner now, Shaper, I demand that you show me its power! Please?" said Leanah.

Grenseal stood up and put a small white hand on her shoulder. "I do not think that you are ready. It is not wise to upset a protector, no matter how attached you are to it." He pushed her back lightly so that she was up against the wall and facing the doors. "Perhaps it is better if we were to sleep. I'm sure we have much to do tomorrow."

That night Leanah had finally gotten the peace and quiet that he wanted. However, Leanah reflected back on what the Shaper had said. Never before had she encountered anyone who knew so much about magick, about the gods. Not unless they had a rune themselves.

No, that can't be.

Leanah rested her head against the pillow, gracefully handed to her from the Innkeeper and looked out at her companion.

Why is he hearing the sword and she was not? She wondered. Certainly she would have been able to detect its power. She was from the village. It was supposed to protect her village, and therefore her.

That mage, she thought. He would be trouble if he stood in the way of her getting what she needed. To protect people, to protect Vamori, she would need power. More power. Power like Grenseal. Power like the Shaper.

The Shaper sat up on the wooden floor and meditated on the

coming events. He did not know what was going to happen, and indeed, even I was not able to discern the source of the next great evil. I knew that this Shadowed Wing had not shown up in his shapings before. Nothing even like it. He was being deceived, he felt. Something dark, something heavy was coming their way. The Shaper felt nothing around him with which to summon the Inspiration of the Elders. For the first time in his entire life, he felt the thrill of not knowing what was going on.

The Shaper let this thought linger in his head, bringing a gradual smile to his face. Sometimes people deserve to be left alone. No burdens. No powers. Just silence.

But why did it appear that Leanah was the great evil they were meant to destroy? Had the Elders fated him with such a task? Destroy the one who is going to destroy the world?

Did she not deserve a chance to be left alone? To make the right decision first?

The rattling of Leanah's bed, her tossing and turning awakened him from his trance. He peered over at the little girl, clutching her bag near her. Her only real connection to her village, her culture and her destiny.

"Go to bed," said Grenseal.

The Shaper turned around to see the man sleeping in his wooden framed bed. His own orange cloak hung neatly from a nearby chair. The rest of his clothes Grenseal decided to sleep in.

"We have a lot of work to do tomorrow," he said. "We cannot afford to have you tired," he said.

The Shaper nodded and smiled. For the first time since he was eight, he had no visions of threats and fortunes. It was freeing, he thought, not knowing what was going to come his way. Though with this freedom came a question that gnawed at him. Why was he devoid of visions now? What kind of magick was at work that would cause him to lose his way? His path?

The Shaper sat in his bed and carefully laid his tired head on the pillow. It smelled of dust and bird down, thought it was definitely more comfortable than what he was supplied by the well-intentioned people of Vamori.

The next morning Leanah watched carefully as Grenseal and the Shaper got themselves ready to continue their journey. Just outside of the cozy town of Bray, bluhorn cows munched on the nearby grass, their heads coming up only to see the whereabouts of the nearby humans.

Grenseal stood on his head again, whispering something and then humming some horrible tune. He closed his eyes and Leanah could see his body wobble back and forth. His feet kicked about and his eyes opened wide. "What, exactly, are you doing, wizard?"

"I told you, I'm a mage!" he said, right before he fell onto the ground with a loud crunch of the grass beneath him.

"Do mages still feel pain?" she asked, laughing at him spewing blades of grass and chunks of dirt from his mouth.

"It is time we leave. The Moon Goddess has spoken to me," he said.

"Really now?" she asked. "And what did she tell you about breakfast?"

With a silly grin on his face he held up a stick from the fire last night. "Fish!" he announced.

Leanah grabbed the sword by the hilt and then swung me around. "I think I will try to fish with this!"

Grenseal began to laugh. "He's not too happy about that," he said.

"There!" she shouted. "He did it again!" She pointed over to the sword's blade and guard, and held it up to the Shaper first and then ran over to Grenseal. "See! Do it again! Loud enough so I can hear."

"Come on," she said. "I'm sorry if I was ignoring you," she said. She dipped the sword into the narrow stream that circled around half of the village. Only the blade, however, and swirled it around. Within minutes the water turned black. "What is going on?" she asked. "What is this?"

"You still do not understand, do you?" said the Shaper.

Leanah swirled the sword around a bit more and then pulled it out. Leanah glanced at the blade, up and down, reflecting what little sunlight she could find.

"My lady!" shouted Grenseal. His orange robes twisted themselves lightly in the wind as he pointed into the water and ran back to us. "My lady! The fish!"

As Leanah turned her head to the riverbed small fish started to bob back up to the surface. Grenseal let out a loud moan that sounded more like a cry and knelt down by the riverbed. He dug his hands deep into the water and pulled out a small handful of fish. They lie motionless in his hands. "I am so sorry, Lord," he said. The fish fell from his hand as he lifted both of them up into the sky. He then looked back to the ground and sat, taking out a handful of water and let it sift back into the river over and over again.

"What did I do?" Leanah screamed at Grenseal. "What did I do?"

"There is nothing you can do, madam," said Grenseal. "These

fish are dead. The power of your weapon may be awakening."

"How do I fix this? I must know now! How?" she asked. Her eyes turned red from the tears forming in the corners. "This rune is supposed to help people! Isn't it? Why is it destroying everything?"

"Its power comes from the user. If the person who uses it is dark, then so will be the powers that stem from the sword," said Grenseal. He dried his hands in his robes. "Likewise, if the sword's master is good, so then will be its powers. Never will a rune be able to bring back life. That is impossible."

"You said that if it's good so will its powers be," said Leanah in desperation. She stabbed the water with the sword and swirled it around. "Come alive!" she commanded. Of course, it did nothing of the sort.

The Shaper held his hand to his mouth and looked away. The color of the water and the smell that came off the surface was too much for his stomach. "I think I'll skip breakfast this morning."

"We must go, Leanah," said Grenseal. Leanah stared at the orange mage, searching for an answer to the dead fish. "It is best that we leave. Now." Grenseal fixed his belt underneath the robe and continued to walk. He whistled and motioned his hand towards his torso. One of the bluhorns came running after him. "We'll be late for our next stop if you do not hurry, Leanah." Grenseal patted it on the head and smiled. "You be good," he said to the bluhorns. "Treat your masters well."

"What next stop?" Leanah asked.

"The swamps of Mrondir are further past the Oaken Forests," said the Shaper.

Grenseal nodded, agreeing.

"If we are to reach the end of these plains, we need to be on our way now," said the Shaper. He reached into a huge pocket on the side of his orange robe and pulled out a tight fist. From between his fingers tiny seeds fell onto the ground.

"What are you doing?" asked Leanah as she tried to catch up. She held the outside, the wind blowing the little droplets of water off of the blade. "Why are you dropping those?"

"These are offerings to the Lady for our accidental trespass into the riverbed," he said, emptying his hand finally as the last of the seeds ended the trail between Leanah and him.

"I do not understand," she said.

"Today we took life. In order to balance, we must give life," he said simply and walked on.

The silence was something Leanah had to get used to after all of the jabbering between them that morning. Leanah was filled with many questions about why the fish were still not alive, why Grenseal knew all the things that he did, and why the sword refused to speak to her. It was the stuff of annoyances if you were to ask her.

The next day they had settled down for another quick rest. The Shaper grew tired and weary carrying the weight of the knowledge with him every day. He would admit to none of this, however, to his companions. As it stood, he needed to ensure that things could change, that maybe they should change for the better.

The orange mage often climbed onto his head and hummed something, whispering something about the stars and the earth and then fell over onto his knees. This was a daily ritual with him.

Leanah asked, "Why are you upside down? Does that not hurt your head? We stop too frequently for this to be useful."

"It is my way of clearing my head and being able to concentrate on the ether around me," Grenseal said.

"I don't understand," Leanah said in a slow and steady sentence.

"When I am upside down I have my energies focused and my mind is able to send it thoughts into the universe."

"That sounds crazy," said Leanah.

"Ah, but it does not matter if it sounds crazy to you. Those who do not hear the beat think the dancers mad, as they say," Grenseal said, his eyes closed and a serene look on his face. He opened one of them and peeked over to the Shaper. "Surely the cloistered monk understands."

"You're a crazy wizard," he said firmly. "I stand by it, despite all we've been together."

"Something is coming," said Grenseal. He opened both eyes but remained standing on his head. "Perhaps it is the beast of which you seek."

"You really expect me to put my faith in your upside down energies trick?" Leanah circled around the group and twitched her ears, focusing on the sounds and sights around her. "I do not hear anything."

"That is because you did not have your ears to the ground," said Grenseal.

"Because I am not a crazy fool," said Leanah. She pulled the out of her pack and held it by the handle, flashing its blade in the sunlight. Though typically it did not reflect light back with its blade, this time it blade lit up with a white aura that seemed to distract Grenseal. He fell down with a dull thud and shook his dusty, red hair. "If you do not believe me, then why are you on guard?"

"Why do you insist on antagonizing me all this way?" Leanah muttered under her breath, "We should have left him for dead."

"That would have been irresponsible of you," said Grenseal. "You needed a guide and I needed help finding my friend and getting some answers. My life is now yours."

"Whatever, you crazy old coot," Leanah said. The air was motionless. All they could smell was the dirt that still clung to Grenseal's orange robe. He dusted off his hair and reached into his belt, pulling out his seeds once more. "Now what are you doing?"

"Speaking with the lands," Grenseal said matter-of-factly. He held the seeds in his hands and pushed them around his palm. His eyes squinted, and he whispered something to them and rested his ear close. He nodded.

"What do you see?" the Shaper inquired.

"They are hesitant to speak," he said. "The earth has been thrown in disarray. There are few things that will shake the will of the earth," he said. "Whatever is coming, and coming soon, has more than the power to do it."

"The darkness? What's coming here?" said Leanah. Leanah felt both of her cold and sweaty palms grip the handle as she swung me back and forth in paranoid arcs in the air.

"Will you let up, please?" asked the Shaper. "The wizard is crazy, we both know that. How do we know that his seeds speak the truth? He knows nothing of the Elders."

As if the Goddess herself heard them, they all turned to the north to the sound of thunderous galloping. At first it was too distant, but this black dot got bigger and bigger as it approached.

"Oh no!" exclaimed Leanah. She held her sword steady in the direction of the black dot and braced herself into the dirt. "It is coming and fast!"

The mage gathered his seeds in a calm ritual and held out an athame into the air. He spoke secret words to the metal blade and moved around in a circle, stopping five times and whispering some more.

"What are you doing?" Leanah felt her own heart beat in time with the approaching gallops. "If this is the demon, maybe we should be prepared for battle!"

"And what do you know of battle, little one?" asked Grenseal. "You are new to this whole thing, or need I remind you." The orange wizard tended to his athame, shoving it deeply into his belt and stood with his hands to his side. He watched the black dot grow increasingly larger as it approached.

"I know plenty! I have practiced in the village and I have studied with the best!"

"You do not even know about the weapon of which you wield! You are going to get yourself killed, you fool!" said the Shaper.

"And why do you care!" she shouted at him.

"I don't very well want to be stuck out here in the middle of nowhere," he said. It was true. If the black dot were to destroy them both, he would be lost or in the custody of some mysterious evil. The Shaper felt rattled deep into his core, the threat of the unknown, an unknown foe and the mystery of defeat or success hung in the air.

"I will not fail. Not with you by my side," Leanah said the sword.

"Perhaps you were not listening the first time, girl," said the Shaper. Just as he was about to admonish this girl some more, Grenseal told them both to hush and held his hands to his face. He had them clasped together, his fingers intertwined and he held his head down. His long auburn hair draped lightly over his hand.

"I shall see what I can do to speak with this creature," he said.

The Shaper had to admit: this man was a fool, but brave.

"Are you so sure it wants to speak to us?" Leanah asked. The dot was again getting darker. We could make out something of a dog, large and black. Its feet were blurry and sometimes disappeared behind a thick brown cloud of dust and grass that was ripped out of the ground. She smelled the dust and a fast-arriving stench that reminded her of the old bluhorns pens that were stashed just outside of her village. The foul, stagnant smell overcame them all and Leanah reached for her nose, closing it with a pinch of her fingers.

"I am not sure about anything right now," said Grenseal. "But perhaps a spell could catch us some time." He brought his hands together at his side and formed his hands around as if he was holding a tiny ball in his hands. The invisible ball grew larger and larger in between his hands and he seemed to be convinced that he was truly holding something massive. In moments he forced the ball in front of him with his right hand.

The intensity in his face both amused and frightened Leanah. Never had she even heard of this before.

Grenseal did not seem to do anything at all, but his face said otherwise. To be a fly on the wall of his mind would be so fascinating sometimes, Leanah thought. "My flame sphere had no effect!" he shouted.

"You did not do anything, you idiot!" the Shaper shouted. "It looked like you were imagining the whole thing!"

"Nonsense! There was magic!" he protested. "Meanwhile, the black dot was growing massive. It appeared to us that the dog was something of an owlbear, large and built like a stone tower. As it moved the light reflected off of its black fur. The stench was horrible as it dug up more and more dirt and grass on its path towards us."

"We did not see anything! You are absolutely insane!" Leanah said. She grasped her sword once again and quivered as she held it out to the owlbear. Her stance was not very threatening, even to herself. It is difficult to be threatened by a quivering spec of a human if you were a twenty-foot tall beast, able to demolish a forest with the slightly flick of your nose.

Grenseal clasped his hands together near his face once more and appeared to be praying.

"I suppose when all else fails the Tomes say that you must stand there and pray like a coward?" the Shaper cried over to him. "You magicians are all ridiculously stupid." He looked over to Leanah's face. Beads of sweat and nervous energy radiated from her face. Her skin had gone completely pale and for the first time he thought she saw her own mortality. The black owlbear was quickly approaching, and by the Shaper's best estimate, was only forty feet in front of them.

"You would do good to listen to everything I tell you," Grenseal warned. "Only together can we destroy this demon."

Leanah nodded—or stood there quivering in fear, the Shaper could not tell which—and gripped her sword harder.

"Great demon owlbear! Hear us! We mean you no harm. We ask that you go back to your dwelling and leave us be," said Grenseal. He held up his hands as if to stop the owlbear by sheer force of will. Needless to say, the owlbear still came charging. From his distance they could feel the ground trembling beneath them. Bump bump. Bump bump. Leanah looked as if she was going to fall over.

"Please tell me you are joking," said the Shaper.

The owlbear charged toward Leanah. She leapt to her right and barely dodged the oncoming rush.

"You must listen to what I say. This is no ordinary owlbear. He has been tainted by darkness, something familiar to my stone!" said Grenseal. "I can feel its powers."

"Maybe we can have this owlbear for dinner?" Leanah stood frozen from her fear. The owlbear realized that it had missed her and turned around.

Grenseal stood with his hands as if he were cupping a ball. Another spell he hoped would not fail. He flung his hands backwards and then threw them toward the owlbear. Again, the Shaper and Leanah did not see anything. Grenseal stomped his foot in disgust. "Again it did not work!" he said.

"No kidding," said the Shaper.

"Plunge it into the demon's heart!" Grenseal screamed.

Leanah held the sword out by one hand. The owlbear came charging at her again.

"It seems to only want you," he said.

Leanah nodded. "Why?" she said.

"Then give it what it wants," said the Shaper. He looked to Leanah, nodding with a smile.

Leanah seemed to have understood his meaning.

The owlbear let out a mind-bending screech that shook the companion's eardrums. Leanah dropped her sword and grabbed her ears.

She screamed.

"What are you doing? Pick it up!" screamed the Shaper. "He wants that!"

Leanah snatched the sword from the ground.

"Yes! Now charge back at him!" the Shaper shouted. As if her legs were connected to her sword, she ran towards the charging owlbear. It was a ridiculous thought, a small girl charging a large black owlbear, she thought, but a danger to her was a danger to her village.

They were so close she could smell the damp, dusty fur. A large wad of snot dribbled from his nose and splattered on the ground. This disgusting beast would be a satisfying meal indeed. As she charged toward the owlbear, Leanah let out a loud wail that was half of a scream and half of a battle cry. Her blood was pumping so hard her face turned red. She felt the moisture coming to her eyes—part sweat, part tears. Her eyes turned glassy and red from the large dust clouds that permeated the air.

The Shaper watched on, protecting his own eyes with his cloak. This was going to be a mess. That was for sure.

The owlbear was a mere three feet from them when Leanah noticed that it seemed to be getting smaller and smaller underneath her. Leanah had jumped up and over the owlbear. She landed on top of it. The bristly fur dug into her naked legs like thorns on a rose bush. She clenched tightly onto its fur. They felt like bristles in her hands, painful enough to make her let go and switched hands from one to the next repeatedly. The owlbear kicked and bucked and tried to get us off. It didn't help that every time the owlbear tried to kick Leanah off, she only grabbed harder onto its prickly fur, which in turn would make the owlbear kick once more. And endless cycle.

"How did I do this?" Leanah asked. With eyes wide open and a face consumed with fear, she asked, "What am I supposed to do now?"

"I didn't know you were going to jump on top of him," the Shaper said.

The owlbear kept kicking and bucking from side to side. Its snout wiped back and forth on the ground, kicking up more and more dust which floated into the humans' mouths.

Grenseal stood by the side and covered his eyes, trying to peek through his fingers to catch a glimpse of the owlbear's fate. The beast kicked back and forth and side to side. Leanah maintained an iron grip.

"Throw it into its side!" Grenseal said. "This beast will fall!"

She twirled the blade around in her tiny hands and held it downwards. She felt the rush of the warm air run all over her. This, she would have to admit, was exhilarating! She could not wait to go back home and tell her father about it.

With a quickness that Grenseal could not even see, Leanah stabbed downwards into the owlbear's side. Just as she did so, the owlbear kicked again and Leanah fell off balance. Instead of going into the owlbear's side the blade slashed into it; however, the cut was not deep enough to slow the monster down and Leanah now hung from the side of the owlbear.

She had fallen in its last kick, a small grasp of hair being the only thing that was keeping her from being trampled underneath the owlbear. Her legs flailed as she kicked herself off of the ground. Her feet could barely keep up and the sword swung madly in her left hand. "Kick off the ground!" Leanah commanded herself. "Kick and get up on top of the owlbear!"

Leanah closed her eyes and clenched onto her sword tightly. Within a second she felt warmth radiating from the blade, then hot, then as if her own hand was on fire. This heat traveled through the sword and into Leanah.

Grenseal had found a way to break his vow of peace.

With a sudden kick, Leanah had managed to leap from the ground and back onto the owlbear. Even this caught her off guard; her body flew wildly into the air and barely managed to land on the owlbear's coarse back. The energy had surprised her, and a toothy grin passed over her mouth, her lips stretched into scarlet red ribbons. "What was that?" she asked, still with a smile.

"They are bonding," Grenseal said. He was not sure he could go into more detail than that. He felt a shift in energy that he could feel and taste.

They still had an owlbear to kill

"Let us give this one more try!" Leanah said and acting just as quickly as she could think, Leanah turned her blade around again and held it high into the air with both hands. Her legs clenched the sides of the owlbear and her both her feet dug deeply into the bristly fur. Her torso shook from side to side as the owlbear tried to buck us both off again. The sword's blade shook around violently.

This black beast was finally going to meet its end. Before Leanah knew what she had done, her sword's blade was buried inside of the owlbear.

The beast kicked around and squealed horribly. The noise grew to be deafening, so much so that Leanah let go of her blade and covered her ears instead.

The owlbear gurgled and screamed and kicked around until it finally fell on the ground, its legs kicking and jerking back and forth. It looked like it was trying to run on its side. The sword, however, was still dug deeply into the owlbear's back. As she sliced into the owlbear's meat Leanah felt the darkness, the energy rising from its being and very soul.

It felt sour in her body, cold; yet, it was not the beast that she was supposed to slay. Somehow, she understood that the sword had not fed.

The sword sucked on the owlbear's dark energy until the owlbear turned from black as a moonless night to the gray color of ashes when a campfire burns out. The beast's sides rose up and down in deep, heavy breaths. The owlbear's black eyes turned the grayish blue you see in clouds of a winter storm, which soon disappeared behind giant black eyelids. The owlbear's heaves up and down slowed down more and more until it turned to a mere wheeze. The wheeze gradually stopped as they crowded around it. Leanah knelt by, leaning on the sword's handle and tried to catch her breath. Her legs were scratched over in at least a dozen places from the owlbear's coarse and prickly fur. She was out of breath and panted, staring at the ground.

She wanted to watch the fruits of her labor. The owlbear's death was something to be proud of. Even she had been impressed with her skills, though she had no idea where it came from. She did, however, have her suspicions.

She grabbed the sword and pulled it out of the corpse. She felt the sword's power, it hungered more.

"We must move on. That was not the beast we were meant to slay," she said.

"Give me a minute," Grenseal said in staccato breaths. He leaned over further, hacking and gargling. "I need to catch my breath."

The final breathe of the owlbear escaped its body, its entire core appeared to collapse.

"I am not used to this kind of warfare," said the Shaper. "I do not want to get used to it."

"I never thought I would have to deal with this," Leanah said, finally standing up.

"You never thought! Period!" Grenseal roared. "You were selfish and stupid. Now we're having to heal the earth twice."

"But you said this beast was tainted," she said. "How was it not supposed to die?"

"We could have helped it," said Grenseal. "We must have been able to." Grenseal shot a glance at the sword, blood dripping off its blade onto the ground. "That's not very funny," he said.

"I didn't say anything," said Leanah.

Grenseal ignored her comment, looking at her. "I am against the taking of life. I see no reason to destroy recklessly."

"This was trying to attack us," said the Shaper. "Surely you can see that."

"I said that I needed you to help save the village. You said that you could do it and Ciaran didn't teach me how to save everything," said Leanah.

"That may be true but you are ignorant of my ways. You have no idea where you are going, what you are supposed to do." Grenseal shouted.

Leanah's eyes flinched every time the orange mage raised his voice at her. Rather than putting the sword away or shoving it back into her backpack like she always did, she stared directly at its face and seemed to start crying. Finally, she was listening.

"I'm sorry to butt in," the Shaper said as he pulled lightly on Leanah's shoulder to get her attention. "But who is this Ciaran fellow of which you speak?"

"He is my village's teacher," said Leanah.

"Ah, so he is a wizard?" asked Grenseal.

"No, not as such in magic. He is powerful in the ways of tek-nolo-jee."

"And what is that?" said Grenseal.

The Shaper shook his head. "He is of those ways, is he?"

Leanah nodded. "He's amazing. Tek-nolo-gee is a metal magic. I've seen him shoot metal arrows out of something called a gun.

He knows of strange and wondrous things, and knowledge like no other." She rested the sword back in her pack and took a long breath. "He was the one who seemed to know about the sword and told me where I should go."

"A tutor, you say?" said the Shaper. He rubbed his chin with his fingers for a bit and then reached into his leather pouch again. "I did not see a tutor in my shapings."

"Interesting," said Grenseal. "And he is not with you because?"

Leanah's eyes lowered to the ground. "Well," she said, her voice lowering to a whisper. "I sort of stole the sword when no one was looking."

"You stole this sacred artifact?" Grenseal said. "You are aware that we will most likely have many people looking for us. Stolen things have a tendency of attracting much attention."

"My father will trust me," she said. "I know he will."

"Is that why you had to steal it? Because he trusted you?"

Leanah had nothing to say.

"And you knew about this?" Grenseal said, pointing to the Shaper.

He nodded, "I was the one who helped her escape."

"We were in danger the minute I set out with you, weren't we?" Grenseal drew up his hood and released more seeds onto the ground. "We face a great trial ahead of us. I have never seen dark, tainted things such as this. This kind of magic is new to me, and I'm hearing new voices, and now you're telling me that we are being hunted by your own father."

"Well, we don't know that he's hunting us just yet."

"But it is a matter of time," said Grenseal. He gathered his things, adjusted his belt, and continued heading south.

"Well, yes, it probably will be only a matter of time," she said.

"Why do you have to make so much sense?"

"I would be weary were I you," said Grenseal. "We are angering the lands."

Leanah rushed up to his side. "You want to be picky and criticize?" she said. "You think you fling fireballs at monsters. No one has seen your mysterious fireballs, you goof. What kind of magic do you practice anyway? Magic does not work if no one can see it," said Leanah. "So right now you do not have a lot of my faith in your abilities, fire magic, or otherwise."

The Shaper pulled up between them, grasping both of their arms in stride. "We need to leave. It will be dark soon, and we're still out in the open."

After a time, the Shaper and Leanah began walking faster, leaving Grenseal behind. The sword remained tucked back into Leanah's pack again.

"My lady, I am merely reporting what I see. The lands and trees show me the path, I merely report it!" Grenseal called out. For a moment he stood on his head once again and closed his eyes. His lips moved as he mumbled something to himself and his eyes opened once again. "Wait up!" I heard him scream out as he trotted along to catch up.

TEN

As the night passed on, Grenseal sat up and observed the rotations of the sky. From this clear evening, he watched as the constellations chased each other from the east to western horizons. His favorite, the constellation of Arryo the Frost Giant, played in his mind as he chased five sister temptresses, who cost poor Arryo his child and wife.

Grenseal was stunned at the deafening silence of the plains. At night it was usually custom to hear the movement of the wind in the trees, or the hunting of snakes or rats in the fields. This evening, nothing shook the grass or rattled underground. This gave Grenseal an uneasy feeling that prevented him sleep.

Even the Shaper, that mysterious fellow whom Leanah had said "made" the rock in his hand at another time, had gone to sleep.

Grenseal smiled. Very well, he would serve as guard duty. As no good came from a lazy guard, Grenseal stood up and watched as the moon traveled across the sky. It was larger now, looking so close and bright he felt he could tickle it from where he stood. Its light illuminated much of the plains, which Grenseal felt thankful for. If there were any vermin, he could catch it and let it loose away from the group before Leanah could kill it.

While he was for the protecting and keeping of his friends, useless death for the sake of killing went against his very core. The act and thought of being a ruthless killer had never come to him.

Even Luca, his trusted friend and perpetual travel companion, had a mean streak in him from time to time, a fact that Grenseal felt complemented his own pacifist ways nicely.

Not even an hour past before Grenseal began to feel the temptation to rest his eyes. A few moments of sleep won't hurt anything, he thought, and he walked back to the tree and laid his hand against it.

"Dear friend, please keep us protected," he said into its bark and then rested his ear against it. "Yes, I know that these two are young and inexperienced, but we cannot judge them so. To do so would be just as callous."

Grenseal stuck his head against the tree again and laughed.

"I'll speak to her about that, I am sorry. Good night my friend."

Grenseal laid his head down on a pillow he made of his cloak and pouches and closed his eyes. As he did so, he felt the snapping of a twig behind him.

The night had been quiet, too quiet, for Grenseal. He smiled, comforted at the fact that he and his companions had not frightened the local wildlife too much

Grenseal's eyes opened quickly, though he dared not move, as a sharp metal edge carved a small path on his cheek. "Do not move," he said.

Looking in front of him, both the Shaper and Leanah had blades against their necks.

"We just want to talk," said the voice above him.

"This is not talking!" Leanah shouted at her captors. Slung over her mysterious captor's back, Leanah pounded her fists into his shoulders. "Let us go or I'll kill you!"

The man laughed, as did the other four men that surrounded her.

"Where are you taking us?" she said. "I demand you tell us."

The men laughed again, a fact that made Leanah grind her teeth. "I am really getting tired of everyone not taking me seriously."

"Calm your nerves, Leanah." The voice came from the Shaper, though she could not see him from her vantage point. "We are all safe for now."

The man holding Leanah chuckled, "'For now,' he says." More laughter from the band.

"Where is my bag!" she demanded. "Where is it? Shaper! Where is the pack?"

Leanah began kicking her feet, twisting and turning, causing any kind of ruckus to make her captor drop her. Her plan, however, failed. When she had flailed about too much, the man squeezed his hands against her side, grabbing hold of her kidney and forcing a bolt of pain to scream through her body.

"Where is my pack?"

"Pipe down there, pipsqueak," said the man. "We got yer stuff."

"Give me the bag at once!" she screamed. "Now!"

"Do yer really thing yers in a position to be making demands now, dear?" said the man. His group laughed in unison, each chuckle and bit of laughter making Leanah more and more frustrated.

And also, more and more tired. Leanah gasped for breath as

the man's squeezes caused less room for her to breathe through her diaphragm. Her stomach felt too full from the food earlier, and the man's thick burly shoulder had begun to dig into her stomach. If she had continued to fight, she feared, she would inadvertently knock herself out.

"Where are we going?" she screamed.

"Pipe down! Last warning." The man squeezed again, causing Leanah to scream out into the night.

"Leanah, please relax. We are not in danger," said Grenseal.

"Grenseal?" she said, her voice weak, airy. "Help us!"

But no help came. Leanah watched at their tree, their protector, disappeared into the horizon. Her friends, she thought, were completely useless.

The bandits brought them to another camp, this one with sentries, masked and holding giant sticks with metal blades that glowed with the flickering orange-red reflections of the torches on the entrance.

Leanah tried to remain silent and still, reserving energy for the perfect moment to escape. She had been the last person, it seemed, in the group, being held in the back. Everyone else may have been in the front of the group, walking perhaps.

Why they could walk and not run, she was not sure. How could they walk into their own deaths?

Leanah sat still and waited. She watched as the sky disappeared behind the roof of an animal skin tent, patched together with thread mad of some kind of thick rope and weaved branches.

"Stay here!" the man demanded. He bent forward and took Leanah by the waist, holding her against a pole. Another man, this one smaller and much, much less muscular came with a rope. He began by roping off her mouth, forcing it between her teeth and then around her head. "This'll shut 'er up."

The rest of the rope wrapped around her shoulders, her torso, and her legs until she couldn't budge a single inch. "And don't go nowhere," the little man said, laughing as he left the tent.

Grenseal stood to her left. The Shaper, to her right.

"Are you all okay?" she said.

The Shaper nodded. Grenseal said, "Yes. You are unharmed?"

"Who are these people?" asked the Shaper.

Grenseal shook his head, pulling it out and away from his pole as far as the rope would let him. "If my suspicious are correct," he said, "these are the men responsible for the lack of caravans and traders in the recent months."

Leanah's eyes narrowed. She worked the rope with her mouth, flexing her cheeks and wetting the piece in her mouth to make it slick. Finally, after pulling her head up, then down, she wedged it out of her mouth, letting it fall down around her neck. "These are the men responsible?" One of the tiniest guards stood near the doorway. "They don't look so tough. Let me at them with my blade, I'll hack them all to pieces!"

"And just where is your blade?" asked the Shaper.

The blade. Of course. "I do not know," Leanah's heart felt squeezed in a tight grip. "I don't know!" she screamed. "I cannot lose the sword!"

"Sword?" asked Grenseal. "The one you used to save me?"

"Where is it?" Leanah screamed. "Where is my damned sword?"

"Will you shut that one up?" asked a guard standing outside. "How'd that rope get off her mouth?"

"Where is my damnable sword?" she screamed again. "Where? Is? It?"

The smaller of the guards came into the tent holding his sharpened staff. From here, Leanah was able to get a better view of her soon-to-be victims. Their clothes were not ones familiar to her, baggy pants that fit tight around their waists but hung low, like sacks around each leg. Their shirts, too, fit tight at the neck and arms but flowed loose around their torso.

"Where are you from?" she asked. "I demand you tell me."

"And I demand you shut up, little girl." The little guard stood directly in front of Leanah and stared into her eyes. "Or we're going to have to get mean."

"You want to see mean?" she said. Leanah made a noise, like clearing her throat, then spit a clear, mucous glob into his face.

"You ignorant wench!" he cried. He dropped the staff and wiped his eyes with the lower half of his shirt. "This witch spat on me!" he cried. He went to the entrance to the tent and stood there, calling out to another of the bandits. "She spat on me!"

The other guards laughed—at first—until the littlest one slapped the others and demanded that they get their arrows.

"Arrows?" Leanah said.

"Did you have to do that?" asked the Shaper.

"No more than he had to take my sword!" Leanah turned to Grenseal. "And where are you in all this? Make with the flames!"

Grenseal's body looked lax against the pole. The only thing hold him up were the ropes wrapped tight around his body.

"Grenseal?" Leanah yelled. "Grenseal? Are you awake?"

"He's been poisoned, I fear," the Shaper said. "Back at the camp. He cannot hear you now."

"Poisoned?" Leanah said. "But we need him! Wake up, you fool!" Leanah kicked at the pole that bound her still.

Another guard followed the little one back into the tent. "That little witch over there!" the man pointed at Leanah. "That's the one!"

The other guard laughed. "All over this little thing?"

"Give me that!" said the little guard. He grabbed the two arrows from the bandit's hands and pointed their tips at Leanah. "Now who's going to get mean?"

Leanah began to clear her throat again, gathering more spit and mucous into the back of her mouth. Until one of the arrows pierced the top layer of her skin.

"You bastard!" she screamed. The man laughed as Leanah squirmed. "Do that again you little bastard! Do it again! I dare you!"

The guard stood backwards, looking at the tip of the arrow that just went into Leanah's chest. "I thought this was supposed to knock her out."

The other bandit shrugged. "Iunno."

His eyes freaking out, and Leanah growing more out of control, demanding that he stick her again with another arrow, the small bandit guard pointed another arrow tip into Leanah's chest and pressed harder.

This time, blood dripped from the puncture wound.

"That's right. And another! Come on!"

The smaller bandit stood backward, smiling at first. It quickly turned into a gaping look of horror as she thrashed about on the pole. "This is not working," he said.

"Give it some time," said the other bandit. "Let her burn it out." The little one, however, had no patience for it and fled the tent. The bandit walked out of the tent and stood by its entrance.

"Leanah!" cried the Shaper. "Leanah! Are you okay?"

Leanah's grunts and kicks quieted down to a dull murmur, her ferocity turning to that of a mild kitten.

"Can you hear me?"

Leanah nodded as best she could. "Uhhh."

"Don't die on me!" cried the Shaper. "Not here. This isn't how it's supposed to be." The Shaper pulled his hands back and forth against the pole, hoping for something that would cut away at the ropes. The speed, however, was not fast enough. "Leanah!" he shouted. "Wake up!"

Other guards, unseen before by any of the group, entered the tent. "The little one, I think," said one of them. He pointed at Leanah and approached with a knife.

"No! Don't!" the Shaper cried out.

"Pipe down!" said the guard holding the knife. He elbowed the Shaper across the face, and then proceeded to cut down Leanah's ropes. "Grab her!" he said to the other guard. They dragged Leanah's listless body outside the tent.

The Shaper stared at the now-empty pole between him and Grenseal, who was still mumbling something incoherent and completely useless.

"We could use a little fire right about now," he mumbled to himself.

Grenseal, however, turned his head toward the Shaper, his auburn hair shifting and draping over his eyes. Out of his mouth came the word, "Burn."

"Let me go," Leanah mumbled. Her feet felt solid ground beneath her, but she felt unable to stand under her own power. Her legs did not want to work anymore. Her eyes appeared just as useless.

This gray and red blob moved from side to side, then around her as he spoke.

"She was the one with this sword?" asked the blob.

"Yes, ser," said the guard.

"Great," the blob said. "Another empty kitchen."

Leanah felt a warm, swift slap across her cheek.

"What is this?" he said.

Something long and gray bobbed in front of her eyes.

"What?" Leanah said.

"This!" the man said. Leanah felt the man's grip in her hair, lifting her head up. The light tickled her eyeballs, but did not hurt. Even the man-blob's grip did not hurt. She felt funny, numb, woozy.

"You're funny," she mumbled.

"Just how much of that stuff did you give her?" he asked.

Another voice—out of Leanah's line of sight—said, "I don't know. Two arrows?"

"Two?" the man-blob asked. "Are you trying to kill her?" He let go of her head, which sunk down to the ground.

Leanah felt sick watching the bright orange blurry scenery turn into a dark green and blue blur in front of her. Her stomach rumbled.

"What was that?" the man-blob asked.

"Uh, I think it was her, ser."

"Her?" the man said. "If she dies in here, I'll kill you next! I swear on your mother's head."

"Ser, you already killed my mother," said the other voice.

"And you'll be next." The man-blob knelt down next to Leanah and lifted her head once again, this time gripping her chin and pushing it up to meet him eye-to-eye. "Your group has nothing else to take, no supplies. No food." He shifted Leanah's head so he could look her right in the eyes. "Tell me, what kind of traveling group doesn't have supplies?" He dropped her head, slapping her face to wake her up. "You have nothing to sell. Nothing to take, except this." He held the sword in his other hand. "Now tell me. What can you tell me about this sword?" he said. He held it close to her head, pulling it forward and backward, watching for a sign that she understood what he was saying.

She mumbled something incoherent.

"She's damn near useless!" he said. The man seized a large chunk of her hair, pulling it back entirely. "This, you wench! This! Where did you get this!"

Leanah tried to focus on the long gray blob in front of her. "M-my."

"Your? Your what?"

"M-mine?"

The man, the leader of the tent, looked at the other bandit guard. "This is almost not even worth it," he cried out. He directed his attention back to Leanah. "Where. Did. You. Get. This?" he asked. "I must know."

"Ser, they appear to be a ragtag bunch," he said. "Merchants, perhaps."

"These are not merchants, Glen." The man rested the tip of the sword into the ground. "This is a unique creation. A sword of interesting power, if I remember correctly. I wouldn't expect you to understand."

"Ser, it's a beautiful sword, sure, but—"

"Get out," the man demanded.

"But, I was complimenting—"

"Get out!" he demanded. He stood up and turned away, but

not before pointing at Leanah's slow, slothful body. "And take this thing with you."

The man went to take the grip of the sword in his hands as he walked away toward his desk, but not before the sword flew out from the ground and toward Leanah's limp hands.

"Grenseal!" shouted the Shaper. "Please wake up! We have to get Leanah! You promised to help us!"

Grenseal's body twitched, flexed, slowly, his head turning left, then right. He made the occasional noise, mumbling something. Then and again, mumbling, "Burn."

"Yes, burn," said the Shaper. "Burn the ropes. Burn us out of here."

A small hiss and pop, the smell of burning oak overtook the tent.

"Grenseal? Please tell me that is you."

Grenseal grunted, but behind him, a thin stream of smoke drifted up into the air, toward the top of the tent. The pole that held him turned to a glowing red, then white-hot beam of charred wood.

The beam to which Grenseal was attached crumbled into a pile of red-hot ash. Grenseal fell forward, catching himself on all fours. He looked up, his auburn hair falling into his eyes. His hands glowed blue, almost white-hot, searing his handprint into the dirt ground.

The Shaper swallowed his fear and turned his eyes up toward the top of the tent. "Please, Elders, watch over us."

"What is this magick?"

In front of the bandit leader stood Leanah, wobbly but standing, grasping onto the hilt of the massive sword in front of her.

"Ser, magick has been gone for centuries!" said Glen.

The leader of the bandits seized a sharp knife from his desk and threw it at Glen. "I know that, you buffoon! I already know!" The knife grazed against the side of Glen's tunic and stuck into a bale of hay used as a seat behind him.

Leanah's foot twitched, then her knee. She groaned as she stood up, forcing herself to use all of her strength to keep her balance. "You will pay," she said.

"Kill her!" screamed the bandit leader! "Kill her now!"

Glen took the knife from the hay and held it, shaking, in his hands. "Come here, little girl." Instead of waiting for her to follow his request, he ran toward the girl, swinging the knife rapidly through the air. The knife's blade made a quick whip noise in the air, moving quickly until meeting its intended target.

"Ow!" Leanah said. In a dull, creepy-quiet voice, she hissed at Glen, "You will be first." Leanah's hand shifted on the hilt, reversing to hold the sword upright. No longer heavy, the blade felt natural in her hands, her strength being just enough to wield the blade with the finesse of a blademaster.

Using little more than the rotation from her shoulders, Leanah thrust the sword upwards, connecting with Glen's tunic and slicing upwards through his chest.

Glen's lifeless body dropped to the ground.

"You little witch!" the bandit leader screamed.

Leanah closed the gap between her and her opponent with

only two steps. With only one hand, she held the sword across the table, pointing the tip of the blade directly into the man's throat. "My friends."

"They're in the over there!" the man pointed behind Leanah. "Over tent!" he said. The man's words felt jumbled, tense. Leanah watched as the lump in the man's throat pulled upwards, afraid, then fell back down toward his collarbone when it touched the Sword of Stone's tip. Leanah smiled and pulled her body forward.

The blade had pressed slightly into the man's throat, causing him to jump backwards. "You crazy witch!" he yelled. "Guards!" he yelled.

But no one came.

Seeing nothing even close to an opening, he gripped the sides of the table nearest him and pulled the table upwards into the air, thereby throwing everything at Leanah and making enough noise to make his escape.

Leanah, however, did not flinch. The feathered pens, inkwells, and paper were not enough to force Leanah to defend herself.

Instead, she turned around, watching the leader try to make his escape. With one smooth motion, a flick of her elbow, she flung the sword from her hand and allowed it to land into the man's back.

The bandit leader gargled, took two steps before falling into the ground. His arms fell over themselves, trying to pull himself away from her, away from imminent death.

"This is more than you deserve," Leanah whispered to the leader and rested her hand on the sword's pommel. With little effort, she pressed downward and felt the crack of the bandit Leader's rib.

Leanah's attention changed to the chaos outside. The other bandits in the camp had seemingly forgotten about her, instead tending to the burning tent that stood down the walking path.

The flames from the tent were small, but had taken over much of the tent's upper half.

Leanah smiled. "Grenseal, you old bastard."

"Get out of here!" the bandits screamed. "Leave!"

The scuttling of the men did nothing to detract Leanah from her path, pushing through the men grabbing armor, clothing, weapons, and food on their escape out of the bandit's camp.

One of the men stopped in front of Leanah. His eyes grew wide, the chaos of the fire, the flaring tongues of flame reflected in his watery eyes. "You!" he said. "You did this!"

Leanah pushed the man out of the way and walked with slow, deliberate steps toward the camp. "Grenseal!" she shouted. "Shaper!"

There was no answer.

"Grenseal!" she shouted again.

A cough. Leanah heard someone—or something—cough and then thud to the ground somewhere around her. Leanah held out the sword in front of her, swinging it back and forth to get the other bandits to avoid her completely.

"Shaper?"

Another cough.

Leanah followed the trail of coughing and hacking back behind the tent.

Another popping, something snapping. Leanah watched at the tent's leathery cover began to glide to the ground.

Leanah did not wait: she grasped her friends by the back of their cloaks and dragged them a full twenty paces away from the fire.

"Leanah!" the Shaper said. "You're—" A hack and cough.

"You're alive."

Leanah smiled and pulled the Shaper to his feet. "Isn't this fun?"

The Shaper shook his head. "Grenseal?" he asked. "Is Grenseal okay? Is he—?"

Leanah pushed Grenseal's coughing body over, exposing his face to the both of them.

Grenseal grabbed his sides and doubled over. There, in his grip, the leather pack that Leanah used to carry the sword.

Leanah looked up at the Shaper. "He'll be fine. Now let's go. This place is coming apart."

The Shaper pushed back Grenseal's hair from his eyes, checking for any scratch marks or tears in his cloak. "He seems okay," he said. "Come, help me."

Leanah snatched the pack from Grenseal's grip and rested the sword carefully inside it. Then, she seized his right hand, but let go immediately. "Ow! Dammit, he tried to burn me!"

The Shaper took Grenseal's left hand looked at it. It was cool to the touch. "He seems to be fine."

"Look!" Leanah said. She grabbed Grenseal's wrist and held his palm facing the Shaper. "It's hot as burning coals."

"I see what's going on," said the Shaper. "Come," he said. "Be careful. You take the left hand. We have to get out of here, soon."

Leanah grabbed the orange mage's hand and dragged him up. "But shouldn't we look for food, for something to take with us? Supplies?"

The Shaper pulled the mage's arm around his shoulder. "Look around us, girl. We do not have the time to look. This place is burning around us."

Leanah reluctantly agreed. The two worked in unison to pull

Grenseal to his feet and haul him out of the bandit's camp.

"What happened?" Grenseal's head raised to see the shadows dancing on the fiery glow of orange and red on the grasslands in front of him.

The shadows belonged to the village that slowly burned to the ground against the nighttime sky. "What smells like barbeque?' said Grenseal.

"That, I'm afraid, is not a barbeque," said the Shaper.

Grenseal's head dropped again. His eyes watched the dancing flames, feeling moist with emotion. "So pretty," he said. "What happened?" He raised his nose into the air and sniffed twice. The dusty smell of dried grass mixed in with the barbeque smell of burning wood behind him.

"You did, big guy," Leanah said with a smile. "That's all you."

ELEVEN

The two companions dragged Grenseal as far as thirty paces before he was able to stand under his own power.

Grenseal's steps were weak, wobbly, from the effects of being drugged by the bandits.

"What did they want from you?" the Shaper asked. He looked on Grenseal, who looked to be losing his balance soon. "Here, my friend," he said and offered his staff to Grenseal.

Grenseal nodded his thanks and gripped the staff with both of his hands. It bore his weight well, he thought.

The moon lit their path as they searched for another safe place away from the bandit's camp.

"With the fire burning," said the Shaper, "more of the bandits are sure to return. It may even attract scavengers, doubling our trouble." He turned to face Leanah. "You," he said. "What was it they wanted?"

Leanah shrugged. "I don't know."

The Shaper slowed his pace. "I'm sorry, Leanah, but I do not believe you." His eyes studied Leanah, watching as her shoulders turned inward, her head ducking down. "They pulled you for a reason."

"It was the sword," she said. "They wanted the sword."

"And you have it?"

Leanah tapped the backpack. "Right here."

The Shaper relaxed his smile. "Good. How are you holding up back there?"

Grenseal held up an unsteady hand, then pointed up his thumb. "Good," he said. "I'm good."

The three companions walked for nearly an hour before settling down at another makeshift campsite. Leanah was the first to fall asleep. She had curled up underneath Grenseal's orange cloak, offered to her to keep her warm through the night. They had decided against a fire this night, deciding that the first must have alarmed and attracted the bandits in the beginning.

Grenseal knelt down onto the dirt ground. He bowed his head to the dirt, kissing it and then spoke to the patch of grass in front of him.

"Do you always speak to the plants?" asked the Shaper.

"Do you always speak to the Gods?" asked Grenseal, poking his head up and watching the Shaper lay down and wrap himself in his own cloak.

"Only because they talk back," he said with a smile.

"You took the words out of my own mouth," said Grenseal.

"The grass speaks to you?" asked the Shaper.

"Should it not?" Grenseal asked. "Does it not speak to you?"

"I cannot say that it does."

"You're missing out. The lands have much wisdom to share with us."

The Shaper nodded and smiled. "The Gods, I feel, are much more responsive."

Grenseal nodded. "Perhaps. But I always better with that face-to-face connection. The Gods, I fear, have been a bit—" Grenseal paused to choose his words wisely so as to not offend his new friend "a bit absent."

"Are you okay, my friend?"

Grenseal shrugged. "I did all of that." He nodded toward the drifting smoke.

"It was under stress. You were not you, Grenseal."

"But it was my power. My will. My fire."

"And if you hadn't, we'd still be in there, held captive."

"How many died by my hands?"

"The Gods will forgive you, Grenseal." The Shaper's voice turned soft, but still grim. "It was from defense, not fear. Not anger. Not even wrath."

The Shaper nodded. "Perhaps we all have our own connections to the world in our own different ways."

Grenseal paused, looking at the grass in front of him. "Maybe I ask you a question?"

The Shaper nodded. "

"Leanah has called you Shaper. That is not your name, is it?"

"It is my title."

Grenseal nodded and smile. "I thought so."

"Have you heard of us Shapers?" he asked.

"Who hasn't?" he said. "When did they change the rules about letting you walk free amongst the lands?"

The Shaper pulled his cloak tighter to his chest. "We're still waiting for those days."

"And yet you run free?"

"I escaped."

"How does that work?"

The Shaper turned away. "I broke free so that I may prevent a horrible disaster. Against the rules of the Citadel, I know, but I could not permit the end to come to us all."

Grenseal sat up. "The end?"

The Shaper nodded. "The Shattering, the twilight of the Gods."

Grenseal shook his head. "Tall tales," he said. "If you ask me, the Gods have been dead for quite some time."

"If that were true," the Shaper said, "then I would not have been able to shape the rock in your hand."

Grenseal glanced at his right hand. The molten rock glistened black and red, embedded nearly halfway into the palm of his hand. The rock, it had been told to him, was made out of volcanic rock. "You had created this rock?" he asked.

"I had shaped the rock," the Shaper said, closing his eyes. "Before we met you, I was overcome with a trance. In the mud that lie around me, I shaped your rock. A prediction," the Shaper yawned and turned away from Grenseal, "I suppose of our eventual meeting."

"That is," Grenseal began to say, but stopped. His sentence had been interrupted by the Shaper's snoring.

Grenseal waited as his two traveling companions fell asleep. Their snores did not bother Grenseal. They were well-earned, especially after their long journeys and the dangers of the bandits.

Still, curiosity grasped Grenseal's interest. The sword, this relic that he had heard about but never clearly seen, had piqued his interest. While Leanah slept, he thought, he could take a peek—just a little one—and see just what all the fuss was about this.

Grenseal crawled toward Leanah's sleeping body. Just a peek, he told himself. Nothing more.

As he approached Leanah, he moved slowly so as to not wake her up. With cautious movements, he poked his left hand into the bag and felt around. His fingernails tapped against something hard and metal.

The Sword.

It felt heavier than he had imagined, but not so heavy as to drag it on the ground. Even now, Grenseal could not remember a time he held an actual sword. Staves were more of his chosen weapon, when he was not practicing the ways of magick.

Grenseal's hand felt for the entire handle and gripped it. With great care, he pulled it out, slowly, slowly, before exposing the entire thing to the moonlight overhead.

The sword was exquisite by Grenseal's eye. The blade, a smooth, blemish-free metal that reflected his own image perfectly. He studied the blade, its unique features and the ornate handle guard, shaped in a heavy, blackened metal into crescents moon. Between the ends of the guard, a few notches etched into the blade. These notches, if looked at without focusing on the finer details, appeared to be the features of a face.

"Fascinating," Grenseal said to himself. "I wonder." Grenseal took his thumb and rubbed it over the apparent face. The notches had a dull texture to them, soft edges and smooth lines. "Hello?" he said.

One eye of the sword opened, then the other. "What is it?" it asked. The voice was male, raspy as if still waking up. "Kaverin?" it asked. "Is that you?"

Grenseal nearly dropped the sword from shock. "Kaverin?" he said. He was not the god of fire. "No, this is Grenseal."

The sword blinked. It had become apparent that while Grenseal was studying the sword, it was in fact studying him as well.

"Who are you?" Grenseal asked.

"What did you do with Kaverin?" said the sword. "Where is he? Why do you smell of him?"

Grenseal shushed the sword, placing his finger along its tiny metal mouth. "I don't know what to say to that. Kaverin is, it is believed. I mean," Grenseal stuttered. How do you explain the state of the world to a sword? "They are, um, not here, it would seem."

"Not here?" the sword sounded disgusted with the answer. "Not here? Bah! Where are they?"

"They are," Grenseal stumbled with his words again. "Am I really talking to a sword?"

"Am I really talking to an idiot?" asked the sword. As it began to raise its voice to Grenseal, he stood up and carried away from the campsite.

"You'll wake up the others," he said.

"And if I do?"

"Then we'll both very much be in trouble."

"You'll be in more than trouble if I do not find out what happened to my friends!" the sword shouted at him, his little voice losing the rasp, turning into a rock-shattering demand.

"Your friend?" Grenseal asked. He sat down, holding the sword in his hands to keep the face upwards in case it would get mad at him again.

"Yes, my friend. Kaverin? Did you kill him? Is that why you reek of him?"

"I don't know what you're talking about." Grenseal gripped the sword with his other hand.

The sword's eyes widened. "No!" he said. "No, this could only mean," he said.

And with this, the sword began to weep. "You are the receiver."

Grenseal looked around his shoulders. Had he been imagining this the whole time? "Who, ser?"

"You!" the sword screamed. "You, you dolt!"

"There is no reason to continue with that kind of name calling or I shall put you back into that pack."

"Pack?" the sword said. "You have been storing me in a pack? How dare you sling such a powerful creature into a pack like a common tool."

"You do know that you are a sword, do you not?"

The sword grimaced. "You will be the first to die, my friend."

Grenseal dropped the sword onto the ground and walked away.

"Wait!" he shouted. "Where are you going? You cannot leave me here!"

"I will return when you are ready to be civil," said Grenseal. "Not a moment sooner!"

The sword let out a loud sigh. "Kragg," he said.

"What?" Grenseal stopped and turned around to face the sword.

"Kragg," he said. "I am Kragg."

"Nice to meet you, Kragg. I am Grenseal." Grenseal knelt over the sword and smiled.

"You already said that."

Grenseal stood up to walk away again.

"No, no, no! Come back!" the sword said. "Come back, please! I'm a little grumpy when I just wake up, you understand."

Grenseal nodded. "Fine, as long as you are quiet and civil."

"Why must I be quiet?" said the sword. "I have been quiet for decades. I believe I deserved a chance to speak a word or two as I see fit."

"You will cause a ruckus, one that was started by you."

"That's not what I understand," he said.

Grenseal paused, gripping the sword so that he may speak directly to its face. "What does that mean?"

"It means that you started the fire, did you not? Is that not what you do?"

Grenseal's hands began to shake. "You were—"

"I was not awake, but aware, yes."

Grenseal blinked. Any words he might have wanted to say left him in that moment.

"You will find, Kaverin's keeper, that I am aware of a great many things."

Grenseal dropped the sword and continued back to camp. "Please keep quiet, for both our sakes."

"Where are we going?"

"I thought you knew a great many things?"

"Sarcasm has not been lost on your kind," said the sword. "Very well."

"Back to camp," Grenseal said. "And if you wake everyone, we'll be off to a horrible start for tomorrow's leg of the journey."

"I see. Very well, I shall keep myself occupied."

As they entered back into the camp, Grenseal walked softly in his leather boots back to Leanah's leather sack.

"I'm going in there?" the sword said.

Grenseal pressed his gloved index finger to his lips. "Shh."

The sword whispered, "I'm going in there?"

Grenseal nodded.

"Please, don't do that."

"I must. If I do not, she will not be happy." Grenseal nodded over at the sleeping Leanah.

"Very well, but can you keep the flap open? For a bit of fresh air?"

That request begged the question of the sword's ability to breathe, but Grenseal swallowed the urge to ask it. "Very well."

Grenseal returned to his place between the two other companions and looked up to the sky. In the distance, smoke still rose from the wreckage of the bandit's village. The night's wind carried the charred wood smell of a bonfire and barbeque over to Grenseal's direction. As hard as he tried to ignore it, he could not.

Grenseal lied down on the ground, curling himself up into a ball. To the ground, he whispered, "I'm so sorry," and closed his eyes to rest.

"I told you to keep your hands off my stuff!" Leanah shouted before beating Grenseal with his own cloak. The edges of the sleeves whipped at Grenseal's face, leaving sharp marks that felt warm like cuts.

He threw his hands to his face to protect himself. "I don't know what you're talking about!" he said.

"Of course you don't!" Leanah said. The whippings continued, even through Grenseal's attempts to stand up and protect himself. "Did you really think I wouldn't notice?"

"Notice what?" he said. Grenseal directed his attention away from Leanah, looking for help. "Shaper! Talk some reason into her!"

The Shaper drew up his hood over his eyes and smiled. "Good luck with that."

"Leanah!" Grenseal screamed. "Stop this! I don't know what you're talking about!"

Leanah began beating him in beats, each whipping of the cloak punctuating the space between her words. "You. Messed. With. My. Bag!"

Grenseal's hand began to flare and he felt the heat flare away in waves from his right hand. "I do not want to hurt you, but if you do not calm down."

Another pass of his cloak across his face, and Grenseal managed to catch it with his warming hand. He released it immediately upon smelling the burning fabric of his own cloak.

"Have you lost your wits?" Grenseal asked. His hand flared into flames, red flames that crackled the air around him.

"You were given direct orders to leave my things alone!" Leanah said. "And you could not even follow those!"

"I did nothing of the sort!" he said.

Leanah pointed at her pack, still half open and facing them. "Is that so? Then why is the bag still half-open?" she screamed and began slapping his forearm. "Tell me that!"

"Maybe someone else opened it! Maybe a critter or rodent?"

"Don't make me laugh," she said. "I know it was you. I can feel it."

Grenseal lowered his guard. "You can feel it?"

Leanah lowered her tight fists to her side, stomping on the ground. "I can just feel it, okay? I cannot explain how I know. I just know."

Grenseal nodded. "Fine," he said. "I admit it. It was me."

"See?" Leanah said and continued to slap at Grenseal's forearms. "I told you it was you! Why did you lie to me?"

Steam and smoke had engulfed Grenseal's feet, the soil burning into a dirty coal smell. Before long, Grenseal began to float upwards, nearly invisible waves of heat radiating from his body. "I said calm down!"

Leanah took a step backwards. "How are you doing that?" she asked. "You can fly?"

Grenseal remained stoic. "Calm down."

"If something happened to that sword, I swear I'll destroy you where you stand."

"You do not have the power, nor the cooperation of the sword to do so." Grenseal dropped back to the ground with a soft thud.

"What did you say to me?" Leanah said. She went to the pack and seized the sword, holding it by the grip. "Say that again!"

"You do not have the sword's cooperation," he said.

Leanah attempted to bring the sword's blade to Grenseal's face, but the weight proved to be too much for her. "Come on!" she said. "You worked yesterday!"

Grenseal smiled.

"I'll slice that smirk right off your pasty magickal face!" she threatened and pulled at her sword's grip. "Come on!" she commanded. The sword appeared to hear her, allowing her to lift it toward Grenseal's face but only for a few moments before dropping again to the ground. "You stupid! Stupid! Little sword!"

"Excuse me!" said a voice.

Grenseal smiled.

"What was that?"

Grenseal pointed to the sword. "Kragg, meet Leanah. Leanah, Kragg."

Leanah's eyes shifted toward the sword. "Kragg?" she said. "You have a name?"

"Don't you?" it asked.

"And you can talk?"

The sword sighed. "Yes, yes. Let's get this out of the way, shall we?"

Leanah dropped the sword, but then knelt down next to it, staring at its hilt. "Where is your face? How do you talk?"

"Up here," it said. Leanah's hands traced the handle, then the guard, until her fingers rubbed against the notches on the shoulder of the blade. "That's my mouth, please."

Leanah jumped back. "Oh Gods!" she screamed. "This is," she ran her hands through her hair. "This is amazing!"

"No more amazing that you talk!" it said.

"But I'm not an inanimate object," she said.

"If I'm talking to you, am I not, in fact, animate?"

Leanah's glances flipped quickly between Grenseal and the Shaper. "I'm arguing with a sword! My sword!" Leanah dropped to the ground. "This is so exciting!"

"No one said anything about anyone belonging to you," said the sword.

"Excuse me?" said Leanah. "But you most certainly belong to me. You came from my village!"

"So you're from Vamori?" it asked. "When did it become a village full of women? Much has changed in the last fifty years."

"It is not a village full of women!" she said. "We have men. My father is still the chieftain."

"And who would that be, my dear?"

"Hibert! The last to hold you and slay the Shadowed Wing."

The sword laughed. The laughter sounded eerie and metallic, like an echo-filled buzz of mosquitoes. "You mean to tell me he's been spreading that lie?"

Leanah stood and stomped over to where her bag lay by Grenseal's cloak.

"What are you doing?" he said.

"I am putting you away. I will not have you speak poorly of my father."

"Oh you little runt. Who's speaking poorly? I've forgotten how pathetic you humans are. No sense of humor whatsoever."

Leanah gripped the sword's handle and dragged it—being unable to lift it herself—into the bag.

"Do not drop me into this bag," the sword demanded.

Leanah buckled it shut. "You knew about this?" she asked.

Grenseal reached for his cloak and punched his arms through the sleeve holes. "I had my suspicions."

"And when were you going to tell me?"

"You wouldn't even let me see it. How was I to confirm my suspicions?" Grenseal sat down in a spot of grass and held his head against it, listening.

"What are you doing? Don't change the subject."

"The forest lies that way," said Grenseal, pointing in the opposite direction of the traces of smoke in the village behind them. "If we move in that direction, we will hit the Oaken Forest."

"Did the ground tell you that?" Leanah said.

"You have talking sword, why is it so impossible to believe the ground may speak to me?"

Grenseal stood up and pulled his orange hood over his eyes. The sun had been particularly bright that late morning. Altogether, they group had almost slept in longer than usual. The events of the last night—the discovery of the sword's secrets, the escape from the bandit's camp—had proven to be too much, too tiring, for the small group of traveling companions.

"Did you grass friends tell you how long this trip is going to take?" she said.

"As long as it takes us to get there," said Grenseal.

Grenseal led the group toward the forest while listening to Leanah's cynical grumbling from behind.

The forest that lay in front of them lay in stark contrast to the plains they were about to leave behind.

"Do we know what lurks in these woods?" Leanah asked.

"I do not. I have never strayed directly into them," answered Grenseal. "Rumors spread of a savage beasts and a bird that cloaks itself in darkness."

"Those are just rumors are they not?" asked Leanah.

The Shaper took the first steps into the darkened wooded area. "Keep faith, Leanah. We will make it through alive."

"I am not worried about being alive," said Leanah.

She looked on as Grenseal followed, taking high steps to avoid crunching the flowers and bushes beneath his footing. "I am concerned about the case at which we will emerge alive."

"There is only one way to find out, young girl," Grenseal said.

Leanah remained hesitant to budge from her position. Her feet remained at the line of where plains met woods—what seemed like a wall of large tree trunks large as the buildings of Deckal. It seemed apparent to Leanah: this was certainly where they acquired their lumber supplies.

"Are you coming or not?" asked Grenseal.

The orange cape of the man gradually became darker and darker still as the two traveled into the forest areas. The canopy above had been dense, letting strays of thin beams of light reach the ground itself.

Beyond the callings of her friends, Leanah heard the buzzing of insects, the chirpings of birds, animals she had never seen before.

Three days ago, this adventure had been a source of excitement. The villagers had all agreed: she was the reason her beloved Vamori village was falling to ruin. Her people, her culture, would fall to destruction without her help.

Thus far, however, she had come across sword that could talk, a man who summoned flames from his hands, and a group of bandits that had been burned to the ground.

"Here goes nothing," she said. Leanah's left foot crept past the long straws of grass that covered the base of the towering trees.

Leanah ran after her group, catching up with them as they left the entrance to the woods. The border where the trees met with the grasslands had completely disappeared over the horizon.

"I guess we have to finish this now," Leanah asked.

The Shaper turned to face her. "Worry not," he said.

"You keep saying that," she said, "but I can't help it." Leanah flipped the pack around her side and pulled out her sword. "Maybe if I have a little bit of protection.

The sword grew heavy in her grip, falling to the ground. Leanah had to turn around and drag it behind her, walking backwards, to keep up with her traveling companions.

"Why are you so damned heavy?" she asked.

"Because I am not about to be used by the likes of you!" it said.

"The likes of me?" Leanah walked over a large rock, on purpose, to make the sword bump against it, then streak over it.

"Watch it!" it screamed at her.

"Then stop being a jerk."

"You stop being a woman!" it shouted.

Leanah gasped. "What did you say?"

The sword's eyes rolled upwards. "You heard me, wench."

"I will put you back in that pack and never take you out again if you do not apologize this instant!"

The sword remained silent.

"You have until two." She waited, tapping her foot. "One."

Another beat.

"That's it," she said. Leanah flipped the sword into the pack and shut it tightly. "Have fun back there."

A muffled list of commands, one of which Leanah understood as having something to do with her mother, rattled out of the pack.

"Keep talking, it'll only tire you out more."

More rattling and muffled screams.

"I cannot tell which I appreciate more," said Grenseal. "The whiny sword or a vindictive little girl."

The Shaper grasped his staff and tapped on the ground carefully, listening for something. "Careful," he said, "we are on strange lands." He tapped with his staff once more. "We do not know what dangers may entrap us here."

"What are you worried about?" Leanah asked. She walked past the other two cloaked figures, falsely confident and charging forward. "We have the sword, we have your powers. We're golden!"

Leanah disappeared behind a tree into the darkness of the deep forest.

Grenseal's hands grew warm, glowing hot. "We must stay on guard," he said.

"Do we even know what type of figure a Shadowed Wing is?"

Leanah popped her head out from behind a tree. "By its name I would judge it to be a bird of some kind."

Something of a muffled laughter erupted from the pack.

"Shut up in there!" Leanah said, shaking the pack.

"How are we to hunt this thing if we don't even know what it is?" asked Grenseal.

"I assumed you knew," said the Shaper, pointing at Leanah.

"I brought you because I thought you knew many things," Leanah said, placing special emphasis on many things. "You are the great and powerful."

"I only know the course of events, Leanah. I cannot tell you specifics."

Leanah stopped shaking her pack. "Then what kind of useless Shaper are you? I thought you were supposed to know things?"

The Shaper dropped his hood and looked out into the trees. "We have an opportunity to find out, I suppose." With that, the Shaper sat down on the ground, in a pile of wet soil that soaked into his pants and cloak.

The Shaper looked up into the sky and his eyes flickered backwards into his skull.

"What is he doing?" Grenseal asked.

"This is what he did when he made your rock," Leanah whispered back.

The Shaper's hands dug into the dirt around him, first making shapes—circles and triangles—then scraping them out and tracing other, more complex shapes.

"Is he drawing something?"

Leanah shook her head. "No, he shapes things."

The Shaper's hands dug deeper into the soil and pulled out a glob of black soil, rich and dark. With his hands, he began to thrust his fingers into it, pushing and shaping, making something that looked like a cup. Then with a sudden grasp of his hand, he balled it up between the palms of his hands, pulling out shapes and training the dirt into a long, oblong shape.

"This is making no sense," Leanah said.

"Just wait," Grenseal said. "He may be finished soon."

Leanah looked around as her stomach grumbled. "I'm going to look for something to eat while he's doing this."

Grenseal had no say in the matter, with Leanah disappearing behind some trees before words could escape his mouth.

Grenseal watched the Shaper's eyes flicker about and his hands moving too fast for Grenseal to keep track.

Leanah took a deep breath of the strange air. These scents were unfamiliar to her, tasting more like the cinnamon that the Shaper had suggested in their first bark meal.

Leanah pressed her nose nearer to the trunks of the trees. They were sticky, something amber colored dripping out of the trunks. "What is—" she asked. Then, taking her fingernail and pulling off some of the sticky gunk, she stuck some of it on the tip of her tongue.

The bitterness made her cough at first. The gunk stuck to the insides of her teeth and left an aftertaste that reminded her of bark.

"Blech."

Leanah scratched at the tip of her tongue and the insides of her front teeth, hoping to remove the memories of the horrible experiment.

"That's not good to eat," she said. Leanah turned and peered back behind her. The scenery appeared to open up behind her, but back where her friends stood remained darkened and threatening. "Hey guy!" she shouted back to them. "This part here is much bigger!"

She caught a glimpse of Grenseal's orange cape fluttering in the breeze, and then his sleeve wavering back and forth. "We'll catch up," he said.

Leanah nodded. Her first priority? Food. Lots of it, she had hoped. And though she knew Grenseal did not eat anything with a face, she could apologize for it later. For now, she needed to sink her teeth into flesh.

Something cracked the dried leaves on the forest floor behind her.

Leanah smiled. "Come to mama."

The Shaper's hands thrashed about in the dirt around him. His hands moved about, shaping an entire scene of little black blobs and three larger blobs.

The blobs, Grenseal assumed, were he and his compatriots.

"Shaper, I have no idea what this is," he said.

The Shaper's eyes fluttered back and forth, and for a moment, Grenseal believed he could detect the Shaper's blue irises before they disappeared into the recesses of his eyelids.

Leanah pulled the sword out of the pack and let it drag in the piles of leaves and twigs behind her.

The sound had come from the insides of a cavern, its entrance covered in windswept leaves and pine needles. In this kind of darkness and environment, Leanah found it difficult to track anything. The smell of animal droppings and dust caused her to cough as it hit the back of her nostrils.

Leanah cleared out her throat. "Come out, come out, wherever you are," Leanah said. The sword made minimal noise despite it dragging pieces of stubborn, hardened sticks and large pieces of bark into the dark soil of the ground.

"I'm pretty sure you sound tasty," she said.

Leanah stopped and listened to her surroundings. With the beating of her own heart, the thrill of the hunt, and her own monologue, she could not hear the traces of her would-be meal.

Leanah's stomach grumbled, leaving her with the thought that for a few more hours, she would have to live with the hunger pangs.

Where once stood three or four tiny blobs of mud quickly erupted into ten and then twenty mud blobs surrounding. Grenseal watched with anticipatory horror as he tried to guess just what was going to happen to them.

"Is this a scene? A symbol? A story?" Grenseal brushed his hand through his hair. He felt as if he were grasping at pieces of sand, filtering through a fishing net. Each guess was just as valid as the one before it. "A trap? Are these rewards?" he said.

The tiniest of the blobs were then dwarfed by a large ball of dirt. With a great speed that Grenseal had never seen before, the Shaper's hands began to mold the ball into another ball, breaking off two half circles and attaching them to the sides.

Grenseal shrugged. "I give up."

"Hello?" Leanah said. She felt the slickness of her own sweat against the sword's grip. She wanted nothing more than to wipe her own hands on her tunic and continue with the hunt, but a moment of cleaning her hands could mean a moment of lost surprise, a feast walking away from her.

Leanah crept forward toward the last crisp snap in the forest. The animal could not be that big, she had determined. Not if it was just making light little snaps. Something bigger would demand a larger space, breaking more twigs and ripping more of the leaves.

Something small, she thought, she could handle.

"Come on out," she said. "I'm hungry."

As she stepped closer to a bush where she believed the cracking to be coming from, she thought she had discovered the quick motion of a black tail, thick like a lizard's with the shimmering scales. In the little bit of sunlight available, the glimmer was

"Here we go," she said. Leanah gripped the sword's handle tighter.

The Shaper's fingers began to create more delicate forms, pressing and kneading the bigger mud ball into rounded haunches like that of a small animal. The Shaper added a neck, long and thick along with a smaller oval at the tip. It began to reflect something of an overweight horse, maybe a black buzzard.

"What, exactly, are you shaping, ser?" Grenseal knelt down over the attempted art sculpture. "Is this, uh, important?"

The Shaper's tilted his head upwards, his eyes replaced with a white film. His face slack, still.

"Okay, then," said Grenseal. He sat down in the mud, crossed his feet, and waited for the creature to take shape.

Leanah gripped the Sword of Stone tighter, pulling it so that the pommel touched her chest. "Now do me a big favor and stay still," she said.

Each of Leanah's footsteps moved slowly, inching toward the unsuspecting creature.

"I've never had lizard before," she said to herself. "I wonder if it's tasty."

"What are you doing?" the sword said.

Leanah nearly dropped the sword. "What is?"

The sword yawned, then blinked while staring at Leanah's chest. "Can you at least give me the common courtesy of knowing what we're going to kill?"

"You can't just start talking whenever you want to," Leanah whispers. She looks up and sees the shimmering tail disappear behind a pair of rocks. "And now you made me lose dinner."

"You couldn't kill it even if you weren't a woman."

Leanah dropped the sword to get a perfect view of the face. "You say that again."

"I believe I made my point."

"You ignorant—" she paused, watching her words before she did something she'd regret. "You cannot believe that. For a second."

"I believe that you are incapable of being a decent warrior. I believe that you have been lied to all your life. I believe that you lack the skill to slay a single slograt!"

"You will regret this."

"Or what can you do? What can you do to a god?"

Leanah chuckled. "A god? You're a talking sword. A parlor trick."

"Can a parlor trick do this?" it asked.

Leanah struggled to keep her hands steady. "What is this?" she cried out. The sword's blade dug into the dirt in front of her. Leanah steeled her feet into the ground, taking a wide stance. Then, with everything she had, she thrust upwards with her shoulders.

The sword did not budge.

It laughed. "Good luck, wench."

Leanah pulled upwards again. Thrusting her legs forward, her shoulders backwards, she pulled. Then pulled again. And again.

Nothing came of the effort.

"How are you doing this?"

"I'm just a parlor trick. A stupid sword. You tell me!" it said.

"And I suppose you want me to apologize?"

"I want you to take me home, wench."

"How can I—" Leanah screamed. She tried to pull up again, barely moving the sword. "Do this without being able to move you?"

The sword's voice wavered. "How are you moving me?" it asked.

Leanah pulled upwards. "You're a parlor trick. That is all." Leanah flashed a snarl. "You're mine, remember that!"

The creature—what once seemed a common lizard—showed its head out of from behind the pair of rocks. It's long, toothless mouth opened, showing a sharp, hooked beak at the end. "Arp?" it squeaked.

"Well aren't you adorable?" Leanah said. She knelt down and held out her hand. "Come here, little guy."

The creature came out from behind the rocks completely. What Leanah saw amazed her. The body was round and short. Bat-like wings flapped in quick succession on its sides. The creature, however, walked on four legs, its black shimmering tale whipping madly from side to side.

"You're a Shadowed Wing?" she said. "You can't be any bigger than a crow!" Leanah held back a squeal of joy for fear of scaring the little thing. "Just you wait until the boys hear about this!"

Leanah held the sword up, pointing the blade toward the Wing. "I bet you taste delicious."

Leanah's sword fell to the ground.

"This is ridiculous!" she shouted. The Wing's head ducked downward, as if dodging her words. It crouched closer to the ground, its tail holding itself still. "Mrr?" it said.

"Just stay there!" Leanah demanded of the Wing. "Get up, you damned sword. Get up or I'll do this without you!" Leanah hoped the sword would not call her out on her bluff.

The final shape of the creature took form. "This," Grenseal said. "This is, what? A creature?"

The Shaper's eyes flickered, turning back to his blue eyes. He blinked, rubbing his eyes, then turned to Grenseal. "How long was I out?" He followed Grenseal's silent gaze at the figure between his legs. "Oh, dear Elders."

"Is those the Shadowed Wings?" Grenseal asked.

The Shaper nodded, then jumped to his feet.

"There can't be that many of them, can there?"

The Shaper pulled his staff close to his chest and held it close. He tipped his head and began to mumble something to himself.

"We don't have time for this, Shaper. We must—"

The Shaper's eyes came back up from the ground, staring directly into Grenseal's "We must go. The end of the World is at hand."

"How have we unlocked the Shattering?" asked Grenseal.

He received no answer. The Shaper had already disappeared in the darkness of the trees.

The sound of Leanah dropping the sword—a metal clang against the rocky floor of the cavern—echoed into the trees outside.

"You stubborn, spoiled little brat!" she shouted.

"Look who spits these lies," says the sword. "Surely you aren't talking about yourself."

"When we are done with this all, you're going back in that chest and staying in there FOREVER!" she shouted.

A second pair of yellowing eyes appeared in the distant darkness.

"Did you bring some friends, lizard?" asked Leanah. She cracked her knuckles and crouched lower to the ground. She had to be ready to spring for the Shadowed Wing at a moment's notice. "Come here."

"You're pathetic," said the sword. "Let me down."

"Kragg, was it?" Leanah said. "Shut up!" Leanah snuck closer to the lizard. She found it difficult to follow both the floor and the motions of her would-be feast. "Now just stay there, okay?"

Inch by inch, Leanah snuck forward. Finding a distance that would make it easy for her to catch it, she leapt at the lizard, thrusting her hands in front of her.

"Do you hear that?"

Grenseal nodded. "That's her." The two followed the echoes of struggles coming from the cavern. Their hearts raced, and suddenly the air tasted sour. "This cannot be good."

The Shaper pushed forward. He dropped his hood and then paused, keeping an arm out to hold Grenseal still. He pressed his finger to his lips as if to tell Grenseal to remain silent.

They both listened, Grenseal closing his eyes and hoping for the best.

A crash, then a thud. The sound of something, not metal, but rock or bone cracking against the walls.

"Dear Elders," said the Shaper. "Come!"

They ran. The Shaper held tight to his staff. Whatever may be up ahead, he was sure it would need a good thwacking.

When they arrived at the source of the noise, they paused. Grenseal let out a nervous burst of laughter, but held ceased with the Shaper's threatening look.

Leanah stood clutching the Wing by the tail and swinging it against the rock. The sword remained three paces from her feet.

"What on earth are you doing?"

She slammed the Wing up against the rock once more. Grenseal noticed the Wing had stopped twitching. Another smaller Wing hid by an outcropping of rocks, its yellow eyes disappearing behind brief blinks. "Fixing dinner," she said.

"Can we eat that?" Grenseal asked. "We can't eat that. Can we eat that? Do we want to eat that?"

The Shaper's staff found the top of Grenseal's foot. "Hush."

Leanah held up the corpse of the black shimmering lizard with a smile. "See guys?" she said. "I did it."

The Shaper nodded. "You did."

"But the point, I believe," said Grenseal, stepping out from behind the Shaper, "was to feed the Sword was it not?"

"Ech!" the sword said. "I do not want to eat that horrid thing."

The Shaper and Grenseal's eyes met each other in confusion, then turned back toward the Sword. "What do you mean?" asked Grenseal. "You don't want to eat it."

"Forget him," said Leanah. "It's a stupid, stubborn sword."

Grenseal held back a chuckle. Sensing what he was thinking, the Shaper held his staff out to Grenseal and shook his head. "Not now, mage."

"But this is utterly ridiculous," he said. "We are to slay this thing, and here she is killing it barehanded." He paused, turned to Leanah. "You're just a little girl from a tiny village. No combat experience from what you can speak of." He turned to the Shaper, hoping he was following. "Just how did you manage to kill that thing?"

Leanah checked on the Shadowed Wing's head, opening its mouth and peering at the eyes. "Do you think this thing is safe to eat?"

"You stupid little girl!" Grenseal said. "Something does not add up here," he said. "Am I the only one to see it?"

The Shaper shook his head. His eyes widened, trying to send the message to Grenseal. "Not now."

"Kree?" The other Shadowed Wing came out from behind its outcropping. It came directly to Grenseal's feet and sniffed.

Grenseal looked up. "What do I do?"

The Shaper shook his head. "I have no idea."

"Kill it," said Leanah.

"But it's just an infant," Grenseal said. "I think." He knelt down and stretched out its hand for the black lizard to sniff. Its wings and tail both began to shimmer, reflecting some of the orange from Grenseal's cape. "I think this is a dragon" he said. "You're a cute little fellow."

"Reeow!" it said.

"I think it just yawned," said Grenseal. "Are you tired little guy?"

The dragon's yawn turned into a screech.

"I think it's calling for help," the Shaper said. "Take the sword. Let's go."

"But my village," Leanah said. "We have to save it!"

"Then bring that bloody thing with you!" Grenseal said and pushed the screeching dragon away from him. "Go home, little guy. It's okay."

"Now!" he said. "Out!"

The trio turned to leave out the way they came in, but the light from the outside became no longer visible. "Grenseal?"

"Got it," he said. As Grenseal stuck his hand out, a spark turned into a low, orange flame that overcame his hand. He held it out in front of them, stepping forward. "I don't remember any rocks being here," he said.

Leanah muttered, "That's not a rock."

Sure enough, the surface felt too soft to be a boulder of any kind. Grenseal held his hand down toward his feet. His fist met with the glowing of iridescent scales and yellow eyes.

"There has to be twenty of them. At least," said the Shaper.

"What have you done?" Grenseal asked Leanah.

"I was saving my village!" she said. Leanah reached into her pack and searched for the sword. "The Sword of Stone! Where is it?"

Grenseal flipped around and held out his hand. He flicked a finger out into the tunnel. A tiny trail of flame sputtered through the air and then fizzled out. "There! On the ground."

Their view of the sword disappeared as more Shadowed Wings flooded the ground.

"Grenseal, can you fireball us out?" asked Leanah.

"If I hurt you," he said.

"What if they hurt us?" Leanah said, nudging toward the sea of shimmering scales and hungry mouths.

Grenseal flung his hand forward, firing off a fireball that attached to a nearby wall and then flared out.

"That was useless," Leanah said. "Do something. Something bigger!"

"I cannot risk killing you. Losing control."

"We risk dying if you don't!"

The Shaper flung his staff back and forth to keep the snapping mouths at bay.

"You are the most useless mage I've ever met," grumbled Leanah.

"I am the only mage you've ever met."

Leanah peered at her orange companion. "We'll talk about this later," she said. "Kragg!"

"What is it?"

"Are you okay?" asked Leanah.

The sword made a sound, as if thinking about the proper answer. "I would have stayed asleep had I but known this was my imminent future."

"All of you!" Leanah shouted.

The crowd of chattering dragons paused, and for a mere heartbeat, there was silence in the caves. "I need to get that sword back!"

"You'll get yourself killed," the Shaper said.

"I can handle one, I can handle them all." Without warning, Leanah rushed forward into the crowd of dragons. She pushed at them with broad swings of her hands, the chattering being temporarily replaced with the screeching of dragon slamming up against dragon.

"Well, let's help her out."

Grenseal stepped forward and summoned another fireball in his other hand. Both flared about, crackling in the cool cavernous air. With a flick of his hands, he fired small fireballs out into the cavern's walls.

"Why are you not aiming for the dragons?" asked the Shaper. His staff swept two Shadowed Wings against the walls. "It's much more effective."

"I do not believe in violence."

"You will get us all killed!" the Shaper screamed, stabbing at one of the Shadowed Wings. It bit onto the end of his staff and pulled backwards. "Let go, you little—" The Shaper snapped it backwards, pulling the dragon with it. It was surprisingly light.

Its wings and claws fluttered about while being held airborne.

Despite its delicate situation, the dragon did not want to let go.

The Shaper swung the staff aside, hoping to fling the beast into the air. It still hung on for dear life. The Shaper sighed and reached out, careful to avoid the claws of the black beast on his staff.

With a careful, but tight grip, he pulled at the wings of the dragon—steady at first, then with a quick jerk. The Shaper looked at his hand in surprise. He held only the wing of the dragon. "Ew," he said.

The Shadowed Wing opened its mouth to cry out in pain and dropped to the ground, releasing the Shaper's staff in the process.

The screech was deafening, nearly stopping the humans from participating in the battle.

Then, a thunder coming from deeper in the cavern.

"Hey, a thought just came to me," said Grenseal. He drew a line of fire that quickly flared into a wall of flame in front of him. "If these little guys are so small and hungry, then they have to be infants, right?"

Leanah grasped the sword's handle, but it didn't want to move. She kicked at a Shadowed Wing from behind her. "I don't follow," she said.

"If these are the children, then where is momma?"

More thunder from the cavern's deeps. As the battle raged on, the sounds and rumbles felt closer, more intense. The ringing of the thunder shook deep inside Grenseal's chest.

"We had best be prepared to move, fast!"

"But I need this!" Leanah shouted. She wrapped her hands around the sword's handle once more, flexing her fingers, then squeezing tight. "Come on!"

The sword would not budge.

"Are you not hungry?" she cried out. "Don't you want to eat

these creatures?"

The sword laughed. "What gave you that idea?" it said.

Leanah paused. "It's tradition!"

"You humans are dumber than we thought!" The sword laughed.

"Come on!" she shouted at it. "Let's go." Leanah threw all of her power into her back feet, pulling at the sword along the ground. Its metal blade scraped against the gray, rocky floor.

"You will ruin my finish!" the sword said. "Unhand me!"

"No!" she cried, pulling back again. "You're coming with us!"

The thunder reached closer, rumbling the rocks on the ground. The dragons began to screech in unison, each of them holding their heads up high.

Grenseal tossed a hand-sized fireball at the back of the cavern. As the ball hit rock, a shadow of something large flashed for an instant. "Leanah, we mustn't waste time."

"Then leave!" she shouted. "I can handle this myself."

The Shaper ran forward and grabbed hold of Leanah's waist. "Come one, little girl!" he said. He pulled at her waist, Leanah pulling up at the same time.

"No! Let me go!" she shouted.

The sword cried out in frustration.

And Grenseal stood paralyzed. The shadow grew bigger, getting closer and yet his friends remained just footsteps away from him, struggling to save a talking piece of metal. "We cannot do this!" he cried out.

Grenseal felt a burning deep within him. The burning traveled outward, his hands not just summoning flame, but feeling the flame. Becoming the flame. Sweat dripped off his brow and made a dark orange trail down his robes. "I'm so sorry," he said.

The Shaper peered upwards upon hearing Grenseal's apology. "For what?"

Before the words could reach Grenseal's ears, a circle of flame erupted from the fire mage's body.

The Shaper seized Leanah's shoulders and he threw himself onto Leanah to the ground. The entire cavern lit up a bright orange, then flashed a blinding white that forced the Shaper to shield his eyes against Leanah's back. He felt the wave of heat travel over him, singing the hairs on his ears and back of his neck.

"You're crushing me!" Leanah said.

The Shaper pressed the girl's head down into the ground. "I've saving you," he said. "There's a difference. Now shut up!"

Leanah grudgingly listened, but reached out for the sword.

The Shaper listened for signs of movement as flesh and fat crackled around him. The dragons—or as many as he could sense—had been turned to crisp.

He raised his head. "Grenseal?" he called out.

The walls and columns of the caverns glowed a brilliant orange, like coals on a fire. Everything around them radiated heat and light, enough to make visible the entire cavern from end to end.

And in front of him, kneeling down and exhausted, Grenseal.

"Grenseal!" the Shaper called out. He scattered to his feet and ran toward his friend. "Are you okay?" he said. He held Grenseal close to him. To his surprise, Grenseal's pale cheeks were cold to the touch. His hair and body held no sign of heat or an explosion. "This is amazing," the Shaper said to himself, then turned to view Leanah stand up. In her hands, the Sword of Stone.

"Leanah!" he shouted. "Stand down!"

She dragged the sword's blade against the rocky floor, but the sword appeared to be weightless in her hands. She had seemingly won the war against the will of Kragg.

"What are you doing?" he called out. "Get back here."

Leanah's shoulders slumped forward. Her head turned to call over her shoulder, "I'll be right back."

The Shaper pulled Grenseal to his feet, who appeared conscious, but unresponsive to any of the Shaper's questions. "Walk with me," he said and pulled Grenseal's arm over his shoulders. "And let's not make a big habit of this, okay?"

Grenseal followed the Shaper's footsteps toward Leanah. "Where are you going?" he called out. "We must leave!"

"We need to finish this," she called back. The sound of the sword's blade scraping against cavern's ground stopped. Leanah had pulled the sword up and in front of her, brandishing it and walking with a confidence the Shaper had never seen in her before.

She had been angry, sure. Blood-thirsty, definitely. But this time, this was a transformation.

"Leanah, don't."

Grenseal lifted his head up to watch as Leanah held the sword in front of her and rushed to face a large silhouette in the back.

The ground shook as a giant black head snapped out at the moving girl.

"Here's momma," said Grenseal.

The Shaper could not help but smile. "We must help her."

"Go," said Grenseal. "I just need a minute." His arm pulled away from the Shaper's shoulder and he stumbled, falling back on his knees. "Or two."

"Are you—?"

Grenseal waved at Leanah. "Go!" The Shaper hesitated. "Go!" Grenseal gripped onto a nearby boulder and pulled himself up. His legs shook underneath him, but he tried to hide his apprehension anyway. "I'll be there soon."

The Shaper drew up his hood and waved the staff about in front of him. "Leanah," he said. "I'm coming."

"I don't need your help!" she cried out. Leanah rushed toward the dragon's head and swiped at it with her blade. The tip just grazed the nose and the Shadowed Wing recoiled in pain. "See?"

The orange walls had turned begun to fade into a pale red, but still emanated enough heat to make the Shaper's clothes itch against his skin.

He stopped, peering over his shoulder. Grenseal stood up on his own two feet, pulling himself toward the struggle by gripping against the wall as support. In front of him, the metallic thud of Leanah's sword against the orange shimmer of the dragon's scales.

"Elders protect us," said the Shaper. He held his staff over his head and rushed into battle. Before he could begin his running start, a fireball shot past his shoulder and smacked the dragon in the eye.

It pulled back and roared at Grenseal's direction, the force of its breath nearly pushing the Shaper backward.

"Don't do that again!" he said to Grenseal, who agreed with a nod, but summoned another fireball anyway.

The Shaper ran to Leanah's side and smashed his staff against the sides of the monster's paw.

"They did not teach us how to fight in the Cloister," he said.

Leanah stepped back while pulling the sword back. "You're telling me," she said. Leanah rushed forward and pressed the sword deep into the foreleg of the Shadowed Wing.

The Wing sat up on its hind legs, hitting its head against the ceiling.

"Watch out!" said the Shaper. Leanah held her sword up over

her head, slicing a falling stalagmite in half.

Leanah flashed a knowing smile at the Shaper, then held the sword over her head again, preparing to slice downward.

"Haii!" she screamed and pressed forward, bringing the blade of the sword down on the Shadowed Wing's toe. "Drink of the blood!" she commanded.

The sword scoffed. "We have not been listening, have we?"

Leanah grasped the sword, holding to her face. "You will feed on this wretched creature, or I will feed you to it!"

The sword remained silent.

Leanah smiled, then gripped the sword and swung it toward the Wing. "Come on! She is injured."

Grenseal fired off another flare, this one sparkling and fizzing into the caverns, landing in the beast's nose.

"What is that supposed to do?" asked the Shaper.

Grenseal smiled.

The beast sat up on his haunches again, this time, sneezing a burst of fire into the ceiling.

"Now can we go?" asked Grenseal.

The cavern's ceiling began dropping giant rocks. "It's going to come down upon us, Leanah! Hurry up!"

"Not until it feeds!" Leanah said. She sidestepped a tail swipe from the Wing and swung her sword, this one digging deeper into the Wing's flesh, exposing white rib bones. "Feed, damn you! Feed!"

Leanah thrust the sword deeper into the Wing's sides, then chest, looking for any fleshy bit to bury the blade.

"Why will you not feed?" she cried out.

The sword remained silent.

A rock from the ceiling landed near Leanah's foot.

"You risk yourself," cried the Shaper. "Come! Now!"

Leanah seized the sword and held it closer to her face. "You had better do as I command!" she growled in clenched teeth. "You will not be responsible for the death of my people!"

She swung the sword yet again, plunging the blade guard-deep into the Shadowed Wing's chest. The Wing let out a piercing cry and collapsed forward. Its strength slowly left its body.

"Leanah! It is dead!"

Leanah gripped the sword in a single hand and slashed repeatedly at the corpse of the dragon.

"That is enough!"

Leanah felt tugging against her tunic. Still swinging her blade, she felt the cooling chill of tears down her face. Her face had grown hot from anger and heat from the walls.

In the distance, the Shadowed Wing grew smaller and smaller as she was dragged away. Her salvation, her people's salvation, disappearing from her view.

Leanah's arms and shoulders grew limp. It was pointless to fight it.

The cavern rumbled as the sides began to collapse. The two had been far enough out of the cavern to not see the fate of the mother Shadowed Wing and her babies. But the last screech and dusty exhale filled in the details of her imagination.

In Leanah's hands, the sword. Its smile remained barely visible to her wet eyes. "Why would you do this?" she asked. "Why?"

Pure sunlight and fresh air enveloped her again. Her cheeks felt cool, the pine needles in the air smelled refreshing when compared to the musty caverns and stench of dragon droppings.

"You!" The Shaper threw his staff at Leanah. "You almost got us killed!"

"Wait just a moment," said Grenseal.

"You're going to threaten me?" Leanah said. She held her sword out, pointing its tip at the Shaper. "You may want to rethink this, prophet."

The Shaper raised his hands and stepped back. His eyes widened. "We can talk calmly," he said, "for now."

Leanah sheathed her blade in the pack and smiled. "That was awesome!" she cried out.

"You had no idea what you were doing," said the Shaper. "Did you?"

Leanah nodded. "Not a clue. But we survived! We survived and we're alive."

"But what about that?" Grenseal pointed at the pack. "Did we get this to feed?"

Leanah shrugged. "It wouldn't feed." Her face turned sour. "Why wouldn't it feed?" She began to wipe away tears.

"Why don't we ask it?"

Both the Shaper and Leanah paused to look at Grenseal and his suggestion.

"Well?"

Leanah gripped the sword and pulled it out of the bag at a speed that almost made her throw it across the forest.

"What was that?" asked Grenseal.

"I thought it would return to being heavy again," she said. "You know, like before."

"Why didn't it?"

"Because it's begun," the Shaper whispered to himself.

Grenseal turned to face the Shaper, but seeing his expression, decided not to pursue the seemingly offhand comment. "I'm sure it will answer us in due time," he said. "It, too, has been through much."

Leanah sat down, laying the sword out in front of her. "You can talk whenever you're ready," she told it. And she sat there, her eyes never wavering from the sword's metal face. "Any time now."

The Shaper grabbed Grenseal's cloak and pulled him away, as if searching for a place to set up camp. "We must speak," he told the fire mage.

"Of?"

"What do you know about that sword?"

"Kragg?" Grenseal wondered just how much of this would sound sane. "He speaks to me, and thinks that I'm someone else. Someone named Kaverin."

The Shaper took a step back, then once calmness overtook him, he nodded. "I see. This is troubling."

"What is the problem, exactly?"

"Grenseal, I escaped from the citadel to prevent a disaster, and thus far, it seems that I have done nothing at all to stop it from occurring." The Shaper understood the look in Grenseal's face to be one of confusion. "When I enter into a trance, I receive messages, from the Elders. They send me messages and I sculpt or create these images. Images of things to be." He pointed to Leanah, still sitting and trying to talk to the uncooperative sword. "Sixteen years ago I shaped the end of the world, on the day that that girl was born."

"And how is a little girl responsible? Look at her."

"That weapon, it's a sentient sword. Never in all of my readings and travels have I heard of an object, a sword, taking on consciousness. It speaks, it thinks. It does what it wills."

Grenseal looked at his hand and then held it behind him.

The Shaper took Grenseal's wrist and held his hand up to Grenseal's face. "I believe that the sword was once an Elder, long past. He recognizes you for the Elder of Fire." The Shaper pointed at Grenseal's right hand. "That, too, was once one of the Elders, Grenseal. You possess a Godpower, the power of Kaverin."

Grenseal knew these things to be truer than he would have liked to admit. "And how do you know such things?"

"I know such things because they have come to me. All of this." The Shaper's voice began to get louder, his eyes wider. "What has escaped me is how does all of this end? How do I prevent the Shattering?"

"The Shattering?" Grenseal's voice got louder as well. He stepped in closer. "We're talking about the Shattering?"

The Shaper nodded. "It's imminent, and I'm powerless to stop it. I've sacrificed my life, my friends, my family to stop this. For nothing."

"What are our options?" Grenseal asked.

"Hey guys?" Leanah wandered into the intimate circle created by the Shaper and Grenseal. "If I was told to go to the Swamps of Mrondir, and the Shadowed Wing was here, then what's at the Swamps?" Leanah's eyes glimmered with a spark of hope.

Grenseal and the Shaper exchanged a glance. Both of them shrugged. "I've not traveled that far, Leanah," said Grenseal. "You?"

The Shaper shook his head. "I've been as far as the Citadel and Vamori. No further."

Leanah flung her pack around her shoulder. "Then it's settled. Perhaps the clue to saving my village is in the Swamps." She took it upon herself to lead the journey. "Come along, if you'd like."

The pair watched as the little girl walked off into the darkness of the forests. "Do we follow?"

"It's the only thing we can do," said the Shaper. "We must keep an eye on her, for she holds the key to the destruction of the lands as we know it."

Grenseal felt a warm glow coming from his hand. It itched deep inside his hand, under skin and muscle. The most uncomfortable place for him to go and impossible to scratch.

"Is everything okay?" asked the Shaper.

"My hand," said Grenseal. "It itches."

"Your God," said the Shaper. "Your God warns you about the cataclysm at hand."

TWELVE

The group walked for nearly twelve hours before pulling aside for camp at the end of the day. The night hand grown cold and silent.

They opted to camp near a series of trees, three of them, close together. This, they decided, would be best in case there were an unsuspected attack. In case of emergency, climb the trees.

"But first," said Leanah, "we'll need food."

The group agreed.

"I'll go get it," she said. "I could use the hunt."

Grenseal exchanged glances of worry with the Shaper. "We'll be here gathering kindling and any berries," he said.

Leanah nodded and withdrew the sword from her pack once again. As before, it seemed light in her hands. Leanah held it deftly, flailing it right and left and reveling in the sound it made as it cut through the cool air.

"Is she getting stronger?" asked Grenseal.

The Shaper shook his head. "I do not know. The Elders have

been quiet lately."

"While she's gone, can you shape something up? Maybe a few answers?"

"That's not how this works, my friend." The Shaper took a few steps behind a tree and bent over to gather fallen branches. "Will this be big enough for kindling?"

"Please," said Grenseal. "Only those that have already fallen off. Do not hurt the trees."

The Shaper shook his head and smiled. "Still on that?"

"I would not tear off your arm to create heat for us," said Grenseal. "Why is it fair to ask the trees to do the same for us?"

"Have you always spoken to nature?"

"Have you always spoken to the Elders?"

The Shaper smiled. "I see what you did there." He dropped a pile of brown and grayed branches into the middle of their camp. "I have always been subjected to voices, to inspiration. At the most inopportune times, I used to sit and dream. When I awoke, my dreams had taken shape in the form of stone statues, mud creatures, whatever I had on hand."

"It is truly a miraculous gift," said Grenseal. "Much more productive than this." Grenseal snapped his fingers and a spark of flame flickered into the air and disappeared.

"But not as helpful," said the Shaper. He nodded toward the pile of sticks.

Grenseal flicked a finger at the pile and it caught fire. Within moments without any stoking, the fire grew to a sizeable flame suitable for warming and cooking.

"Now that," said the Shaper, sitting down on a felled trunk, "that is a neat gift."

Grenseal sighed and sat down next to the Shaper.

"Tell me," the prophet said. "Why do you search for your friend?"

"We made a promise to search for something," he said. "We split up with a plan to return." He looked to the fire, the orange glow lighting his facial features. The Shaper noticed Grenseal's exceptionally smooth skin and eyes that seemed to change color as the flames flickered into the air. "I returned, he did not." He sighed. "Now I fear for the worst."

Grenseal heard the cracking of twigs and branches behind them. Leanah was still on the hunt.

"My friend and I," said Grenseal, "we were both gifted with these abilities. Mine was fire, emanating from this rock. My friend was gifted with a water gift."

"So there are more like you?"

Grenseal nodded. "That was our question. We needed to know where these gifts came from, why we were chosen."

"The Elders appear to have a plan for themselves," the Shaper said.

"Why do you believe they allow for such horrible things to happen?" asked Grenseal, poking at the black rock embedded into his hand. "Do you believe they relish in destroying the lives of humans?"

"I believe the Elders themselves are jealous and bored. We live the lives of mortals. To us, life has meaning and worth. Even money and gold loses its value after you have so much of it."

Grenseal turned to view the source of more broken twigs getting louder. "Have we food to eat?" he asked.

"We do," said Leanah. She held two furry corpses of rabbits, small bunnies to be precise, in her hands. "I do not know what to feed someone who will not eat animals."

Grenseal stood up. "It's just as well," he said. "I could afford a small walk to clear my head."

Leanah placed the rabbits along the trunk which the Shaper sat on. "They look delicious, do they not?"

"Do you feel," the Shaper stopped, unsure of how to ask this question. "Different?"

"Different how?" she asked. Leanah held her hands out to the fire to arm them.

"Just different? Than normal?"

"I feel just fine," she said. The fire flickered in the cold air. "Why do you ask?"

"I've been a little under the weather, I suppose." He watched Leanah's actions as she sat down by the fire. Her shoulders appeared stronger, wider. Her eyes reflected a confidence she didn't have before. Even the way she spoke was powerful and unwavering.

"Have some meat," she said. Leanah stood up and searched. She stopped and tossed a long, pointed stick at the Shaper. "Here," she said. "Barbeque."

Leanah took her sword and cut into the rabbit's fur, peeling off the skin like it was a banana. In one quick motion, she impaled the corpse with the pole, shoving it from end to end, and held it over the fire to roast. "I hope he comes back soon."

"What do you hope to see in the Swamps?" asked the Shaper.

"You're the fortune teller," she said. "You tell me what we should expect."

"That is not what I asked," he said.

"We won't know until we get there." Leanah flipped the rabbit. Even the Shaper had to admit, it began to smell good as it roasted on the fire. "I just hope to find something that will help us save this village." She flipped the pack off her shoulder with one fling. "If this thing ever decides to talk, we'll get some more answers."

Grenseal arrived back into the camp, cupping berries in his hands, along with two light green apples.

The three sat down in silence, staring into the fire and watching as the night passed by. Moments later, Leanah had decided to turn in, gripping her pack and holding it close to her.

"I'll stand watch," said Grenseal. "You two get some rest. If I need you, I'll wake you."

The Shaper nodded and rested on a bed of leaves, not far from where Leanah lay.

Grenseal sat by the fire, feeling it cool as the night progressed. He had no need to seek out more kindling. As the fire began to die down, he just flung another finger at the glowing embers and the fire would start again.

The stars moved throughout the sky. The edge of the forest should only be a few hours away, he had guessed. And with any hope, they would be in the Swamps and back at Deckal before the end of moon's cycle.

Then, maybe he would find Luca. He would know what to do, he thought. Luca always knew what to do.

"Psst."

Grenseal sat up, looking back at his companions. "Shaper?"

"Psst."

"What is it, Shaper?"

"Psst."

Grenseal stood up and searched where the Shaper slept. He was not awake.

"What is this?" Grenseal said.

"Psst."

Grenseal's hand grew warm and then became engulfed in a

blue flame. "I will protect myself," he said.

"Kaverin!" said the voice. "Kaverin, old friend, get down here."

Grenseal looked at his feet. The strap to Leanah's pack lie just underneath his toe. "Kragg?"

"Get me out of here," said the sword.

"But Leanah—"

"That horse is asleep," it said. "Take me out."

Grenseal gripped the sword with his stone hand and pulled it out.

The sword's face had completely opened up, his eyes bright and wide. It smiled. "This feels great!"

"Keep it down!" warned Grenseal. He held his finger to his mouth to shush it.

"You worry too much," Kragg said.

"Maybe you worry too little." Grenseal carried the sword ten paces across the campsite, hoping to keep some distance between them and Leanah should she happen to awaken.

"Kaverin," it said. "It's been ages."

"I told you I am not Kaverin," Grenseal said.

"Nonsense," said Kragg. "I can sense your life force. You are none other than the Lord of Flame."

Grenseal blushed. Even if he were not the true Elder Kaverin, it was always nice to get a compliment or two. "What do you want?"

"It's good to see you, old friend."

"Yes, yes, I know. Listen, Kragg, I need to know. What is it that you know about the Swamps of Mrondir?"

"The Swamps?" Kragg's voice raised in excitement. "You mean we're going home?"

Grenseal nearly dropped the sword. "Home?"

"I'm sure you remember," he said. "That's where I lived before the Dallheim Wars. Those wretched humans and their lust for power. No respect for that which they seek."

"What is this?" Leanah rubbed her eyes and approached Grenseal. "Why have you my sword?"

"It was speaking to me," he said. "Tell her."

Kragg yawned and then looked at Leanah's direction. "Go to sleep, little girl."

"You are mine to command, sword! You will come back to me at once." Leanah held out her hand. Grenseal felt the tug of the sword against his hands. His grip grew tighter around its handle.

"What is this?"

The sword appeared to grimace, then muttered, "Very well."

The pull became too much for Grenseal and it flew out of his hand and into Leanah's. "Do not ever take the sword again, fire mage. Or I shall slit your throat in your sleep."

"Leanah, please."

Leanah turned away to return to her bed. "And you!" she scolded the sword. "Don't you ever do that again."

Grenseal watched as Leanah snuggled up to the sword and fell asleep with an eye open, watching him. The thought had crossed his mind to wake up the Shaper, to warn him of her anger, the sword's message. For some unforeseen reason, Leanah was being led to take the sword back to its home.

Why? What purpose did it serve other than to destroy the Vamori Village?

Grenseal had decided that he could not sleep, even if his body was not rattled by the death threats—which he took very, very seriously—of his traveling companion. She appeared angry, serious, irrational. If she were to slit his throat, he doubted he would ever receive another warning.

Night turned into daylight. The sun began to glow a warm red over the hills to the east. Beams of sunlight penetrated deep into the forest and cut into the sleeping companion's eyelids like a dagger's blade.

"Wake time already?" said the Shaper. He stood up and chewed on the leftover bunny meat at his side. Curled up in leaves, it was dry but still tasty.

Grenseal stood sitting over the burning embers of a fire long forgotten.

"Have you gotten no sleep at all, my friend?" The Shaper went to Grenseal's side and sat down. "We have a long journey ahead of us," he said. "You should have gotten rest."

Grenseal agreed. "She said she would kill me."

The Shaper gripped his gnarled staff and peered over at Leanah, stuffing her pack with the leftover meats and berries of their dinner last night. "She grows worse."

"I believe we are taking Kragg home," said Grenseal.

"Who?"

"The Sword of Stone. Kragg is his name."

The Shaper ran his hand over his bald head. "This is growing stranger by the moment," he said. "Why would she be driven to take it home? Did she not need it herself?"

"Are we ready, gentlemen?" Leanah had thrown most of the supplies over her shoulder and appeared ready for movement. "We're wasting time here." Even though she had not appeared to have grown, she seemed taller than Grenseal last remembered her.

"Yes, yes, let's get on with it," said the Shaper. "I saw the way she looked at you." The Shaper pointed at Leanah. "What did you do?"

"Kragg—the sword—it asked to speak to me. And she found

out." Grenseal's eyes lowered to the ground and never wavered.

It had become clear to the Shaper that Grenseal had truly become worried for his life. Something in the way Leanah had threatened him had frightened the courage out of the fire mage. As destructive as he could be, this roaring tiger was reduced to a kitty cat.

Their travels to the Swamps remained in silence. The air of uneasiness only seemed to be felt by Grenseal and the Shaper. Leanah, who walked ahead of the group, appeared to be in high spirits, walking and skipping and at times, even laughing and talking to herself.

The Shaper had considered several times to ask for the sword, but the thoughts quickly fluttered away as if carried away by butterflies. The look on Grenseal's face, the sudden morose feelings and his unwillingness to talk pulled at the Shaper's own heartstrings.

Could she be trusted? Would she turn on her own group? The answers were difficult to see, even for one as gifted as the Shaper.

"The ground," said Grenseal. "It grows wet, almost muddy."

It was true. The Shaper's staff sunk into the ground as they reached further and further away from the solid darkness of the forests.

"More moisture!" said the Shaper. "We approach the Swamps!"

The Swamps had also been known as the Lowlands, not just for the elevation from the water, but also for the type of company it attracted.

The Swamps of Mrondir, specifically, was not frequented by many humans, at least none that have ever returned to tell the tale. It was believed that both the lands and waters held dangerous secrets, secrets such as hiding places of large animals with even larger teeth.

"Why are we coming this way again?" Grenseal asked. His voice wavered as he scraped off the mud from the bottom of his shoes. "This will only get us sick," he said, "if it doesn't kill us first." Their feet—with the exception of Leanah—were covered with either sandals or soft leather boots. If they risked getting the boots and sandals wet, they could be destroyed and allow in the wet and the cold. "We'll need something to get us across."

As the group continued, all of them could not help but notice that the grounds were getting increasingly wet, until they were faced with a stopping point.

"How do we cross this?" asked the Shaper.

Leanah let out a loud groan and walked along the wetlands.

In front of them lay a shallow swamp overrun with greenery, shrubs, and reeds that stuck out of the water's surface.

"We won't get through this without a boat," said Leanah. "Where do we find a damnable boat?" she asked.

"How about there?" asked the Shaper.

Down the flowing river that fed into the lake, three low-rimmed gondolas rowed along. The boats were simple, painted a white color that allowed them maximum visibility in the greenery of the swamps. It wasn't anything that was meant for stealth, the Shaper thought.

In each of the gondolas stood three men. One pushing the boat along with a large oar, one wearing gilded armor, and one who appeared to be something of a merchant. All three were filled with pouches and bags of various foods and objects.

"Perhaps we can acquire some goods," said Grenseal.

"We have no coin to spend," said the Shaper.

"You don't have coin. But I do." Grenseal stuck his hand into a small pouch that hung from his belt. He withdrew a small handful of coins and let the light reflect off them. Twisting the coins, Grenseal attempted to throw the light into the direct path of the merchants. "If we can get their attention, we can maybe get some decent food."

Leanah held up her sword and waved it to catch their attention.

The merchants pulled up nearer to the shore, slowly at first. The Shaper gripped his staff near the top, resting along. His eyes studied the boats and their contents. They were already hijacked by bandits once. He did not doubt that they would try again.

"Lo!" the merchant from the first boat said. "What have we here?"

"Are you selling?"

"We have goods, yes." The merchant snapped his fingers at the guard in his boat and pointed at the shore. The guard nodded and snatched up a bag and brought it to the shore. "What is it you are looking for?"

"Fresh water? Maybe food?" said Grenseal.

"Food?"

The guard dug into the pouch and pulled out a small bag of yellow fruit. "We have these citrus," said the merchant. "For you, one bit."

"Coin is hard to come by," said Grenseal. "For us, two bags for one bit."

The merchant pointed at Grenseal with a smile. "I like your style, and I do not just mean your cloak," he said. "Let us first see your coin."

Grenseal held the coin between his index finger and his thumb, rolling it back and forth.

"Give this to them," he said to the guard. The guard tossed the yellow fruit to the mage and held out his hand. "Your turn," said the merchant.

As he held out his hand, the guard snatched up the coin with one hand and gripped Grenseal's elbow with the next.

The other companions held to a defensive position. Leanah pointed the tip of Kragg at the guard. "Let him go."

"Leanah, is it?"

She nodded.

The merchant nodded toward one of the men in the other boats and an arrow flew through the air, hitting Leanah in the cloak.

"Try that again," she said.

"And if we do?" said the merchant. He stepped off the boat and walked toward Grenseal. "We need something of yours, Leanah."

"How do you know my name?" she asked.

"You know, I was afraid we'd have to take all night to do this." He carefully analyzed Leanah and her friends. "Your father commands that we take the sword back home."

"He did not send you!" she shouted.

The merchant laughed and reached into a pouch strapped to his leg.

Leanah stepped forward and brought the tip of the sword closer to the guard's arm. "Make a wrong move and I strike."

The merchant laughed. "You should calm down, little girl. All of that tension, not good for the heart." He pulled something small and silver out of the pouch. "This," he said, "will prove to you we mean business."

The brooch landed on the muddy sand, its sharp edge cutting into the ground. Leanah pointed her sword at the guard. "Pick that up!" she commanded.

The guard laughed and held his hand tighter around Grenseal's neck. "You're hardly in a position to bark orders, girl." Leanah watched as Grenseal's neck turned white around the guard held his grip. If he squeezed any tighter, Grenseal would surely pass out.

"Do as I say, and you won't be hurt," she said.

"Leanah, pick it up yourself," said the Shaper. He took small, gradual steps to the metal object before pausing at the command of Leanah.

"You will let him pick it up, or he will lose his hand," she said.

Grenseal felt a chill pass through the man's body. The guard was taking her seriously. This made Grenseal breathe a sigh of relief. There was solace in knowing that someone else—even a trained warrior—found that little girl threatening.

"Well?" she said.

The guard looked at the merchant, then at the point of Leanah's sword. The merchant nodded. The guard released the sword and Grenseal fell to the ground, coughing and gasping for breath.

"Are you okay, my friend?" asked the Shaper.

Grenseal nodded, but could not speak. He crawled on all fours to sit beside Leanah's threatening stance.

"Pick it up!" she demanded.

The guard bent down and picked up the silver piece. From his hands, the group saw that the piece was circular with an intricate design etched into the surface.

"Does this convince you now?" asked the merchant.

The guard held the silver circle out to Leanah to take. When she refused, he tossed it at her feet.

"Return the sword to us, come along if you'd like, but I'm under strict orders."

"I will not leave my village to perish."

"Little girl, your father is concerned for your safety. Return with us and I promise no harm will come to you or your friends."

"No!"

"You saw the brooch. You know I come with your father's warning. Now stop being stupid and get in this boat."

"But why are you dressed as merchants?" asked the Shaper.

"Disguises," said the merchant. "We could not let the world know that we were looking for the Chieftain's Daughter of Vamori Village."

Leanah's eyes narrowed. "Or did you just want this sword?"

The merchant looked to the two other boats, then motioned for them, too, to make shore. "If you want to do this the hard way, we are authorized to use force."

"Come get me, then," said Leanah. She flexed her muscles, swinging the sword across her chest with the finesse of a trained warrior.

The Shaper stepped forward. "Leanah, we can talk about this, you know."

"We can do talking after I do some cutting," she said. With that, Leanah pushed the Shaper out of the way and ran toward the guards. Each one of them seized their swords and prepared for battle.

Grenseal finally found the strength to stand, then held his hand upwards and let a flare fly into the air.

All action paused.

"Wha—?" the merchant said. "How are you—?"

"Leave us be, or there will be bloodshed like you have never seen."

A guard inched toward Leanah.

A fireball shot from Grenseal's finger, passing directly over the guard's shoulder. "I said stop right there."

One of the three guards threw down his sword and held his hands up high. Through an opening of his cloak, the red and yellow uniform of her father's guard poked out.

"You!" she said. "You are from my father!" Leanah stabbed the sword into the ground. "You listen and you listen well!" She pointed at the merchant and gritted her teeth, trying to hold back all of her anger. "Tell my father I will return with the sword when I have finished my quest to preserve Vamori. Then, and only then, will I return home safe and sound."

The merchant nodded. "How do I have your word?" he said. "I cannot return without your sword. I hope you understand."

"So I can be tossed to the side, but this," Leanah held up the sword again, clutching it tightly, "this is more important?"

The merchant shrugged, then nodded. He feared any response would cause her to become angrier.

"Tell him this, then," Leanah said. With inhuman speed and precision, she sliced down one of the guards across the chest and watched as the man fell to the ground. "Father can come and take this sword when I am good and ready."

The merchant looked upon with horror at his dead traveling companion. One fallen, one running away, this merchant had begun to recount his losses. "As you wish, Leanah. But know this, I cannot be held responsible for what Hibert does with this information."

"Then tell him to come. I'll be ready." Leanah placed the sword in her pack and turned to walk toward the river. "Wait!" she cried, holding up a hand. "I am in need of one more thing from you."

THIRTEEN

Grenseal waved at the last of the guards while the Shaper pushed the boat away from the shore.

"You will never cease to amaze me," said the Shaper.

Leanah nodded with a laugh. "They had something we wanted, did they not?"

"But how are they going to get back home and tell your father what you did?"

"Reeds and swamp water, our problem. No boat, their problem."

Grenseal had to give it to her. It was difficult to disagree with that simple logic. "But you are aware that they will be coming back?" asked Grenseal.

"Aware?" she said. "I'm counting on it."

The Shaper rowed the boat across the river's edge and into the murky, swampy waters of the Mrondir. The sun had begun to climb over the horizon, and soon it would be too difficult to remain in the shade. Leanah had begun to envy Grenseal and the

Shaper for their own cloaks and the hoods that came with them.

"Can we row faster?" she asked.

"Not much faster," said the Shaper. He pushed his staff into the water and felt around. "The ground is soft, but getting closer as we get deeper into the swamps." The Shaper waited for a sense of acknowledgement from Leanah, but she did not appear to follow. "We may be nearing another piece of land. An island, perhaps."

Leanah nodded and shielded her eyes from the sun with her hand. "Why would he send someone after me?"

Grenseal opened his mouth to correct her, but remembered her threat.

"If he wanted me to return, he would have sent a more serious note."

"Maybe he was just sending a warning?" said Grenseal. "That group was not that serious about taking you in, it appears."

"My father is a coward," she said.

"Tell me about it," said a voice coming from the pack.

"What do you know about it?" said Leanah.

"Much more than you'll ever know, little girl." A muffled cackle came from the pack that drove a shiver up the Shaper's spine.

"Do we even know what we're looking for?" he asked.

Silence.

"I only know that I was supposed to come here and slay something," she said. "Now that the Shadowed Wing is dead, I don't know what more I need to do. Or why he said to come here to begin with."

"He?" asked the Shaper. "Who is this he?"

"He, Ciaran," she said. "My tutor."

"He is knowledgeable of these things?" he asked. The Shaper passed a worried look to Grenseal. "What more did he tell you?"

"Only that I needed to feed this sword, to come here and slay a Shadowed Wing."

"Leanah, may I see that sword?" asked Grenseal.

"What did I tell you?" Leanah stood up, seized the sword from her pack and held its point at Grenseal's chest.

"But we need answers, do we not?" Grenseal motioned around him. "Look at us, we are in the middle of a swamp. We don't know what we're looking for. We have a sword that talks and doesn't seem to like you."

"But you're suggesting that it'll talk to you?"

The Shaper clung tighter to the oar as he felt his muscles begin to tense.

"I'm merely suggesting that he will speak with me."

"What the fire mage says is true," said the sword. "Allow him to speak."

Leanah's attention turned to the sword. "You're a traitorous piece of—"

"Don't be jealous, dear," said the sword. "We'll only be a minute."

Leanah dropped the sword onto the boat and sat down. The motion of the sword hitting the bottom of the boat caused it to rock back and forth. The Shaper, still standing at near the aft, gripped the sides of the boat to keep still.

"Can we not do that again, please?" he said. "This is a small boat. Any large motions will tip us over."

"How did they even get this far in something this small?" asked Grenseal.

Leanah looked out north over the river. "We are on the Thames," she said. "This river goes directly to the outskirts of Deckal."

"But I thought the river dried up."

"It did," she said. "Or does."

Leanah gripped the sword back into her hands. "Enough talk," she said. "Where do we go, sword?"

"Kragg."

"We go to Kragg?"

"No, you dolt. We go home. My name is Kragg."

Leanah held the sword over the open pack. "I swear if you continue to play with me, you will find yourself in the pack for the rest of the journey."

"But we are almost home," Kragg said. "Yes, almost home."

"Tell us about this home."

"It is a place much older than this world, a place where things go to grow, live, die."

"Things?" said Leanah. She lowered the sword into the pack. "I grow tired of this."

"You would not understand without my showing you first," he said. "This I promise you."

"And why would Ciaran send us here?"

"Ciaran?" he said. "I don't know any Ciaran. What kind of name is Ciaran?"

"What kind of name is Kragg?" she said. She dangled the sword over the pack again. "If you so much as lead us astray, you will suffer the consequences, do you hear me?"

The sword chuckled at the threat. "You are not going to do anything to me. You simply cannot do anything. You need me."

"I do not need you any more than I need these others in the boat."

Grenseal looked over his shoulder. It became even more apparent that things were going to get uglier before they got easier.

"Just tell us when we get there," she demanded.

"I will not listen to a girl," he said.

"You will listen to me, for I am your master. Your owner. You belong to me."

The sword laughed again. "You really believe that, don't you?"

Leanah dropped the sword into the pack and flung it over her shoulder. "Oh shut up."

"Is that an island up ahead?" asked Grenseal. He stood up, careful not to rock the boat too much, and pointed starowlbeard.

"Indeed, it is," said the Shaper. "Is this where we go?"

"Could we ask the sword?"

Leanah dismissed their comments with a wave of her hand. "Just steer the boat, we'll go anyway."

The Shaper nodded and dug his oar into the water and paddled faster. The boat flowed along the current that seemed to pull them to the shore of the island. The island was little more than a lump, not much bigger than a hundred paces in any direction, and covered with a thick green grass, greener than anything, grass or otherwise, she had ever seen. Along the center of the island, almost directly in front of them, lay a rocky outcropping.

Leanah squinted. "From the look of things, it appears that's where we're going." Leanah pointed at the pile of rocks and waved for her companions to leave the boat.

The companions took everything off the boat that they felt they could need. The group had lucked out when Leanah demanded their boats: supplies from the supposed merchants were left in. Food and water were plentiful—or at least for the next day or two. Any more than that and they would have to make do with whatever they found.

The group walked to the shore and took inventory. All three

held bags of items, the food carried by Leanah herself. "In case I get hungry," she said. "You wouldn't want to see me when I'm hungry."

It took little convincing to allow her to carry the food. The tools, however, were left behind in the boat.

"We make for that group of rocks," said Leanah.

A muffled sound erupted from the pack.

"Shut up in there!" she shouted. "You had your chance." She shook the pack. It quickly grew silent.

"And what do you suppose we'll find in these rocks?" asked Grenseal to the Shaper.

The Shaper shook his head. "Your guess is as good as mine. It feels as a wild snape chase."

"We go forward until we have saved the village," she said. "We go until I know that I can reverse this curse."

Unintelligible words came from the pack.

"I said shut up!" Leanah demanded.

The crew walked further onto the island. Sounds of buzzing—animals or insects Leanah had never heard of before—rang in their ears. This entire area was a vast, uncomfortable difference from the rocky environment of the Vamori village.

"Does anyone live here?" she said. After some silence, she shouted, "Hello?"

Her words echoed out into the trees, absorbed by the leaves and water.

"Anyone here?" she shouted.

"Is this truly wise?" asked Grenseal. "We will only attract more people who want to kill us."

"Let them come," she said. "We will be ready."

"And just how are we going to be ready?" asked Grenseal.

The Shaper held out his hand to Grenseal. He shook his head. "Don't," he whispered.

"You think I don't know what you're thinking?" she asked. Leanah turned around, digging her feet into the ground. "You think I don't know what you whisper amongst yourselves? You think I am truly that ignorant?"

"I think you don't know what you're doing, what you're saying," said the Shaper. "You have changed so much," he said.

"You have become a tad bit frightening," added Grenseal.

"A mage with the powers to control the world of fire is afraid of a little old girl?" she said. "Do not speak about me. I will always find out." She turned to face the rock's outcropping. "For now, we work together to solve this problem, to save my village." Leanah pointed at Grenseal. "But you, you can leave whenever you want to," she said. "I don't remember inviting you here."

"I owe you a debt," he said. "For saving my life."

"Then consider your silence an integral part of your debt," she demanded. "Now do we move on forward or have you more rumors to spread about me?"

Grenseal looked down at his feet, ashamed of the conversation that just took place. The Shaper, however, remained stoic, pushing forward past the vines that hung from the giant green-trunked trees.

"The rocks are just up ahead," he said.

When the group had reached the rocks, they stopped. "What now?" the Shaper asked.

"Now we look for clues?" said Leanah. She pulled the sword out of the pack and held it out to face the rocks. "What is this?" she said. "Tell us what to find."

The sword smiled. "Home!" he said.

"You live in a pile of stone?"

"Lived," he said. "Yes. Before."

"How do we get inside?" she asked.

"We do not go inside," he said. "We are inside."

Leanah looked about her, searching for walls and a ceiling that made some semblance of a home. "This looks nothing like what I had imagined," she said.

"You're pathetic," he said. "You have no creativity. You believe in gods, in a cataclysm, but your refuse to acknowledge that a home is whatever you make of it."

Leanah slammed the sword's blade into the stones. "What game are you playing, Kragg?"

The rocks began to shift with a loud rumble beneath their feet.

"What is this?" said Grenseal.

The ground had begun to open up, a flashing of light appearing deep beneath them. The Shaper held onto his staff and attempted to shield his eyes from the oncoming light.

Leanah felt her feet begin to slip. "Where is this? What's happening?"

"My homecoming!" said the sword.

Leanah's grip on the sword weakened, allowing for the sword to slip out of her hands and down into the white light of the hole.

"No!" she shouted. Leanah stepped off the cliff and down into the growing hole beneath them. "You will not escape me so easily."

The Shaper stepped back, watching as Grenseal pulled himself out of harm's way by grabbing onto a low-hanging branch in a nearby tree.

"Shall we?" he said.

Grenseal shook his head. "We shan't."

"Come on," the Shaper said. "This will be fun." He grabbed

Grenseal's hand, yanking it off of the branch. "With me," he said.

The Shaper took a step off of the cliff and let his foot dangle over the bright light. From this angle, the light had begun to fill up all of the Shaper's vision. Grenseal's face had no longer seemed to exist, only a pale gray outlining of Grenseal's head. The Shaper pulled his other foot forward and stepped into the white void beneath them.

Grenseal's hand remained stiff, almost clawing into the Shaper's own soft hands. The Shaper knew his mouth was open. He was almost sure he was screaming, or saying something, but no sound rang out, everything disappearing into the whiteness around them.

Feeling a quiet, solemn calm around him, the Shaper held on to his cloak and closed his eyes, waiting to land.

A warm slap across the Shaper's face woke him up. The rush of blood to his cheek made him feel faint, sweating under the embarrassment of losing control.

"Where are we?" he asked.

Leanah stood over him. "We're in Kragg's home," she said, looking around. "I think." She extended a hand out to the Shaper and helped him stand up. They appeared to be in a cave, but brighter.

"Another cavern?" Grenseal said. "I thought we were done with these things."

Leanah embraced the sword, ready to attack. "Be prepared for any visitors or dragons."

Grenseal sighed. "Right. Dragons."

The Shaper dusted off his brown cloak. "We are here because

the sword brought us here?"

"It would seem," said Grenseal.

"You can calm down now," said Kragg. "We are safe. We are home."

"You're home, maybe," said Leanah. "But not mine."

The sword chuckled, then said, "That's not as true as you'd like it to be."

Leanah gripped the sword by its blade, holding it near her face. "I'm growing tired of your riddles. When Vamori is saved, I'm melting you down into scrap."

"Oh, you humans are so much fun!" said the sword. "If you'll kindly place me down."

"I will do no such thing," said Leanah. "Why are we here?"

"You are here because you're supposed to be," said the sword. "It was always here you were taking me."

"What is that supposed to mean?" she asked.

"You wanted to get answers?" he asked. "Then you can have answers."

"Then why was I sent to kill a Shadowed Wing?" she asked. "What is this all about?"

The sword's blade began to glow a light blue. "That I cannot tell you. But I do not consume the blood of vermin." The sword shivered. "Shadowed Wings. Terribly disgusting things."

"You're glowing," said Grenseal.

The Shaper pointed at Grenseal's hand. "As are you."

Grenseal held his hand out in front of him. The light glowed a bright blue, a color Grenseal himself had never seen come from his body. A dark blue, orange, white, yellow, red...all of these were colors of flames he summoned. This blue, the color of pristine ice crystals, was all new. "Why are we glowing?"

"Forward," the sword said.

Leanah followed the glow of the sword, tracing the walls of the cave with her hands, watching along the floor. "Where are you taking us?" she said.

"Answers," he said. "All of these, answers."

The group wandered deeper into the caverns. The walls appeared to glow with the light coming from roots and vines that grew along the sides of the cave.

Grenseal placed his hand against the walls and listened to the vines. "They speak with a weird accent. Their words are unusual."

The Shaper patted the mage on the shoulder. "If anyone would know anything about unusual…."

"Hey!" he shouted back and caught up the group. "What, exactly, are we looking for?"

The sword began to glow brighter, illuminating the entire cavern.

"I believe we are about to get our answer," said the Shaper. He clung to the sides of his cloak and pulled his hood up over his head. Its edges fluttered in the sudden gusts of wind that came from somewhere in front of them.

"Wind?" asked Leanah. "In a cave?"

"Almost," said Kragg. "Almost."

The wind grew more intense as they progressed into the cave. The walls of the caverns glowed with the phosphorescent lighting of the vines, but at this point of the cave were smooth like river rocks.

"What is this place?" Leanah said. The wind had carried her voice further back to the rest of the group.

As the wind picked up, the noises became increasingly harder for everyone in the group to hear. If anyone had said anything to answer Leanah's question, no one could tell.

Trying to keep a firm grip on the ground despite their gradually deteriorating shoes and sandals, had exhausted them all. And, inexplicably, there was no more wind. The sound had returned to normal. If anything, the group felt warmer.

"What is this?" Leanah stepped forward into the small part of rock that jutted out over the scenery.

"This is your answer," said the sword.

After struggling for the last few feet, they reached the edge of what looked to be a cave entrance overlooking a valley. Something appeared to be leaning up against the walls, something black with thick shadows that masked all features. While light came in from the very green scenery outside, it appeared to be absorbed by the figure.

"You took your sweet time," the figure whispered, its raspy voice sounding more male than female.

Leanah seized the sword. "Who are you?"

"Put the sword down, Leanah." The figure stood up from the wall and extended a long, thin arm. Clawed, shadowing fingers curled into a fist and then released into an open palm. "Give me the sword."

"Go into the Void!" she shouted.

"You always were stubborn!" the voice said. The body grew bigger, reaching out into the sides of the walls, seemingly connected to the shadows and absorbing the light of the cavern.

In what seemed to be a blink of an eye, the entire cavern grew pitch black.

Leanah flung her sword in front of her, caring not who would stand in her way. "Come out, demon!" she shouted. "Come fight like a real beast!"

The walls echoed with laughter, a deep laughter that rattled the insides of the humans as well. "You're getting more stupid as the time goes on, Leanah. You cannot control that sword for long. Give it to someone who knows what to do with it."

Leanah felt something press down on the sword's tip, flicking it back up into the air.

Whatever this demon was, it was only playing with her.

A nasal, sniffing sound came from sword. "I know you. Somehow."

"Why aren't you glowing again?" Leanah demanded. She tried to keep her feet still, for fear of falling off some something or bumping into a weapon in the shadowy darkness.

"What do you think I've been doing all this time?" said the sword. "It's not working," he said.

Leanah felt something dull tap her spine.

"Sorry," said the Shaper.

"Where are you?" Leanah demanded. "Watch out, everyone."

"Watch out for what?" said a voice—probably the Shaper, but Leanah had stopped paying attention. She lowered her stance, pushing her shoulders and elbows out beside her to minimize hitting anyone she might have known. "Duck!" she said, hoping that everyone would actually do as she demanded for once.

"Raawr!" she grunted and swung her sword completely around her. Her blade sliced through the air in a smooth motion. Nothing standing in her way.

"Damnation!" she shouted. "Where the Void are you?" she shouted. "Show yourself."

A grunting, someone being hit, followed by a sound of a body being slammed up against the walls.

Leanah felt her palms begin to sweat. "This is not funny," she said.

"Oh, but it's freaking hilarious to me!" whispered the shadow into her ears.

Leanah screamed, turned her body and sliced toward the sound of the whisper. "Die!" she screamed. "Die! Die! Die!" Her blade whooshed through the air, nothing more.

Another dull slam, the meat sound of another of her companions hitting the walls.

Leanah swung her sword ferociously through the air, turning in every direction. She knew she risked the lives of her teammates, but this was life or death, the end of their journey if this man got his dark clutches on the sword.

"That's it!" the sword shouted. "Darque!"

The Shadow cackles echoed into the caverns. "You're an idiot, Kragg. And I had such high hopes for you, too."

"Darque? What happened to you?"

"I happened," said the Shadow, pulling at the sword's blade. "I've been waiting for you to return back home. Back to my own command."

"You know you cannot command me," the sword said. "I have already been chosen."

The pulling ceased, though Leanah's grip did not lesson on the Kragg's handle.

"You pathetic pile of ore!" said the Shadow. "You wouldn't know your own master if it bit you on the handle!"

Leanah felt the clawed hands of the shadow grab her tunic and push her forward. The fresh air of the outside touched her face, but she could see nothing. How close she was to the edge of the outcropping, she had no idea. This, however, spurred her on. Leanah turned around and swung her sword into the darkness.

Leanah's body stopped moving—the blade had snagged onto something. "Die, you monster!" she shouted. She pushed the blade into the snag, twisting her shoulders to add leverage and power to her blow. Leanah tried to pull the blade back, to free it and let loose another hack, but it stuck.

"You stupid, stupid little girl."

Leanah gripped the handle tightly, then lifted a leg, reaching into the darkness. She felt the tight flesh of what she hoped was her opponent and kicked off. It had delivered the effect she wanted: the blade slipped out, but forced Leanah to fall backwards.

Leanah tried to pull herself around, to steady her fall and brace for impact, but she had kept falling. In this darkness, she had no way of knowing if she was falling or standing still. The room began to spin, though form what, she was unsure.

"No!" Leanah screamed. As she peered downward, something—a flicker of light—caught her eye. The flicker of light came from the floor against a wall.

Grenseal.

"I'm trying!" His voice sounded weak, in pain.

Leanah turned her sword around, holding it so that her blade faced downward, and she stabbed repeatedly hoping for the blade to snag into the wall and keep her steady.

Her body began to slow down, the spinning almost stopping.

"What is this?" she screamed. Leanah hacked at her surroundings, but something heavy and muscular grabbed her waist and wrapped itself around her. "Unhand me!" she shouted.

She was moving, though in the darkness it felt impossible to know in what direction.

The flare that Grenseal had first begun to summon turned into a steady flame, one that began to grow against the walls, now visible to Leanah.

"How are you cutting into the shadows?" she asked. Her hands gripped the shadowy tentacle and tried to push it away from her. "Let me go!" she shouted.

The fire at the wall turned into a big enough flame to reveal the bodies of Grenseal and the Shaper, sitting against the wall with their legs stretched out in front of them.

"Can you hit it?" she asked. With her sword, Leanah stabbed at the tentacle.

A laughter began to echo down the caverns, feeling distant, cold. "I expected more from you, Kragg."

"Darque!" said the sword. "You will suffer for this betrayal!"

More laughter. "You will never learn, will you?"

The sword's blade began to shimmer light blue.

"You're doing it!" Leanah said.

The sword grunted, then the shimmer faded. "I do not have the power." Then, louder, "Darque! Your power is fading! You're getting weaker!"

Leanah took this moment to stab the tentacle with her blade, slicing into something and releasing a putrid stench that made her turn her head.

However, out of the corner of her eye, Kragg began to glow brighter a gradual brightness that increased.

Leanah stabbed further into the tentacle, hacking it blindly. With each cut, each time the blade went deeper, Kragg's blade would glow brighter and more brilliant.

"You're feeding?" asked Leanah.

The sword muttered something that was interrupted by an explosion that lit cavern briefly, muted as it was against the magickal darkness that took over the cavern.

"Do it again!" Leanah demanded. "Again!"

Against the darkness, a ball of fire, this one yellow, not orange or red, grew and was flung into the air.

The Shadow seemed to retreat, its ruby eyes growing smaller as it ran further away into the darkness.

"Don't you worry," said the Shadow. "I got what I wanted."

The voice of the Shadow echoed into the caverns as their villain seemed to run away. As he did so, light began to gradually return to the area.

"I never thought I would be so happy to see that bright orange cloak again," said the Shaper. He stood up and extended his hand to pull up Grenseal.

"Nice to see you, too!"

Leanah pointed Kragg down the darkness of the hallway. "Come on!" she shouted. "He's wounded. We must finish it!"

"We have other things that matter first, Leanah," said the Shaper. "We must save your village. Here, your sword promised answers."

"You cannot be serious! That—that—thing still walks this earth! We must destroy it!" Leanah's eyes narrowed, her teeth gnashed together and looking decidedly sharper to the Shaper's keen eyes.

"I believe we must take time to regroup, to learn of this place," he said. "I believe him that he'll come back. I say we be ready for him."

"And wait to be ambushed?" said Leanah. "I will not wait to die!" She turned to run down the entrance to the tunnel, but froze at a flash of light. Leanah held up her arms to shield her eyes and face from the intense heat and light of the wall of flame in front of her.

"Even you would stop me?" she said.

"You're better alive than dead," said Grenseal. "The Shaper has a point. Our goal was to save your village, not destroy something we don't understand."

"But I felt it," she demanded. "I felt the power when I cut into it. This sword hungers for more."

"I do not think it is the sword that is hungry," said Grenseal.

Leanah rushed to Grenseal and gripped his cloak, pressing him against the wall.

She grew so close to him that he could smell the stench of adrenaline in her veins.

"Give me a good reason why I should not slit your throat right now," she said through closed, gnashed teeth. She drew Kragg's blade closer to the mage's throat, tickling the stubble that grew along his neckline. "Just one reason."

The Shaper's staff tapped Leanah on the shoulder. "Because if you do, I will cease to help you and your village will be laid to waste."

The angry little girl pulled her sword back, still clutching it in a tightly curled fist around the handle. "You're saved this time," she said.

Kragg's blade grew a stronger blue. "Now that we have the dramatics out of the way," it said, "you can see what we came to see."

The group turned their attention to the opening of the cavern's wall. Outside, a different scene than the one before, a rocky hillside and a small village. Strong grey walls, marbled with red streaks of ore encircled the village. A pair of men, both with rust-colored beards pulled their bluhorns to the gate's opening. "Let us pass!" they shouted.

"What is this?" Leanah said. "What kind of magick is this?"

The sword smiled. "These are your answers."

"Is this," the Shaper paused, searching in all directions of the cavern's opening, "Vamori?"

The sword grunted a yes. "About a few years ago," he said.

"A few years ago?" said Leanah. She pointed into the picture. "That's my father! He has to be just barely older than me!"

"Yes," he said. "He would be about fifteen."

"That's nearly twenty years ago," she said.

"Time passes by quickly when you're asleep for decades," he said. "Sorry."

"He looks so young. So handsome," said Leanah, as if seeing her father for the first time.

As the companions watched on, a group of horses and war bison began to rattle the ground. The earth trembled and rocks shook nearby the village. Shortly thereafter, a large army of men marched onto the village, firing arrows of fire.

One of the men—the general of the Dallheim—led rode in front of his army shouting words in a language none of the companions appeared to understand. "What is he doing?" asked Leanah. "What?"

The general held his hand up toward the sky and then flung it forward, pointing to the Vamori gates. Fire arrows and bolts of a purple magic shattered against the walls.

"See? Nothing can break through!" Leanah stood firm, her smile reflecting the pride she still held for her people.

"I would not be so sure of that," said the sword. As he said this, the walls began to crumble, a war bison attacking the walls with its head. With each thunderous strike, the walls crumbled a bit more, the cracks deepening in the walls.

"But...but..." Leanah could not finish the sentence. She watched as her village fell, the raid completely overcoming Vamori, its people, and its defenses. She looked on as if this were happening now, presently, in front of her eyes, as if she were powerless to watch her village fall to ruin—the same fate she had promised to alter, if not delay.

"But we survived," she said. "We survived."

"Some of you, yes," said Kragg. "Look on."

As parts of the wall fell, pale figures escaped from the village. Climbing the walls and pulling each other through, one of the leaders of the group standing tall on top of the walls and pulling women and children over. His hair grew wild with red, rust-colored hair.

"Father?"

"Your father was a coward, only living to see another day because he ran with the women and children," said the sword.

Leanah shoved the sword back into her bag and watched on.

"You lie."

"Do I?" he said.

Hibert escaped, holding the hand of his soon-to-be wife. The handful of humans ran toward the southern forests to flee from the rule of the Dallheime.

"So he lived to fight another day," said Leanah. "Big deal."

"It's not your father's life that's important," said the sword. "It's what he did with the life he spared."

The scene changes in front of them, a great wind carrying and pushing images and pictures in front of them. The ledge overlooks a darkened forest, the Oaken Forest, as the group traverses the area, looking for food and picking from bushes and trees.

"It was when your father stumbled into a trap that things

turned for the worse."

Leanah's heart began to beat faster. She felt the blood rush and the heat of her anticipation in her chest. "Just show me already!" she demanded.

The sword smiled. "As you wish," he said. Kragg's metal face blinked, turning the scene in the cavern to a hunt.

Hibert held to a thick wooden stick, a sharpened rock tied to the tip. He held the spear as if willing to throw it at his target. "Stop!" he screamed.

In front of him: Leanah's mother, running at top speed, faster than any human.

Hibert's face grew moist and red, not from exhaustion but from fear and loss. He tracked her down through forests and through mazes of protruding rock until finally stopping at an entrance. A deep, black entrance.

Hibert analyzed the ridges of the entrance.

"Runes," said Grenseal. "Darkness waits for the bold."

"You can read that?" said the Shaper.

"So can I," Leanah said. "But why?"

"Because of me," the sword muttered.

Hibert entered the cavern and ran toward the end, following any sound of his beloved's footsteps. "Serah!" he screamed into the darkness.

A pair of ruby red eyes returned an answer.

"Serah?" asked Hibert. He followed the pair of eyes, seemingly floating along the walls until Hibert stumbled upon a rock, cracked along the side, but not enough for it to fall apart.

The ruby eyes fluttered along until finally resting on the rock. Then disappearing inside.

Hibert seized his spear and thrust the rocky end into the crack.

"I'll save you, Serah," he said. Tears fell down his face, falling into darkened wet spots on the ground. Hibert's shoulders and arms appeared to flex harder as he dug into the rock. Deeper, each banging of the spear taking more and more rock away until finally, like the sound of an egg hatching, something cracked open.

Pieces of the stone fell to the side, inside, the Sword of Stone.

"That's—" Leanah said, then stopped. "You?"

"You were hatched out of an egg?" said Grenseal.

"So to speak," said the sword, a smile in the tone of his voice. "You could say that."

"But what's he doing?"

Hibert took the sword and held it close, attempting to hide it in the lower hangings of his tunic. As he took the sword, Hibert's eyes and face turn darker, redder, than before.

"What's he doing?" said Leanah. "I thought were you were the village's guardian? Its protector?"

"In a matter of speaking, I am. Your father used me to destroy the Dallheim, but in doing so, pulled me from my rightful resting place."

"It angered Darque, didn't it? Your removal?"

The sword said, "Yes, but it had to be this way."

"Why?" asked Leanah.

The Shaper lowered his head, "Because the Elders have demanded it."

The companions turned their gazes to the Shaper.

"What is that supposed to mean?"

"We've been tools all this time," he said. "We are the reasons why the world is going to fall apart. I was not supposed to help the village, I was supposed to help destroy the village."

The Shaper fell to his knees, holding on to the walls as if trying to hold himself steady.

"You mean…?"

"We've already started something that cannot be unbroken."

"What do you know?" Leanah said, putting the blade against the Shaper's head. "What do you know that you're hiding from me?"

"This is your doing, isn't it?" said Grenseal.

The sword appeared to sigh. "Yes."

"Then the Shattering?"

"The Shattering will happen whether we want it to or not."

Leanah rested the blade against the Shaper's cheek. "Lies!" she shouted. Her voice rumbled the room around them. "All of this is lies! Everything! My father was a hero, not a thief!" Her grip on the sword tightened, her hands wavering as it gripped the Shaper's bald head. "You tell them all that you were lying! Manipulating us!"

"There are no lies here, only truths, Leanah," said the sword. "We stand at the Crux of Planes. Where lands collide."

"I will destroy you myself!" said Leanah. She threw the sword against the wall and watched as it merely dented the wall. "Destroy you myself!" she shouted again, picking up the sword and smashing it against the walls and rocks over again.

"Destroy!" she shouted.

But with each strike against a rock, the sword appeared to be stronger, angrier. The Shaper was not sure if this was illusion or reality, but he swore that the sword's blade grew with a faint red glow. "Leanah! You cannot destroy the sword! You cannot destroy a god!"

The sword spoke, "You cannot defeat me here. This is where I was born, where all of the lands come together. There are magicks and powers here that you cannot comprehend, cannot control. I am the Sword of Stone, little girl. If you destroy me, you destroy this place!"

Leanah's fists clenched into tight balls. She took strong, gentle strides toward the sword and picked it up. Holding it, gazing into the Sword's face, she said, "I can do whatever I please."

"Leanah, perhaps you should let go of the sword, let us carry it for safekeeping." Grenseal searched for the pack, then offered one of the storage pouches from the boat. "Just put it in here."

Leanah smiled, then silently shook her head. "You dare challenge me?"

"This was not a challenge," said Grenseal. He held up his hands and stepped backwards. "Just a suggestion. Okay?"

Leanah looked up at her companions. "If I cannot be strong enough to kill a god, then I must become a god myself."

"Don't be ridiculous, Leanah," the Shaper stepped forward. "Think of your village. Think of your family."

"My family is filled with lies. My village, damned. Only I can save it." A sudden look of contentment waved over her as she looked back at the tunnel that led to the entrance of the cavern. "It is my responsibility. No one else's."

"Leanah, I think we just need to calm down here," Grenseal said. "We can go back to the village and bring the sword and make everything okay."

Leanah's eyes turned a dark green, reflecting the darkness in the cave. "I do not need you." Leanah, as if carried on by the wind, fled from the cavern, down a darkened tunnel passage.

Grenseal and the Shaper watched on as she fled.

"How is she running so fast?"

The Shaper drew up his hood and grabbed his staff. "We are

watching the sword infuse with her soul."

"The Sword made her do that?"

"Just like that rock makes you do fire. Come," said the Shaper. His sandals made flat flip-flop noises as he ran down the tunnel passage to follow Leanah.

As he ran, he noticed a sudden burst of heat, then the roar of a dull crackling of air. "What is this?"

Grenseal flew next to him, standing, but traveling forward.

"How are you doing this?" the Shaper asks.

"Need a ride?" said Grenseal.

The Shaper held out his arms and closed his eyes, still running at top speed. "Just please don't kill me." Grenseal's hands felt warm, but not scorching hot, counterintuitive compared to the waves of nearly invisible heat radiating from the body of Grenseal.

"Learned that I could heat up the air around me," he said. "Seems to make me fly like a bird. But you know, with less flapping."

The Shaper nodded, and drew his legs up around his body. "Can we watch for the rocks?" he said.

Grenseal's face seemed to have a white halo around him. "I can try, but I've never carried anyone before."

The two flew through the caverns and eventually pulled out of the cave, hitting fresh, cool air like a running into a spider's web. They flew into the air, nearly thirty paces into the air. From up here, the Shaper could see far into the distance on either side of him. "This is beautiful," he muttered to himself. Then, the sudden feeling of having your intestines travel upwards into your lungs made the Shaper flex his stomach and pull his feet upwards. They were falling back to the ground.

"Don't you worry," said Grenseal, a slight strain in his voice. "I've got you."

"Where are we?" asked the Shaper.

Grenseal looked around him and slowed his speed. "We are—" he peered around. "I don't know where."

"She has to be nearby," said the Shaper. "We were flying too quickly for her to be ahead of us."

The Shaper looked to the sky and noticed its direction. It was over halfway across the sky. "It is after midday," he said. The Shaper looked to his right. "We are to go that way," he said, pointing north.

"Then north it is," said Grenseal. The two took off by foot. "I hope you don't mind walking a little bit. I cannot continue that type of use for too long. It tires me out."

"I'm just thankful for the experience. We will need everything we can to stop her."

The two ran as fast as they could, sparing no time or energy. The Shaper, however, had begun to feel the pangs of hunger and a pulling along the back of his muscles. He was hungry and tired, and the stress of the travels, of the emotional betrayal, all of this was too much for a cloistered monk.

"We may need to stop," he said. "We cannot continue this pace for long."

Grenseal's feet burned as he touched the ground. The Shaper wondered if he knew he was burning through his own power, so to speak.

Grenseal nodded. "We can take some time," he said. "But we shouldn't wait too long."

"A Shaper is not meant for this type of physical activity," he said. "Please forgive my weakness."

Grenseal slowed his pace to a stop and waited for his friend to catch up. "We don't stand a chance, do we?"

"If we can stop Leanah, we may be able to prevent the Shattering."

Grenseal looked behind them at the swamp waters. "Shall we go back? Get something to drink?"

The Shaper shook his head. "That we cannot afford to do," he said between panting for more breath. "We cannot go backwards." The Shaper felt the burning in his lungs, of the muscle just beneath his lungs, a fire that traveled to every sore muscle in his body. It was true that he was a cloistered Shaper for all this time, he was not cut out for such physical exertion. "If only I had stayed in the cloister, allowed for the messengers to carry my readings for me."

"Stop speaking like that," said Grenseal. "I believe that bigger forces are at work here. Bigger than you, me, or Leanah. All of us put together, really."

"So we're starting to have a stronger belief in the Elders, are we?" The Shaper managed a smile amid the pain.

"I'm starting to see how the Elders are real bastiches themselves. While I do not condone Leanah's anger toward the Elders, I certainly understand."

As if reacting to his statement, Grenseal felt a flare in his hand, but no fire. A sudden pain stabbed into his palm.

"Are you okay?"

Grenseal gripped his palm and doubled over in pain. "I'm fine," he said. "I just felt heat, an extreme warmth."

"You do conjure fire. Is it that?"

Grenseal shook his head. "When I create fire, I feel no fire myself. My hand remains cool to the touch."

"Perhaps it is the Elders, trying to tell us something."

Leanah felt the power of stone over her feet, her every step carrying her further than she had been able to run before. She felt the energy of the earth travel in her blood, carrying her soul to her desired destination.

It was this same power that allowed her to come to a screeching halt at the sight of her father's image in the shadows of the trees.

"Coward!" she shouted. "It took you too long to come and get me yourself."

Hibert stepped out of the shadows and crossed his arms. "You are messing with forces you do not understand, Leanah." He held out his hand. "Surrender the sword and you will not be punished more than a few weeks of hard chores."

Leanah barked forth a strong laughter. "You cannot order me around anymore," she said. "You are so, so far beneath me that any words from you are like the buzzing of a mosquito!" Leanah drew the sword and turned it around in her hand, extending the hilt out to her father. "If you want this so much," she said. "Come take it from me."

"Don't be stupid, girl." Hibert stepped forward and pointed at the ground. "Drop it first and come back home with me."

"You lied!" Leanah shouted. Tears streamed down her face. "You lied about everything!"

"I did not lie!" he screamed back. "I did what I had to—to protect your mother!"

"And you let me take the fall for this? For the bad things happening to the village?"

Hibert's face began to turn a dark red. He wiped away a tear from his eyes. "You were not supposed to find out like this."

"Then how?" she said. Leanah took small steps forward.

"Then tell me just how I was supposed to find out, Father? How would you tell your little girl that you are a liar, a thief? That your daughter felt guilty for things that were out of her own control?"

"You don't understand," Hibert said. "You will never understand. You're just a child."

Leanah flipped the sword around and thrust it at her father. "I may be a child, but I have the power of a God!" she said.

"The sword is corrupting you!" said Hibert, running backwards and sidestepping all of Leanah's attacks.

"I control the sword," she said. "The sword does not control me!" She sliced into the air, nearly connecting with her father's foot.

"That's what I thought," he said. "We have to put the sword back, bury it where no one can find them again."

"I can't do that!" she shouted. Leanah threw the sword at her father and held out her hand, watching it come back and slicing off strands of her father's hair. "This weapon holds the key to protecting the people I love."

"Is that why you are trying to kill me?" he asked.

"I'm not trying to kill you, I'm protecting you," she said. "I must save our village, make the Gods answer for their crimes!"

Hibert stretched his hands out to the side. "Leanah! Listen to yourself! What would your mother say?"

"Why do you even care?" she said. "You're a liar! A thief! You let your own daughter take the fall for your misdeeds!"

"You're imagining things, Leanah." Hibert showed his hands, unarmed, and stepped forward from his position. "If you want to finish this, then come forward and finish this. Kill me!"

"You are putting words into my mouth!" she said. "Stop confusing me!" Leanah's face twisted into something darker, angry.

"I am protecting you! Protecting!" she said.

She slammed the blade into the ground and watched as the rocks began to tremble under her feet. Then, peering up at her father, she smiled and sliced upwards with her sword. The rocks' trembled traveled to her father and knocked him down.

"You're going to destroy yourself, Leanah." Hibert tried to stand up, but failed. The trembles kept coming, each one stronger than the rest. "We must take that sword, hide it forever! Why do you think I had it hidden in the treasury all this time!"

"Lies!" Leanah screamed and pulled back her sword.

The Shaper and Grenseal stopped in their tracks. "I think I heard her," said the Shaper.

Grenseal nodded and pointed toward the edge of the forest. "That way!" he said. With a burst of heat, he blew himself upwards to scout. "They are up there," he said. Grenseal landed on the ground. "They are over there."

"They?" asked the Shaper.

"Leanah and some old man that looks like her young father."

The Shaper said nothing, but just ran. "We must hurry now!"

Leanah pulled the sword back above her head and jumped toward her father.

Hibert did not move away, instead closing his eyes and nodding. "Do what you must. I have already lost my daughter."

Leanah withdrew the sword over her head and kept her eyes

locked on Hibert's chest.

"I'm sorry," said Kragg.

Leanah brought the sword across her father's chest.

"What did you do?" screamed the Shaper.

"Your own father?" Grenseal said.

Leanah twirled the sword in her hand. "You're next?" she asked.

The Shaper began to run toward Hibert's body, but was held back by Grenseal. "Do not get too close. You'll only risk your own life as well."

The Shaper still pulled forward, free from Grenseal's grip, and slid to Hibert's body.

Hibert's mouth lay open, gasping for breath. The blood had already soaked much of Hibert's tunic and leather armor, glistening in the sun. "I'm so, so, sorry," he said. "I wanted to protect against this," he said.

"I promise."

Leanah lowered her sword and continued to run toward her village.

"We must go! Now!" Grenseal shouted. "We lose daylight!"

The Shaper held Hibert's body watching as his mouth opened, then closed, struggling to speak.

"Shh," said the Shaper. "Shh. Save your energy." He held Hibert's head on his lap. "Have your peace," he said.

As the last breaths of Hibert left his body, the Shaper brought his hands to his chest, raising his index and middle fingers. "Rest with the Elders, Hibert of Vamori. You deserve peace."

The sun cast an impatient Grenseal's shadow over the two figures. "We can bring him with," Grenseal said. "But we waste time."

"We cannot bring him with," said the Shaper. "He will only

slow us down."

Grenseal nodded. It was about time the Shaper began to see things his way. "Then it is agreed. We leave for Vamori."

FOURTEEN

The race toward Vamori would have to wait until sunrise for the last of the companions. The night brought with it troubles and the unknown, and for unskilled warriors such as them, it was doubly so.

The two traveled through the night, unspeaking, running through the afternoon and through the woods as best they could. It was Grenseal's idea that they do not camp in the woods, but rather just outside of it.

"The plains allow for an easier vantage point," he suggested. "In the woods, we are surrounded by shadows, and we all know what lurks in the hearts of shadows."

The Shaper could not agree more. His sides felt aflame, burning from the running and traveling. Too little food and too little rest for the would-be prophet. Any rest was a gift from the Elders themselves, especially in such perilous times.

The moon shined down at its highest peak in the sky upon the two travelers. At long last, Grenseal agreed to rest.

The Shaper watched as the fire mage sought out a perfect place to camp. "I've only done this once or twice before," he said while pressing his hand against trees and whispering to their trunks. "Please forgive me."

"What does it feel like? When they talk to you?"

Grenseal turned his head and raised an eyebrow. "I don't understand."

"The trees, you said they speak to you. What does it sound like? Feel like?"

"I imagine not too unlike when the Elders speak to you," said Grenseal. "He rested his head against the tree and listened again." After getting what the Shaper assumed was his answer, Grenseal whispered something to the tree trunk and bowed his head. "This tree said that Leanah is heading north still, but moving slower."

"Then we have time to rest?"

Grenseal nodded. "They believe that she will tire soon. You cannot raise war with a village and with the gods on without rest." Grenseal rested his head against the tree. "What was that?" Grenseal smiled.

And so did the Shaper. "They have a sense of humor as well?"

Grenseal nodded. "These trees are the funniest I've spoken to in a long time." Grenseal patted the bark on the tree. "Even in times like these, they have a sense of humor."

"Then I suggest we rest. I am unfit for this type of activity."

"Aren't we all?" said Grenseal. "I do not see any bushes, no berries around us."

The Shaper shook his head. "No, it seems that we are without food for the evening."

Grenseal, "Without fresh food, perhaps." He reached into his storage belts and withdrew nuts and berries and slivers of dried meat from the packs. "Leanah may have the lead, but we have the food," he smiled.

The first multi-course meal in nearly a week, the Shaper bowed his head to Grenseal and took a handful of berries and nuts. "With any luck, we will be back in Vamori soon."

"If not, I fear what we will return to," said Grenseal.

Leanah's veins carried blood like lightning to the rest of her body. Striking every part of her body, she felt she was invulnerable to harm. Her body breathed in air differently, her muscles felt stronger, bigger, thicker.

"What is this?" she said, still running through the Oaken Forest.

"What is what, master?"

Leanah slowed her running, too distracted by her sword's sudden sense of respect.

"Master?" she said with a laugh. "I think I like that."

"I believe it is best that you get used to it," said the Sword. "The way things will be for you, the future will accelerate you to a place of power. Of untold riches and untold destruction."

"There will be no destruction as long as I have power," she said. "As long as I have you."

The sword sighed. "And your father thought the same thing. Look how far that got him."

Leanah dug the sword back into her pack and noticed immediately that her running pace had begun to slow. Her muscles grew tired as if her strength were being sucked from her.

"What is this?" she asked. "What's going on?" Leanah pushed

on harder, pressing her feet, her knees, harder into the ground. Her speed, however, did not increase. "Why am I so weak?"

Leanah slowed from running to jogging to walking quickly. Finally, her legs could move no longer.

"What is this?" she said. "Why?" She gasped to catch her breath.

The sword began to laugh. "You're too stupid to figure it out, it seems."

Leanah flipped the pack from her shoulder and tossed it onto the ground. "Tell me the secret!" she said. "What am I doing wrong?"

"You do nothing wrong," it said, "only that you do not listen, pay attention."

Daylight began to turn a dark blue, then purple as Leanah walked to the edge of the forest. "Where did my strength go?" Having only walked a few hours, she should not have felt this weak, this winded, she thought. I must sit. Sit down and rest.

Leanah's pack had become heavier in the process, almost too heavy as if the sword had been made out of cast iron instead of the magical stone as before.

"Tell me," she said. "Tell me of this Shattering."

"You will find out soon enough," said the Sword. "I refuse to help you further."

Leanah gripped the sword and held it high, coming face-to-face with its guard. "Where is this coming from?" she said. "Now you turn on me, too?"

"I will not be the source of destruction amongst my people."

"Destruction?" Leanah stood up and stabbed the ground with the Kragg's blade. "Is that all you can speak of? Destruction? I am trying to save the world here. My world." Leanah felt the terrible pains of hunger in her stomach. "I will keep those I love safe and free from deceit. From hunger. From lies."

"And you plan on doing this, how?" said Kragg. "By destroying those you love?"

"By destroying those who lie. Who cheat. Who steal."

"If you are to save your village soon, Leanah, then you must make way for your village quickly. There is still a threat that needs us to contend with."

"Then I will vanquish it," she said. "I will do what the Gods have failed to do."

The sword scoffed and then grew silent. Leanah attempted to grab the sword. "I have never been asked to save a village, girl!"

Leanah's hand paused. "And if you are correct," she said.

"How can you be correct about history, little girl? It either happened or it did not!"

Leanah shook her head. "If you are correct, and you were never in the hands of my father for the sake of saving a village, what were you asked to do? Why do you exist?"

"I exist to kill."

Leanah nodded. "If I cannot destroy you, then I will control you. If I cannot have your power, then I will control your power," she said. "This," she said. "This is my will."

Leanah grasped the sword and felt the familiar surge of energy in her arms. A lightning strike of warmth through her body, her muscles no longer felt fatigued, no longer tired. "This is your secret?" she asked.

"But with every secret comes a price," Kragg said.

Leanah laughed. "I will pay the price to get what I want."

"I was afraid that you would say that."

The town of Deckal lay just ahead, the last major stop before she would be able to make it her own hometown.

Leanah had decided that it might be a good idea to stop, slow down. She had already acquired the sword. No one knew she was going to return. It was something that maybe, just maybe, she could get the upper hand for a chance and not have to worry about being killed or lied to.

She especially hated the lies.

Leanah's footsteps were quiet, slow. She peered from side to side looking for a particular street that she had stumbled across just a week earlier. The same street that had the most delicious of orange fruits.

Leanah felt the sting of a sharp object against her back. "If you want to stay alive, you will do as I say," said the voice. Leanah smiled, but did what the voice said anyway. It was a woman, from the sound of it.

As she walked forward, they entered into the busier part of town, the hustle and bustle that Leanah had never liked the first time she came across it.

At times she felt the footsteps of her would-be abductor against her heels, pulling on her shoes. "Would you mind?" she said.

"Sorry," said her abductor in a somewhat seductive voice, but digging the dagger even deeper into her Leanah's back. "Keep going."

Leanah reached the center square and wanted to move forward, but the dagger and a tug onto her jerkin told her to move right instead.

Leanah followed, watching and smiling at the passersby until she felt a sudden pull into a nearby alleyway.

"Where is it?" said the woman. Her face was hidden in a black cloth, only a lock of brown hair hung above her forehead.

"Where is what?" Leanah asked.

"The object?"

Leanah stood up, dusted herself off. "You'll have to be more specific," she said.

"The sword of stone," she said. The abductor pointed at the pack on Leanah's shoulder with her dagger. "Whatever is in there."

"Whatever is in there is mine," Leanah said.

"It belonged to your father first," she said. The abductor pulled the pack off Leanah's shoulder. "If you don't mind," she said.

"My father didn't send you," she said. "He's dead." Leanah allowed for the woman to go digging into the pack.

Another person, a man, came from behind Leanah and pressed another dagger into her side. "If you scream," he said. "We kill you on the spot."

Leanah nodded. "This dagger thing," she said and twitched her backside, "it's a little redundant, no?" She appeared to be unshaken by the events that were transpiring in front of her. Neither of her robber-abductors appeared to be entertained. She sighed. "Fine. Do as you will," she said.

The dagger dug deeper into her side. "You're awfully smug," said the man behind her. "I think you're hiding something."

Leanah smiled. "Is that what you think?"

The dagger pierced the outer layer of her tunic. "If you try this again," he said, "we'll kill you on the spot. Now what are you hiding?"

The woman pulled the sword out of the pack, but as soon as she tried to show it to the man, the sword fell to the ground, with the woman's hand still hold it.

"Sorcery?" asked the man. He brought the dagger up to Leanah's neck and held it closer. "Undo the spell," he said. "Undo it now!"

The woman's hand remained crushed against the ground, pressed between the rocks of the cobblestone and Kragg's hilt.

"This sword," she said. "It's enchanted?"

"You can say that," said Leanah. Watching the frustration in her voice, Leanah began to smile. Twist the knife a little more.

"Call off the spell!"

"Let me leave and I will," said Leanah.

The woman and the man exchanged glances. The moment of silence held thick in the air, waving between the two. "Fine!" said the man. "Let her go!"

"I have your word you'll leave me alone?" said Leanah.

The woman cried out in pain. "Yes!" she said. "Call off your sword."

Leanah walked to the sword and grabbed Kragg by the hilt. "Let the poor girl go," she said.

As Leanah picked up the sword and dusted off its blade with the end of her sleeve, she saw the man coming from behind.

Leanah turned around swiftly and knocked the dagger out of his hand, then kicked him down. The woman, grabbing her wrist lowered her eyes away from Leanah. "Just go!" she cried. "Please."

"Who sent you?" Leanah screamed. She grabbed the man by the back of his throat. "Tell me."

"I can't," she said. "He'll kill me."

"So it's a man," she said. "Got it. Who is it?"

"Our employer," she said. "I don't know. He's dark. Never showed himself." The girl sniffles back some tears. "He stayed in the shadows all this time."

Leanah flipped the sword around in her hands playfully. "Thank you," she said with a smile. Leanah grabbed her pack from the ground, tucking it back over her shoulder, and placed the sword back inside. "And tell your employer if I find out who he is,"

"Ha!" said the lady, "If we see our employer without you, we won't have any time to explain before he kills us."

Leanah walked to the edge of the alleyway and peered out into the sunlit crowd. The people were still busy, even during this time of day, midday. It would be a perfect time to get lost, she thought.

"Yeah," Leanah said. "Good luck with that."

Leanah placed her hand on the strap of the backpack and walked out of the alley and into the crowd of people. As she walked to the edges of the city, she realized that the city seemed more crowded than usual. People, especially poorer people appeared on the edges of the city streets. Beggars held out their hands and pots asking for coin or food.

Leanah paused at one of the groups.

"Coin, please madam?" said a little girl, no older than ten years old by Leanah's accounts.

Leanah tapped around her person before saying, "I don't have anything, I'm sorry. Where are you from?"

The girl paused and looked back at another woman—her mother. She wore dirty, flame scorched clothing, a cloth shirt that was more of a piece of long cloth with a neck hole in it, folded over her shoulders. "I, uh…"

Leanah knelt down. "You can tell me, you know. I won't kill you."

The girl's eyes widened and she backed away. "Kill?"

The older woman stepped up, standing to be quite taller than

Leanah's smaller frame. "You had best just leave us alone, ma'am. We are not looking for trouble."

Leanah extended a hand out to them to reveal that she did not hold any weapons. "I did not mean anything by this," she said.

"Please, we did not mean to cause you to threaten us," the woman said. She pulled a piece of cloth over her shoulders. "We hold only a few spare pieces of food. We'll need more soon."

Leanah raised her hands and bowed. "I understand ma'am. Good luck to you."

FIFTEEN

Emerging from her night's sleep, Leanah wielded her sword and peaked across the horizon. Her eyes spied something distant, a wispy gray cloud hovering over the north.

"It looks like rain," she said. "Maybe things are starting to look up."

"Think again," said the sword.

Leanah put out the last of the embers of her fire and started to the north, holding her sword in her hand to feel connected to the constant surge of power. Her pace quickened to a jog, then a full-force run. As Leanah traveled over the great distances through the plains, she noticed the clouds were moving up, not across, the sky.

"What is this?" she said.

The sword sighed. "And so it begins."

Leanah flipped the sword to speak to it face-to-face. "What begins?" she said.

"My child, the worst has happened."

Leanah's eyes grew bigger. She knew the answer before she

could even ask the question. Her feet traveled faster, barely touching the surface of the ground. She ran faster than the bluhorns of the Karavano.

"I've grown stronger," Kragg said.

"What do you mean?" she asked. She pushed the sword back into the backpack over and over again, still not quite getting it that I just wouldn't fit.

"As you grow stronger so do I. Our connection has given me, or given us depending on how you think about it, more power."

Leanah scratched her head and then smiled after a little thought. Her companions could almost see the spark of her thoughts above her head.

"It is nice to see that a mortal can stop being so dense," said the sword.

"So you're saying as I get more powerful so do you?"

"I believe I just said that, yes."

"But why did we get more powerful? What happened?" she asked. Her questions were good questions.

"I have more faith in your abilities. I have been fed, and in this trust our connection grows," it explained. "There are only so many different ways that I can explain this thing over and over again. If only Kaverin, could help me. Or that Shaper fellow."

Leanah's feet began to travel slower, now down to a walk.

"I have been asleep for over a century, I have grown tired of explaining myself, but it appears that we were meant to be together. The deaths have fed my hunger."

"If that happens when I feed you, what happens when you defeat the great evil?" she asked. Her voice was slow and somber. "Does that mean that you get even more powerful?" A veiled enthusiasm hid behind this question.

"That depends on who wields the weapon," said the sword. Leanah's smile grew bigger. "Some have fallen, others have risen to greatness before falling. The Shaper says you are destined for the latter."

"Fallen?" Leanah asked.

"You are destined to fall into the darkness after achieving greatness. You will become a wonderful warrior only to become the most feared human, man or woman, in the land of Terra." The sword did not bother to look up as he said this. It was as plain as day to him, a simple fact of life.

"That's impossible!" she screamed. "I am not evil!"

"Are or are not; that is not the question here. It is what you will become that is important."

"Well, then, I will not become evil. I just want to save my village and go home. That's it."

"Power corrupts, my lady."

Leanah's feet came to a full stop, she held the sword over the pack again, threatening to drop it in "And just what is that supposed to mean?"

"Quite simply," said the sword, "that those who are given power are doomed to succumb to it. It is a trait among all humans that you are not able to handle power. Power and the possibilities of forging the world in our image are attractive to the human mind. To get what we want every time we want it; that is the power of evil."

Leanah shook her head. "But Caeran said you were a savior, that you would help us." She looked up to the sky. "You know, during the wars."

"That was the reason that our ancestors fell a millennium ago. The runes all have a dark side to them."

"Then how come Grenseal has not gone evil? He has one of you, does he not?" Leanah asked. Her heels tapped

"His is a rune of power. His rune must not be flawed," he said with a smile. "At least as far as he knows."

The thought did not seem to linger in Leanah's mind long as she observed the mountains that were growing increasingly thicker and thicker along their path. She was almost back home.

"This ridiculous behavior of yours. It is a trait of your rune," the sword said.

"Ridiculous?" she said. "You, too?"

"You would dare to question a rune?" the sword said. Its handle began to grow warm.

"Ease up there," said Leanah. "But I don't see what you're talking about. Everyone says that I'm this big bad person, but all I'm doing is saving myself and my family." Leanah tucked the sword into her belt and began to walk again toward the mountains. "I'll show you," she said.

"You will show much in the coming hours, Leanah."

Leanah ran until she could barely catch her breath, and then pushed harder. The muscles in her legs burned, felt like ropes ready to snap, collapse to the ground.

The fire, the lightning in her veins, it coursed through her entire body.

Leanah spotted hills, perfect for a better view. She traveled up the lowest of the hills and peered to the north.

"No!" she screamed.

The village of Vamori was burning to the ground.

Leanah said nothing more but grasped the sword closer to her body as she ran to the gray-red dusty grounds of the Karavano. Her village lay just over the hills, but the clouds and become dark, threatening.

Leanah peered overhead and listened. People had been running in different directions. The crackling of burning wood of the village gates.

"What is this?" she said. "Who did this?"

Leanah ran to the village gates. Flames of orange and red had already overcome the walls. Gaping holes of fallen lumber, now glowing ash, lay on the ground just outside the place she once called home.

Leanah felt the cool drippings of her own tears on her cheeks. The sight was something she could not pull away from. Everything she had known, everything she had loved, burned in front of her.

"No," she said. Leanah felt the urge to fall to her knees, to watch as everything she had struggled to save was pulled from her grasp. "Grenseal," she said. "I know you did this."

Leanah seized the sword, ready for war, and ran down the hills.

A man wearing black, the lower half of his face covered with a thick gray cloth, though he spoke loud enough for Leanah to hear. "Stop!" he screamed.

Leanah looked over her shoulder to the man and his horse. "Do not tell me what to do."

"By order of the Chieftain's wife," he said. "You are not to enter."

Leanah walked toward the entrance anyway. "I'm here to help, you fool."

The man's horse approached Leanah, its rider drawing its own spear. "I said," he said, but his words were ended when he hit the ground, clutching his side.

Leanah pulled the sword and rested it against her side. "I said I'm here to help."

Leanah gripped the sword and placed her hand against the flaming wood of the village's walls. She felt the incredible heat against her flesh, but she did not melt.

This sword, she thought, it has some incredible secrets.

Leanah pressed forward, pushing the wood of the gates down in front of her. The walls collapsed behind her in a pile of flaming ash and sparks.

"Leanah!" screamed a voice. It was Frondir. "Leanah! You have returned!" He dropped himself to his knees. "Please, I beg of you," he said. "Return the sword to its rightful place. Return it so that we may live."

Leanah held it closer to her chest. "But it will save us," she said.

Frondir stood up and leaped toward Leanah. "Give me the sword! You did this! You did all of this!" There was a madness in his eyes, ash and streaks of black across his forehead and cheeks. Leanah had never seen him so maddening. Sure he was a jerk and never cared much for Leanah, but this was a different person.

Leanah pushed her sword forward into Frondir and pulled out. The body dropped to the ground, lifeless. Leanah stepped over the body and continued to her own house.

The building of her home had been completely set aflame. Leanah watched on as the chickens fled from the insides of the house out toward the gates. They, too, thought Leanah, they will suffer as well.

"What are you doing?"

Leanah turned around to see the source of the question. Serah held to a chicken in her hands. "Where is your father?" Serah watched as Leanah's eyes told her the story without saying a single word. "He's?"

Leanah nodded. Serah did not need to know how.

"But he was to go get you, save you." Serah slapped her daughter's face. "You endangered this village with your stunt!" she shouted. Leanah's room had begun to catch fire. "You took the sword? You took our protector and our savior?" Serah turned around, presenting the burning house to Leanah's eyes. "Do you see what you did?"

"I was going to fulfill the prophecy," she said. "I was going to save us."

"You damned us, Leanah. That is all you managed to do."

The flames overcame all of Leanah's house. Where once was Leanah's room, now lay something akin to a funeral pyre.

"What have you done to us, Leanah?" Serah's eyes glowed with the intensity of the fires around her. The reflection of the flames in her eyes, to Leanah, it was as if she witnessed her own mother, her own family, burning alive in her eyes.

"We're too late," said the Shaper. His knees began to buckle. All he could do to keep from falling was to grab his staff and hold himself steady. "We have failed."

"Not yet!" Grenseal said. "Look!"

Down below, dark figures moved around the village, destroying and setting fires. Only a few of them, from their vantage point, but the dark figures moved about quickly on horses.

"Did Leanah...?" Grenseal asked.

The Shaper held his hands up to silence his friend. "There is no knowing. But we must help the people get to safety."

Grenseal nodded and pulled his hands from the sleeves. "I cannot pull in fire, but I can control it," he said. "Let's see what we can do."

The Shaper clutched his staff harder and ventured down the hills, careful to look for solid ground to step on.

"Why would she lay waste to her own village?" asked Grenseal. "It doesn't make sense."

"She's been tainted by the sword. Right now, many things will not make much sense."

Grenseal held his hand out to the fire as they stepped down the hills. "And this is the will of the Elders?"

The Shaper did not know what to say, so he chose to be silent. Instead, pointing at the fire. "Help them!"

"Mother!" Leanah said, grabbing Serah's shoulder. "Mother, I need for you to leave, flee with the other villagers." Leanah pointed at another hole in the gates. A group of villagers fled, carrying chests and armfuls of bags. "Go with them," she said. "I will find you."

Serah shook her head. "I cannot leave. I must help."

"Mother! You are in no position to help," she said. "You must leave. You are too important."

"It has reached you, too, has it?" Serah's eyes analyzed Leanah's. They darted from side to side, looking for something, anything, Leanah did not know.

"What are you talking about? It's me, Leanah." Leanah pulled her head away from her mother's hands. "You need to go. Help the others."

"We've already lost," said Serah. "We lost the moment you took that sword into your hands."

"Mother!" Leanah growled. "You will get yourself to safety if I have to carry you myself!"

Leanah's mother nodded and walked toward the village. "I have nothing left," she said. "Today, I lost a husband and a daughter."

"Mother!" Leanah shouted.

Serah began to run to the flames that were eating at her house. "Mother! Stop!"

Leanah reached out for her mother, but it was too late. Her mother had made it into the house and disappeared into the wall of flames.

Leanah watched, reaching out into the flames, trying to resist the heat. But, it was too much. The loss of her village. Her mother. Leanah felt the pressure of her anger forming in her chest.

She looked around, listening to the hiss and pop of the fire against the stone and wood. Leanah walked the center of the village, unusually devoid of fire.

From here, she watched as the last of the people fled the village. Men wearing black, their faces covered, and riding horses carried off with cloths and gems from the houses. No doubt one of them had her father's gold, maybe an important painting or weapon.

"Take it all," she said. "Just take it." She stood firm in the center. Her eyes wandered to the stars, the dog constellation chasing the moon around the sky. "Just take it all from me."

"That was the intent," said a voice.

"Ciaran?" Leanah looked down. The figure in front of her looked skinner, darker. "Ciaran? It is you." Leanah rushed to his side to give him a hug. The last person she had expected to be alive stood right in front of her. "I'm so glad you made it out okay."

"Is this the one you were looking for?" Another masked man approached Leanah. He drew his spear and pointed it at Leanah's face.

Leanah's shoulders dropped as she let out a sigh. "Of course," she said. "You too."

Grenseal held out his hand to help the Shaper reach the last step onto solid ground. "What do we do now?" he asked.

Grenseal shook his head. "We start with making sure the people are safe," he said.

The Shaper held his breath as he looked around. So much of the village was already destroyed, burned to the ground. There was little he felt he could do, and he certainly was not trained for this in the his studies at the Citadel.

"But I don't know," the Shaper began to say, but was silenced by Grenseal.

"We helped to cause this," Grenseal said. "We must help to stop it."

"It's too far gone," said the Shaper. "We've already lost."

Grenseal shook his head and took a few steps toward the fire. His right hand began to glow again, a nearly invisible wave of heat radiating from his fingertips. With a wave of his hand, he pulled the flames from the bridge and moved them to the rocks, where they died out.

"That's a neat trick," said the Shaper.

"Go! Now!" Grenseal said. "Help the villagers!"

Two dark men on horses approached the companions. "Go no further."

"Go!" shouted Grenseal. He pointed at a direction around the horses toward a hole in the village wall. The Shaper nodded and ran. He felt a sudden surge of heat behind him, them the screams of the horses.

Grenseal pulled his hand back into his cloak as the horses, tails aflame, fled into the mountains. His hands radiated with heat and itched for more fire, more destruction.

The dark men stood, pulling small sharp weapons—daggers perhaps—from pouches on their legs. The smallest of the men threw a dagger at Grenseal. It landed in shoulder, causing Grenseal to scream aloud and grasp his shoulder.

As the Shaper touched the fence, about to lower his head and go in, he heard Grenseal's scream. Should I? he thought. Do I go back and help?

The Shaper paused to see the battle. His jaw dropped open as he watched fire flare from the open wound on Grenseal's shoulder. Something glowed a bright orange-white before trickling down his cloak. Grenseal's entire body appeared to be covered by a wall of orange flame that hugged his body tightly. Grenseal walked toward the man and grabbed his shirt. Upon impact, it exploded into flames and Grenseal walked past him, panting, but moving nonetheless.

His friend, the Shaper had decided, would be fine. He needed to get people to safety.

"This was all you?" said Leanah.

Ciaran nodded as he approached Leanah. His own dark brown cloak turned black, like invisible arms wrapping around him and covering every piece of his body. When Ciaran stopped just short of arm's reach, he had become completely covered in the same darkness as Darque.

"You're Darque?"

An arm of the darkness peeled off of Ciaran's body and grabbed Leanah by the throat. "You're awfully slow for my brightest student," he said.

Leanah tried to hold up the sword, but another shadow arm snapped it out of her hand while the first one wrapped itself tighter around her body. "Thank you, by the way, for bringing this to me, nice and ready for me."

Leanah felt the strain of the tentacles around her throat too much to be able to speak.

"Yes, ready," he said. Ciaran reached down to grab the sword, but a bright blue flash around its handle reflected his hand. "What is this?" he said.

"You know the rules," said Kragg. "One at a time."

Ciaran's distraction with the sword had caused his arms to weaken. Leanah seized the moment—she pulled the tentacle around her mouth and bit into it, hard.

Ciaran screamed in pain. "You little witch!"

The arm wrapped itself back around his body and then peeled itself out again. "Where there was one are now one hundred," he said. More arms peeled away from Ciaran's back, flailing in the air. "You really do have so much to learn."

All of the arms began to whip at Leanah at once, smacking and slapping her across her face, her body, her arms. Leanah felt the warm snap of her jaw, now just hanging—intact, but weak—from her mouth. Leanah screamed, but even that caused her jaw to sear in pain.

"This is almost too easy," said Ciaran. "You threw me off when you decided to go to the Swamps of Mrondir despite meeting the Shadowed Wing."

Leanah's eyes opened wide as she collapsed to the floor. The air smelled thick like smoke, her lungs struggled to breathe and her body felt broken. To move caused her pain like she had never been prepared for. Leanah looked around on the ground. The sword still remained on the ground. If only…

"And I really didn't expect you to kill your own father. Good job there," he said. Ciaran's shadowy form began to absorb the light of the fires around him, creating a fuzzy walking shadow where Ciaran's body should be. He reached over for the sword once more time. "Now if you'll excuse me, I'll take what's mine."

"Fine," Leanah muttered despite her broken jaw.

Ciaran's hand froze in place. His head tilted toward Leanah's broken face. "What was that?"

"Take it." Leanah fell to the ground completely, covering her face with her hands, trying to hold her lower jawbone still and free from pain. "Just take it."

Despite the slurring of her words, Ciaran appeared to know what he was saying. "You're understanding now," he said. "This was never meant for you." He reached down to the ground and tried to take the sword again. His hand was pushed back by the force of a blue light around the handle.

Ciaran looked to the sky and screamed. "You would do this to me, wouldn't you?" Ciaran stepped back and tried to grab the sword with one of his shadow arms. Like a flowing black liquid, it whipped around the ground trying to grab the sword with thick, dark fingers.

Every attempt failed. A bright blue flash of light blinded the area, pushing back Ciaran's shadowy arms at every try.

"But you were supposed to unlock it for me!" he said. "You were supposed to be ripe for the taking!"

Ciaran thrust his hands out into the sides and his body became covered in the thick, liquid-smooth shadows like a set of body armour. He threw his body onto the sword in frustration.

A blue flash, brighter than the fires that surrounded them, flared into the air without any noise. Ciaran flew backwards, into the fires that burned a nearby house.

Leanah reached out to stand up. It hurt move, to breathe, to think. But the sword. She must have the sword. It became apparent to her as she got closer and closer to the sword.

"What are you doing, little girl?" Ciaran cried out.

He can't take it, she thought. Ciaran didn't know what to do with it. But she did. She knew its power.

Leanah reached the sword and grabbed it closer to her chest. The power, it traveled through her like heat, then cold. The pain that had been traveling in her body disappeared, replaced with strength, with a burst of energy. With bloodlust.

"What are you doing?" Ciaran cried out. "That's mine!"

From the flames, more shadow arms flailed out. They whipped at Leanah, who blocked the arms with the blade of the sword.

"This ends!" she shouted.

Ciaran appeared from the flames, unscathed, walking as if emerging from a warm shower. A broad white smile appeared across his face, ruby eyes flashed brightly before more arms flailed about. When Leanah deflected them with her swords, she pressed forward, charging at the shadow.

But Ciaran disappeared into the fires. Melting—it seemed—into the shadows cast upon the ground.

"Get out here!" shouted Leanah. "Come out here now!" Leanah swung at the shadows and stabbed at the flickering darkness on the ground. With each stab, another grunt, another scream.

"Leanah!" shouted the Shaper. "We found you!"

Leanah looked up. Her friend looked thankful, smiling with his bright blue eyes. "What happened?"

Leanah started to call out to the Shaper, but a hand reached from a shadow near Leanah and pulled onto her leg, causing her fall to the ground and scrape her cheek against the rock.

The Shaper started to charge forward, but stopped out of fear and self-preservation when he watched the figure he only knew as Darque appeared from the shadows.

"You're a tricky girl to kill," he said. "More powerful than I thought you'd be." His shadow arms flailed around his body, stabbing at Leanah's body like angry snakes. "But again, you have a lot to learn."

Leanah rolled over to her side and deflected the stabbing shadows, each one faster than the other. "You will fall, Ciaran."

The Shaper readied his staff for battle, if she needed his help.

A large arm swung from Ciaran's body and swiped at Leanah. She grabbed at it, hugging it tight against her body, and was lifted off into the air. It swung about, trying to fling her into a fire, maybe a building.

Leanah, however, did not let go. As she braced herself, pulling it tight against her, she felt the strength of the Sword, the sword's stone energy covering her body, fortifying her muscles.

Leanah squeezed her legs around the tentacle. She struggled to keep her eyes on the arm as it whipped from left to right, then in circles. Then, locking her ankles together underneath, she pulled the sword up and stabbed into the shadowy arm.

Ciaran screamed and withdrew his arms back to his body, completely covering him again. He was nearly doubled over now, from the pain and frustration.

Leanah landed on her knees and pressed herself off the ground. Both she and her opponent were breathing heavy now, striking a balance between hitting hard and falling over would prove to be a difficult decision for Leanah.

The first to fall loses, she thought to herself.

"You will stop this senseless violence!" came a scream from Grenseal. Two pillars of fire shot across the village, one hitting Leanah, the other hitting Ciaran.

Leanah fell to her side yet again, barely holding herself up. The sword had taken some of the damage for her, but some of the flames and heat pushed in through her sword's protection. The smell of singed hair—her hair—twisted her face into anger. "More betrayal!" she roared.

Ciaran stood up, shaken from the hit. The shadowy armour seemed to bubble and pop on Ciaran's body.

Leanah looked, smiled. This would be her secret. She stood up. "Grenseal, you old dog," she said. "Get over here."

Leanah walked away from Ciaran, his body still reeling from the pain of having been hit with the fire. From her vantage point, it appeared that he was boiling in his own shadows.

Leanah struggled to keep walking in a straight line to the source of the fire pillars. "Where are you, old friend?" As Leanah approached the front of the gates, she slowed her pace to a stumble and then, upon reaching the end of the gate, stopped. She rested her hands against the gate and peeked her head out into the surroundings.

There, on the ground, sitting, bent over, and nearly falling over, was Grenseal's smoking body.

"You're okay," she said. Leanah approached Grenseal's body while keeping her sword close to her chest.

Grenseal looked up, his body fought its exhaustion to stay up.

"What," said Grenseal, gasping for breath, "are you doing?" Grenseal held his hand out to his side to keep from falling over. This did not appear to help, however, and he fell over, laying completely on his side and watching as Leanah came closer.

His eyes widened.

Leanah's heart paused, watching Grenseal's expression shift from exhaustion to horror. As if he knew—he must have known—what was coming to him.

Grenseal shook his head, weak and slow. "No," he whispered.

"I need you," said Leanah. "I need your power."

The Shaper ran to Grenseal's side. "Leave him be, girl. He has suffered enough." The Shaper knelt down in front of Grenseal, pulling his friend's face up toward him. "Look at me, buddy. Look at me."

Grenseal's eyes wandered from side to side, peering, looking, as if looking through the Shaper.

"No, it can't be like this. Not like this."

The sound that came from Grenseal was more carnal than a scream, a cry for safety out of fear and knowledge that he, too, will be lost forever.

Leanah's leather boot pressed into the Shaper's back, and then shoved him off to the side, strong enough to shove him nearly five paces from where he sat. "I need him for a minute."

Leanah knelt down and rubbed the hair away from Grenseal's eyes. "You know I need this," she said. "You can help me, can't you?"

A tear escaped Grenseal's eye.

"Look at me!" she demanded. Grenseal's eyes listened, narrowing in on her own. "Good." Leanah stood up, and held the sword up in front of her.

"I hope this works," she said and brought the sword down upon Grenseal's neck.

The Shaper stood up. "Grenseal! Stand up!" he shouted. "Stand! Kill her!"

But as he wiped the tears from his eyes, the headless body of Grenseal leaned forward, his orange robes tainted with the bright red of his own powers, his own blood.

Leanah knelt down in front of the corpse and bathed the sword's blade in the blood. "Taste good, buddy?"

The sword made something of a sniffing sound, then muttered, "I'm sorry, Kaverin."

The Shaper's muscles grew tense with rage, his hands gripping his staff so hard his knuckles grew white. White hot. The Shaper had never known a rage such as this. Without warning, without thought, he rushed at Leanah, pulling his staff high above his head, ready to swing it down and beat this little girl to a senseless pulp.

The rock from Grenseal's right hand popped out of his palm, rolling along the ground.

The Shaper grew nearer to Leanah, but then pushed back by a wave of heat. The Shaper threw his hands up over his face and tried to push forward, but the heat turned into a burning. He began to smell his own clothing catching on fire and he drew back.

Leanah bent down, grabbed the stone and allowed it to embed itself into her right hand. Leanah turned to face the Shaper, pulling the heat back into her body and then smiling. Her eyes turned a bright orange, almost as orange as the hair on her father's chin. "I wouldn't do that," she said.

Her eyes flared orange, giving off the heat of a dozen torches. This wave of heat pushed the Shaper even further back into the debris of a burnt down house.

Finding no other recourse, no way to fight Leanah, he pulled withdrew his staff and pushed the rocks to the side. There, he buried himself and watched on until the struggles had finished. Then, he had decided, he would take care of Grenseal's burial rights.

"Well isn't this fancy," said Darque. His body took shape amongst the shadows of the rubble in the village. "I see you took care of your flaming friend for me. Thank you."

Leanah turned to face Darque, who immediately withdrew. "You couldn't have. It's impossible," he said. Ciaran pulled back and attempted to flee back into the shadows, but Leanah held up a hand, showing her palm and the rock embedded into it. A ball of fire flew from her palm into the rock, destroying it and scattering the shadow among the million pieces on the ground. Ciaran stood, unprepared. As he closed a fist, a cloak of shadows embraced his body and absorbed the light of the flames around him. "What is this?" he said.

"This is your death," she said. "This is what protection looks like."

Ciaran threw his hand in front of him, a trail of darkness unraveling from his arm and stretching out to grab Leanah. She reacted by summoning a wall of fire around her.

The darkness, seemingly alive, squealed and pulled back to Ciaran's body. "You joined two powers?" Ciaran played a desperate move. "You cannot do that! It's against the rules of magick!" he shouted.

All of the shadows pulled from Ciaran's body and thrust themselves toward to Leanah. His dark hair and pale body reflected the heat and fires around him. He dripped sweat, but kept throwing his hands in front of him, moving his tentacles as a puppeteer moves a puppet. Each throw more rapid than the last, attempts to stab, cut, kill.

Leanah, however, brandished her sword and summoned the power of flame over Kragg.

Ciaran paused. His eyes widened. On instinct, he summoned the shadows to pull back to him, wrapping around him like a security blanket. Not an inch of him was left exposed.

With nothing else to do, he ran toward the village, back toward its center.

Leanah followed after. Her feet left deep, burning marks into the dirt as she traveled faster, picking up speed with each kick off the ground. "Don't run," she said. "We're just getting started."

Leanah pulled the sword to her side and then grabbed it with both hands. She held it lower than her chest, the blade on fire and pointed downward.

"No!" he shouted. "You cannot do this! You cannot!" Ciaran threw himself into a nearby shadow caused by a crevice of rock and ground. Leanah, however, caught up and seized his foot with a flaming hand before he could complete his jump.

Leanah yanked him to the side and watched as Ciaran's body flew to the flaming ruins of her old house. "This is for the lies. The torture. The death."

Ciaran pulled himself from the wreckage, but sat back, resting. "The death, the torture. That was all you, my dear."

Leanah shot another fireball at Ciaran, pushing his body backwards along the rubble.

"The truth hurts, does it not, Kaverin?"

Leanah threw another fireball at him, walking steadily toward Ciaran. "I am not Kaverin."

"Ah, but you are. You are the fortunate host of two Elders," he whispered. The force of his own words exhausting what was left of Ciaran's energy.

"You are Kragg, you are Kaverin. You are now the avatars of the elders," Ciaran whispered. "But that was supposed to be my honor! My destiny!"

Leanah pointed Kragg's blade at Ciaran. "You confuse me with someone else," she said. The sword caught aflame.

Ciaran closed his eyes with a smile.

With a flick of her wrist, Leanah flung the sword toward Ciaran's relaxed body. It traveled through the air until its flaming blade was slowed, then stopped, by the shadowy cloak of Ciaran.

Ciaran opened his eyes, his mouth dripping with a red goo, so dark it's black. "The Elders are waiting for you, young Leanah." Ciaran's shadows escaped from his body, seemingly absorbing inside him the way a cloth absorbs water.

Leanah approached Ciaran's body, rested her foot against Ciaran's shoulder, and pulled the blade out of his chest. Ciaran slumped over, falling face first into the ground below.

Leanah turned around, her eyes flaring a ruby red and her chest covered with a black cloak. Leanah's glowing eyes looked up and held her flaming blade threateningly to the sky.

"Elders, if you can hear me, listen and listen well. If you cannot protect these people, then I will. If you will not seek revenge on those who harm others, then I will do what you won't. Fear me, Elders, for I am not afraid of you."

Leanah lowered her sword and watched as the sky turned to darkness and the glowing embers of her city faded to thin streams of smoke.

The air grew silent. The last of the villagers had to have

escaped by this point. Leanah wondered for a moment where they all traveled to.

It didn't matter, she figured. These people were already lost. Lied to. Their lives destroyed.

Leanah wandered to the burning rubble of her house, taking in the fallen walls of shops and homes around her. Everything used to be so pretty, so wonderful.

This, rubble, this was not how it was supposed to be.

Leanah kicked over the body of Ciaran, still bleeding along the rocks that used to be her front door. His body slumped over, with Leanah kicking it to one side.

One last look, she thought. Just one last reminder.

Leanah stepped over the rubble, the pieces of wood and rock that made up her living room.

There, in the back, her bedroom. Further back, what used to be her chicken pen.

The chickens. Leanah had almost forgotten about them during her adventure. She looked down to the pen. The hen house remained standing, miraculously, with some eggs intact inside.

Leanah smiled. The eggs were probably gone, too far heated with no mother to look after them. Leanah sighed, looking toward the sky for the course of the moon. The mountains, she thought. She had never been there.

"I'm coming for you," she said.

SIXTEEN

The threat of smoke loomed over the horizon. Luca pulled his war bison behind him. "Hurry up, Clea," he said. "I think someone's in trouble."

Clea yawned and grunted as Luca pulled on her reins. Clea's steps rattled the pots and pans that were packed up against her sides. If anything was true, Luca could over prepare for just about anything. He had won the tools on Clea's back only a moment ago in a test of strength.

It's a shame that they never even saw it coming. Luca peered at the sky. The steady stream of smoke seemed to get thicker as he approached. He was getting nearer.

Where there was smoke, there was almost always fire. However, this made him smile. Fire had always reminded him of his friend Grenseal. Buddies since they were only thirteen years of age, they had discovered much of life together, war, philosophy, the gods.

They had realized early on that they were to be adventurers. It was only five years ago that each of them had acquired a special object, hidden from the other's view for fear of ridicule and a loss of each other's friendship.

Luca, Grenseal had always argued, got the better of the deal, for Grenseal had acquired a rock. Luca, an earring in the form of a seashell.

Luca rested the memories long enough to arrive at the edge of the burning town. Smoke rose from anything that could be set on fire. Luca's heart nearly stopped in his chest. Nothing recognizable had been left from the attack, whoever or whatever it was. Luca pulled his shirt over his face to protect from smoke and walked into the walled area of the town.

"Hello?" he called out. The chances seemed slim to him considering the view. "Hello?"

Something from behind him rattled. Luca turned to view a piece of rock shake. On top of it, gripping the rock and shaking it back and forth as it struggled to get up.

"Hello?" he said again and ran toward the moving rock. He laughed. "Someone's alive!" Clea, still standing on the hill, brayed back to him. "Yes, I know girl, I know."

Luca pulled the rock backward. There, panicked and hunched over, his face covered with black dust, sat a man concealed in a dusty brown cloak.

The man held his hands to his face. "No!" he shouted. "Stay back! Stay back!"

Luca looked back to Clea, who began to step down the hill. "No, no, Clea, stay there."

Luca smiled and extended a hand to help the man up. "It's safe, I promise you."

The panicked man stopped and allowed his eyes to meet with Luca's own eyes. "Who are you?"

"I'm Luca," he said. "A friend."

The man's eyes widened. A sad smile came across his face. "I'm Shaper. Well, a Shaper."

He looked around the destruction and rising smoldering rubble. "I'm so sorry," he said.

Luca surveyed the burning town from where he stood. "Was this you?" Luca stepped back.

"No, no, this wasn't me. It was another man. Darque. Ciaran."

"I don't know who those men are," said Luca. "Never heard of them."

"Not men. Man." The Shaper stood up and dusted himself off. "Is Leanah here?"

Luca shrugged. "I don't believe anyone else is here," he said. "This entire place looks deserted." The Shaper began walking toward a clearing just outside the walls. "Excuse me," he said.

"Do you know of other survivors?" asked Luca. "Where are you going?"

The Shaper said nothing. He walked until reaching a point just outside the walls. Luca heard something that sounded like a sobbing.

"Shaper?" he said. "Shaper?" He followed the Shaper to arrive at a pool of blood, dried into the rocky ground. From just behind the Shaper's legs was a bright orange cloak.

"No," Luca said to himself. He began walking, then running, to the spot where the Shaper stood. "No no no no no."

Luca's fears were very real.

Luca fell to his hands and knees, gripping Grenseal's cloak in his hands. "No," he said. "I just found you." Luca grabbed the cloak and pulled it closer to his body, wiping his face with it, feeling the textures against his skin again.

"Who did this?" Luca's eyes moved slowly across the landscape, unable to meet the Shaper in his own eyes.

"She did it," said the Shaper. "Leanah."

A long silence as Luca took the cloak from the body and wrapped it up, folding it in half, then fourths and kept it between his belt and his own tunic. He let out a sigh and wiped the tears from his face. "I will need to see this Leanah."

"I will come with you," said the Shaper.

"Aren't you due back in your Citadel?"

"I cannot return. That has long been forbidden. As a matter of fact, they may be looking for me."

Luca waved over for Clea to come. The slow animal stepped slowly toward her master, as if sad herself.

"Then as long as we have common goals, we can travel together," he said. Luca knelt down and took some rocks in his small hands. He placed them on the body, inch by inch and allowed for them to rest along the corpse's primary joints. One on each shoulder, the neck, the hips. Then, with a wave of his hand, Luca summoned a hazy mist that covered the corpse. The mist grew as Luca's concentration grew, eventually taking up the entire corpse, white crystals forming on every inch of the body.

"You can do magick too?"

Luca did not turn away from his concentration. The body's skin turned tick, pale, and rubbery until finally consumed by the frost.

SEVENTEEN

The Shaper and Luca looked over the river south of now destroyed village of Vamori.

"You, you were the friend, the one he was looking for."

"We had made a pact," Luca said. His eyes looked upon the horizon as the Grenseal's frozen body disappeared down the river, floating on a charred piece of wood. "In time we would meet at Deckal and discuss our findings."

"Findings?"

"We had hoped to find clues to the source of our powers. Grenseal had power over fire."

The Shaper nodded. "A power he feared."

Luca looked at Shaper and smiled. "Yes, you did know him. He feared his power. He never saw the potential that we had, the things we could do."

Grenseal's body disappeared over the horizon, at which point both Luca and the Shaper bowed their heads in respect.

Luca continued, "It was my fault." Luca tried to hide his sobs from his new friend. "If I hadn't let him leave, we could have faced her together, or been far away from here."

"You would have no way of knowing," said the Shaper. He rested his hand on Luca's shoulder. His words served no comfort to Luca, who shoved off the Shaper's attempts to be friendly. "I understand what you're thinking. I was there. I saw it all. And all I did was nothing. I watched him die."

Luca turned on the Shaper.

"You watched it?"

"I was paralyzed. I had never seen so much power. I'm just a powerless monk. What do I know of fighting?"

"It was his idea, you know. To seek them out."

"Who?"

"The Gods. We had believed our gifts to be from the Elders themselves. We wanted to find out why and how. He went to the east to follow rumors of a stone."

"A stone sword?" asked the Shaper.

"Yes, you know of it?"

"Leanah owns it. Along with powers beyond our comprehension. We are in a dark, dark world now."

Luca turned to gather his things and feed an apple to Clea. "My journey was to the east. I had heard rumors of other, how should I say, interesting things happening around the world. We were searching for them, maybe to see what we may know."

"If I may, I would like to seek some answers myself," said the Shaper. "If you'll have me. I would like to seek atonement for what I have done myself."

Luca looked to the Shaper for an answer, but received nothing more than a simple nod and coy look away.

Luca nodded. "Then it sounds like we have some answers to get and a god to kill."

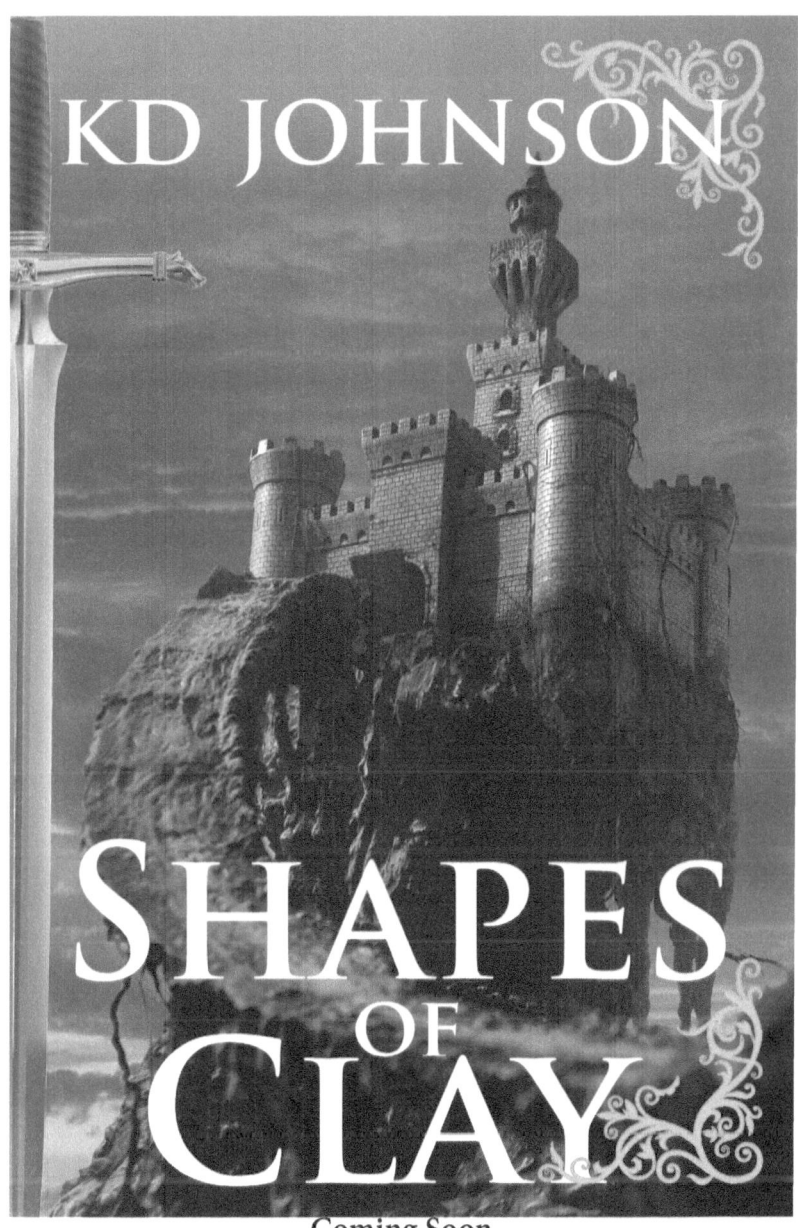

KD JOHNSON

SHAPES OF CLAY

Coming Soon

Angered by the destruction of the Vamori Village, Leanah declares
war on the Elder Gods themselves. Meanwhile, the Shaper and
Luca, still saddened by his lover's death, come across others whose
mysterious pasts have ties with Luca's own godpower.

Also by KD Johnson, available soon in ebook and paperback

The Shattering Series
Shapes of Clay (Book II)

Also by Akusai Publishing, available in ebook and paperback

Dark Fantasy
Mr. White
Savior
Gifted

Psychological Suspense
Wannabe
Echoes
House of Braddock

Contemporary Dark Fantasy
Exiled From Hell
Reign From Heaven
Across the Realms

Visit the publisher at www.akusaipublishing.com

ABOUT THE AUTHOR

KD JOHNSON lives in the Seattle area. While this is his first foray in the sword and sorcery fantasy genre, he writes under different pen names to satisfy the various creative itches that strike him at random moments in his life. When he's not teaching, he's slaying dragons in his favorite caverns in *Dragon Age: Inquisition* or kicking ass on drums in *Rock Band*.

www.ingramcontent.com/pod-product-compliance
Lightning Source LLC
Chambersburg PA
CBHW030648260626
47157CB00007B/2550